The Case of the
Curious Bride

The Case of the Curious Bride

Erle Stanley Gardner

G.K. Hall & Co. • Chivers Press
Thorndike, Maine USA   Bath, England

This Large Print edition is published by G.K. Hall & Co., USA
and by Chivers Press, England.

Published in 2001 in the U.S. by arrangement with
Thayer Hobson & Company.

Published in 2001 in the U.K. by arrangement with
Thayer Hobson.

U.S. Softcover   0-7838-9432-5   (Paperback Series Edition)
U.K. Hardcover   0-7540-4535-8   (Chivers Large Print)
U.K. Softcover   0-7540-4536-6   (Camden Large Print)

The text of this Large Print edition is unabridged.
Other aspects of the book may vary from the original edition.

Set in 16 pt. Plantin by Rick Gundberg.

Printed in the United States on permanent paper.

British Library Cataloguing in Publication Data available

Library of Congress Cataloging-in-Publication Data

Gardner, Erle Stanley, 1889–1970.
   The case of the curious bride / Erle Stanley Gardner.
      p. cm.
   ISBN 0-7838-9432-5 (lg. print : sc : alk. paper)
   1. Mason, Perry (Fictitious character) — Fiction. 2. Large type
books. I. Title.
PS3513.A6322 C87 2001
   813'.52—dc21
                                            2001016730

Cast of Characters

Chapter 1

The woman was nervous. Her eyes held the eyes of the lawyer for a moment, then slithered away to the book-lined walls, as the eyes of an animal survey the bars of a cage. "Sit down," said Perry Mason. He studied her with a frank scrutiny which had been developed by years of exploring the dark recesses of human minds — not only of witnesses, but of clients.

"I'm calling," she said, "on behalf of a friend."

"Yes?" asked Perry Mason tonelessly.

"My friend's husband has disappeared," she said. "I understand there's an expression known as 'legal death' that covers such matters, isn't there?"

Perry Mason didn't answer her directly. "Your name," he asked, "is Helen Crocker?"

"Yes."

"Your age?" he inquired abruptly.

She hesitated a moment. "Twenty-seven," she said.

"My secretary thought you were a bride," the lawyer went on.

She squirmed uncomfortably in the big leather

chair. "Please," she said, "let's not discuss me. After all, my name or my age doesn't make any difference. I told you that I was calling on behalf of a friend. You don't need to know who I am. I'm simply a messenger. Your fee will be paid — in cash."

"My secretary," Perry Mason went on, "doesn't usually make mistakes. She felt quite positive you had been recently married."

"What ever gave her that impression?"

"Something about the way you fingered your wedding ring, as though it were new to you."

She spoke with quick desperation, after the manner of one who is reciting a speech which has been learned by rote. "My friend's husband was in an airplane. It's been a good many years ago. I don't remember the exact location, but it was somewhere over a lake. It was foggy. Apparently the pilot was trying to come close to the water, and he hit the water before he knew what was happening. A fisherman heard the plane but couldn't see it. He said it sounded as though it was just a few feet above the surface."

"Are you a bride?" Perry Mason asked.

"No!" she said with swift indignation.

"Are you," asked Perry Mason, "certain the plane was wrecked?"

"Yes, they found some wreckage. I think it was what they call a pontoon — I don't know much about airplanes. They found the body of one of the passengers. They never found the body of the pilot, nor the other three passengers."

"How long have you been married?" the lawyer inquired.

"*Please*," she said, "leave me out of it. I have already explained to you, Mr. Mason, that I am trying to get information for a friend."

"I take it," Mason said, "there was some life insurance, and the insurance company refuses to pay until the body has been recovered?"

"Yes."

"And you want me to collect the insurance?"

"Partially that."

"What's the rest of it?"

"She is wondering about her right to re-marry."

"How long since her husband disappeared?"

"About seven years I think, perhaps a little longer."

"No one," asked Perry Mason, "has heard from the husband in the meantime?"

"No, certainly not. He died. . . . But, about the divorce."

"What divorce?" the lawyer inquired.

She laughed nervously. "I'm afraid I'm getting the cart before the horse," she said. "This woman wants to re-marry. Some one told her that unless her husband's body had been discovered she would have to get a divorce. That seems foolish. Her husband is dead, all right. It seems foolish to get a divorce from a dead man. Tell me, *could* she re-marry without getting a divorce?"

"It's been over seven years since the disappearance?"

"Yes."

"You're positive of that?"

"Yes. It's been more than seven years now . . . but it wasn't when . . ." Her voice trailed off into silence.

"When what?" Mason asked.

"When she first met this man she's going with," Helen Crocker finished lamely.

Perry Mason studied her with calm, contemplative appraisal and did not seem conscious of the fact that he was staring. Helen Crocker was not beautiful. There was a touch of the sallow about her complexion. Her mouth was just a bit too long, her lips too full. But she was well-formed, and there was a sparkle to her eyes. Taken all in all, she was not hard to look at. She bore his scrutiny calmly, a touch of defiance in her eyes.

"Was there," asked Perry Mason, "anything else that your friend wanted to know about?"

"Yes. That is, she's curious about it, that's all — just curious."

"Curious about what?" Mason asked.

"Curious about what you lawyers call the *corpus delicti.*"

Perry Mason became rigid with watchful attention. His eyes stared with cold steadiness as he asked, "What did she want to know about it?"

"She wanted to know whether it was true that, no matter what evidence they had against a person, they couldn't prosecute her for murder unless they found the body. Is that right?"

"And she wanted to know," said Perry Mason,

"just to satisfy her curiosity, is that it?"

"Yes."

"So this friend of yours," Perry Mason went on, with steady, remorseless insistence, "finds it necessary to produce the body of her dead husband in order to collect the insurance and be free to re-marry, and, at the same time, has to keep that body concealed in order to escape a prosecution for murder. Is that it?"

Helen Crocker came up out of the chair as though she had received an electric shock. "No!" she said. "Certainly not! Not at all. It's just curiosity that made her want to know about that last. She'd been reading a book."

There was a scornful smile in Perry Mason's eyes. His manner became that of a big dog who has condescended to amuse himself for a few minutes with the gambols of a puppy, and, having wearied himself of the purposeless playing, walks toward a shady corner with an air of complete dismissal. He pushed back his swivel chair, got to his feet and stood looking down at her with a patient smile. "Very well," he said, "tell your friend if she wishes to have her questions answered she can make an appointment through my secretary. I'll be glad to discuss the matter with her."

Dismay flooded Helen Crocker's features. "But," she protested frantically, "I'm her friend. She sent me to find out. She can't come herself. You can give me the information and I'll give it to her."

11

Perry Mason's eyes continued to hold a smile. There were mingled contempt and amusement in his manner. "No," he said, "that's a poor way to get legal information to the ears of a client. Tell her to come in and see me — I'll talk with her." Helen Crocker started to say something, but checked herself with a single quick intake of the breath. The lawyer walked across the office, twisted the knob of the door that led to the corridor and held it open. "You can," he said, "get out this way."

His face held the expression of a poker player who calls the bluff of an opponent. But that expression underwent a sudden change as Helen Crocker elevated her chin, clamped her lips together, said, "Very well," and swished past him through the open door and into the corridor. Perry Mason stood in the door waiting for her to turn, but she did not once look back. Her heels clicked down the corridor with quick, nervous steps. A descending elevator cage caught her signal almost as soon as she jabbed her thumb against the button. Her back was still to Perry Mason as the cage door slammed shut and the elevator dropped smoothly out of sight.

Chapter 2

Della Street, Perry Mason's secretary, looked up inquiringly as he opened the door of his private office. Automatically, she picked up a pencil and reached for a daybook in which was entered the names and addresses of those who called, the amount of time they consumed, and the fees received. Her eyes showed inquiry. Those eyes dominated her face. They were clear, steady and unafraid — the eyes of one who saw far beneath the surface. The lawyer faced the calm scrutiny of those eyes, and explained: "I gave her a chance to come clean and she didn't."

"What was the trouble?"

"She tried to pull the old line on me, the one about a mysterious friend who wanted certain information. She asked me several questions. If I'd given her the answers, she'd have walked out and tried to apply the law I had stated to the situation that terrified her. The results would have been disastrous."

"Was she frightened?"

"Yes." Between Della Street and Perry Mason was that peculiar bond which comes to exist between persons of the opposite sex who have spent years together in an exacting work where success can only be obtained by perfect coordination of effort. All personal relations are subordinated to the task of achievement, which brings about a more perfect companionship than where companionship is consciously sought.

"So what?" asked Della Street, pencil still poised over the book.

"So I quit playing," Mason said, "and told her she'd better tell her friend to make an appointment with me. I figured she'd weaken and tell me the story. They usually do. This one didn't. She sailed out of the office and didn't once look back as she went to the elevator. She fooled me."

Della Street's pencil made irrelevant designs in the upper corner of the blank page. "Did she tell you she'd been recently married?"

"No. She wouldn't even admit that."

Della Street's nod of the head was a quietly emphatic assertion. "She's a bride, all right."

Mason slid his right leg over the corner of her desk, pulled a cigarette case from his pocket, took out a cigarette and said, almost as though thinking out loud, "I shouldn't have done it."

"Done what?" she asked.

"Done what I did," he mused. "What right have I got to sit back with that 'holier than thou' attitude and expect them to come clean with a total stranger? They come here when they're in trouble. They're worried and frightened. They come to me for consultations. I'm a total stranger to them. They need help. Poor fools, you can't blame them for resorting to subterfuges. I could have been sympathetic and drawn her out, won her confidence, found out her secret and lightened the load of her troubles. But I got impatient with her. I tried to force the issue, and now she's gone.

"It was her pride that I hurt. She knew that I'd pierced her subterfuge of lies. She knew that inwardly I was mocking her; and she had too much pride, too much character and too much self-respect to come clean after that. She came to me for help, because she needed help. When I refused her that help, I betrayed my calling. I wasn't playing the game."

Della Street moved her hand toward the cigarette case.

"Gimme," she said.

Absently, the lawyer extended the cigarette case to her. Their companionship was such that no apology from Perry Mason for having helped himself without proffering the cigarette case was expected. On the other hand, there was no necessity for the secretary to ask permission to smoke during office hours. In more formal law offices, where results were subordinated to methods, a secretary would have stood in apparent awe of her employer, an awe that would have been but a thin and spurious veneer covering inner amusement and a complete lack of respect. But Perry Mason specialized in trial law, mostly criminal law. His creed was results. Clients came to him because they had to. There was no repeat business. Ordinarily a man is arrested for murder but once in a lifetime. Mason realized that his business must come from new clients, rather than from those who had previously been acquitted. As a result, he ran his office without regard for appearances or conventions. He did what he pleased when it suited him to do it. He had sufficient ability to scorn the conventions. Lawyer and secretary lit cigarettes from a single match.

"She'll go to some other lawyer, chief," Della Street said reassuringly.

Perry Mason shook his head in slow negation. "No," he said, "she's lost confidence in herself. She'd rehearsed that story about her friend. God knows how many times she'd rehearsed it. Probably she didn't sleep much last night. She went over this interview in her mind a hundred times. She planned a breezy method of approach. She was going to try and be casual about it. She could be hazy about names, dates and places because her 'friend' had been a little hazy with her. Lying awake last night, staring into the darkness, turning the situation over and over in a mind that had become weakened by worry, it seemed a perfect scheme. She thought she could get the legal information she wanted without tipping her hand. Then I ripped off the cloak of her deception so easily and so casually that she lost confidence in herself. Poor kid! She came to me for help and I didn't give it to her."

"I'll make the charge just the amount of the

retainer," Della Street said, making notes in the daybook.

"Retainer?" Mason echoed blankly. "There isn't any retainer — there isn't any charge."

Della Street's eyes were troubled. She shook her head gravely. "I'm sorry, chief, but she left a retainer. I asked her for her name and address and the nature of her business. She said she wanted some advice, and I told her that I presumed she understood there would be a charge. She became irritated, opened her purse, jerked out a fifty dollar bill and told me to use that as a retainer."

Mason's voice held self-reproach. "The poor kid," he said slowly. "And I let her go." Della Street's sympathetic hand dropped to his. Fingers — fingers that had grown strong from pounding typewriter keys — squeezed a message of silent understanding.

A shadow formed on the frosted glass panel of the outer door. The knob clicked. It might have been a client with an important case, and it spoke volumes for the manner in which Perry Mason conducted his office and lived his life that he made no effort to change his position. Della Street hastily withdrew her hand, but Perry Mason remained with one hip resting on the corner of the desk, smoking his cigarette, staring with steady, uncordial eyes at the door.

The door swung open. Paul Drake, head of the Drake Detective Bureau, regarded them with protruding, glassy eyes which held a perpetual expression of droll humor, an effective mask, covering a keen intelligence which passed upon life in the raw. "Hello, folks," he said, "got any more work for me?"

Perry Mason managed a mirthless grin. "God, but you're greedy! I've been keeping your whole detective agency busy for the last few months, and now you want more!"

The detective moved away from the door, let it click shut behind him. "Did a little jane in brown, with snapping black eyes, leave your office about six or seven minutes ago, Perry?" he asked.

Perry Mason slid from the desk, and turned to face the detective, his feet spread apart, his shoulders squared.

"Spill it!" he said.

"Did she?"

"Yes."

The detective nodded. "This," he said, "is service with a capital 'S.' That's what comes of maintaining friendly relations with a detective bureau that's in the same office building. . . ."

"Cut the comedy and give me the dope," Mason ordered.

Paul Drake spoke in a husky, expressionless voice. He might have been a radio announcer droning through a list of stock exchange quotations, utterly insensible to the fact that his words spelled financial independence or economic disaster to his listeners.

"I'm coming out of my office on the floor below yours," he said, "when I hear a man's feet coming down the stairs from this floor. He's running fast, until he hits my floor, and then he forgets he's in a hurry. He saunters over to the elevator, lights a cigarette, and keeps his eye on the indicator. When the indicator shows that a cage has stopped at your floor, he pushes the down bell. Naturally, the same cage stops for him. There's only one passenger in it — a woman about twenty-six, or seven, wearing a brown suit. She's got a trim figure, a full-lipped mouth and snapping black eyes. Her complexion isn't anything to write home about. She's nervous, and her nostrils are expanded a bit, as though she's been running. She looks frightened."

"You must have had binoculars and an X-ray machine," Mason interrupted.

"Oh, I didn't get all this in the first glance," the detective told him. "When I heard this guy tearing down the stairs, and then saw him start to saunter as he hit the corridor, I figured it would be a good plan to ride down on the same elevator with him. I thought I might be drumming up a job for myself."

Mason's eyes were hard. Smoke seeped through his nostrils. "Go on," he said.

"The way I figure it," the detective drawled, "was that this guy was a tail. He'd followed the jane to your office and was waiting in the corridor for her to come out. He was probably parked at the head of the stairs, keeping out of sight.

19

When he heard your door open and the jane go out, he gave a quick glance to make sure it was the party he wanted. Then he ran down the stairs to the lower corridor and sauntered along to the elevator, so he could catch the same cage down."

Mason made an impatient gesture. "You don't have to draw me a diagram. Give me the dope."

"I wasn't sure she'd come from your office, Perry," the detective went on. "If I had been, I'd have given it more of a play. The way the thing stacked up, I thought I'd see what it was all about. So when they got to the street, I trailed along for a ways. The guy was tailing her all right. Somehow, I don't figure him for a professional shadow. In the first place, he was too nervous. You know, a good tail trains himself never to show surprise. No matter what happens, he never gets nervous and ducks for cover. Well, about half a block from the building, this woman suddenly turns around. The man that was back of her went into a panic and ducked for a doorway. I kept on walking toward her."

"You think she'd spotted one or the other of you?" Mason asked, his growing interest apparent in his voice.

"No, she didn't know we were living. She'd either thought of something she'd forgotten to ask you, or else she'd changed her mind about something. She didn't even look at me as she went by. She turned around and started back toward me. She didn't even see the chap who was standing in the doorway, trying to make himself look inconspicuous, and making such hard work of it that he stuck out like a sore thumb."

"Then what?" Mason inquired.

"She walked fifteen or twenty steps and then stopped. I figured that she'd acted on impulse when she turned around and started back. While she was walking back, she got to arguing with herself. She acted as though she was afraid of something. She wanted to come back, but she didn't dare to come back, or perhaps it was her pride. I don't know what had happened, but . . ."

"That's all right," Mason said, "I know all about that. I expected she'd turn and come back before she got to the elevator. But she didn't. I guess she couldn't take it."

Drake nodded. "Well," he remarked, "she fidgeted around for a minute and then she turned around again and started down the street once more. Her shoulders were sagging. She looked as though she'd lost the last friend she had in the world. She went past me a second time without seeing me. I'd stopped to light a cigarette. She didn't see the chap who had been sticking in the doorway; evidently, she didn't expect to be tailed."

"What did he do?" the lawyer asked.

"When she went by, he stepped out of the doorway and took up the trail."

"What did you do?"

"I didn't want to make it look like a procession. I figured that if she came from your office and was being shadowed, you'd like to know it, but I wasn't certain she'd come from your office, in the first place; and I had work to do, so I figured I'd tip you off and let it go at that."

Mason squinted his eyes. "You'd know this chap, of course, if you saw him again — the one who was trailing her?"

"Sure. He's not a bad looking guy — about thirty-two or thirty-three, light hair, brown eyes, dressed in tweeds. I'd say he was something of a ladies' man, from the way he wore his clothes. His hands were manicured. The nails were freshly polished. He'd been shaved and massaged in a barber shop. He had that barber shop smell about him, and there was powder on his face. A man usually doesn't powder his face when he shaves himself. When he does, he puts the powder on with his hands. A barber pats it on with a towel and doesn't rub it in."

Perry Mason frowned thoughtfully. "In a way she's a client of mine, Paul," he said; "she called to consult me and then got cold feet and didn't. Thanks for the tip. If anything comes of it, I'll let you know."

The detective moved toward the door, paused to grin back over his shoulder. "I wish," he drawled, "you two would quit holding hands in the outer office and looking innocent when the door opens. I might have been a client. What the hell have you got a private office for?"

Chapter 3

Perry Mason stared somberly down into Della Street's flushed face.

"How did he know," she asked, "that I was holding your hand? I moved it before the door opened, and . . ."

"Just a shot in the dark," Mason told her, his voice preoccupied. "Something in your facial expression, probably. . . . Della, I'm going to give that girl a break. I'm going to back up. If we accepted a retainer from her we're going to see it through."

"But we can't do it. You don't know what she wanted you to do."

Perry Mason nodded and said grimly, "That's all right; she was in some sort of trouble. I'll get in touch with her, find out what it is and either give her her retainer back or help her. What's her address?"

Della Street took a sheet of yellow paper from the file.

"Her name," she said, "is Helen Crocker. She lives at 496 East Pelton Avenue, and the telephone number is Drenton 68942." Without waiting for comment from Mason, she plugged in a line and spun the dial on the telephone. The receiver made noise, and Della Street frowned. "Drenton six-eight-nine-four-two," she said.

Once more, the receiver made squawking noises. There was a moment's pause, then Della Street spoke into the transmitter. "I am looking for a telephone listed under the name of Crocker. The initials I'm not certain about. The former number was Drenton six-eight-nine-four-two. That number has been disconnected, but it was listed under her name." The receiver made more sound. Della Street said, "The address is four ninety-six East Pelton Avenue. What have you listed there? . . . Thanks very much — probably a mistake in the number."

She dropped the receiver into place, pulled out the plug and shook her head at Perry Mason. "Drenton six-eight-nine-four-two," she said, "was listed under the name of Tucker, was disconnected more than thirty days ago. There isn't any four ninety-six East Pelton Avenue. Pelton Avenue is a street only two blocks long. The highest number on it is two hundred and ninety-eight."

Perry Mason jerked open the door of his private office, and said over his shoulder, "She'll get in touch with us again somehow. She forgot about leaving that retainer. Whenever she calls see that I have a chance to speak with her." He strode through the door, glowered savagely at the big leather chair in which the young woman had sat while she told her story. Light streaming in from the window caught something metallic. Mason stopped to stare, then walked to the chair and bent forward. A brown purse had slipped down between the cushions, only the clasp visible. Perry Mason pulled it out. It was heavy. He weighed it speculatively in his hand, turned and jerked open the door. "Come in, Della," he said. "Bring a notebook. Our caller left a purse behind her. I'm going to open it. I want you to inventory the contents as I open it."

She jumped to wordless obedience, bringing notebook and pencil, pulling out the leaf of the desk in a matter-of-fact manner, opening the notebook, holding the pencil poised.

"One white lace-bordered handkerchief," Perry Mason said. The pencil made pothooks over the pages. "One .32 caliber Colt automatic, number three-eight-nine-four-six-two-one."

Della Street's pencil flew over the pages of the notebook, but she raised startled eyes to the lawyer. Perry Mason's voice droned on mechanically. "Magazine clip for automatic, filled with cartridges containing steel-jacketed, soft-nosed bullets. A cartridge in the firing chamber of the gun. Barrel seems to be clean. No odor of powder discernible."

He snapped the magazine clip back into the gun, closed the mechanism, replaced the ejected shell in the firing chamber, went on in the same droning monotone: "Coin purse containing one hundred and fifty-two dollars and sixty-five cents. A bottle of tablets marked 'IPRAL.' One pair brown gloves, one lipstick, one compact, one telegram addressed to R. Montaine, 128 East Pelton Avenue. Telegram reading as follows: 'AWAITING YOUR FINAL ANSWER FIVE O'CLOCK TO-DAY EXTREME LIMIT — (Signed) GREGORY.' A package of Spud cigarettes, a package of matches bearing advertising imprint, 'GOLDEN EAGLE CAFÉ, 25 WEST FORTY-THIRD STREET.' "

Perry Mason's voice ceased the droning inventory. He held the purse upside down over the desk, tapped on the bottom with his fingers. "That seems to be all," he remarked.

Della Street looked up from the notebook. "Good heavens!" she said, "what did that girl want with a gun?"

"What does any one want with a gun?" Perry Mason inquired, taking a handkerchief and removing any fingerprints which might have been on the weapon. He dropped the gun into the purse, picked up the other articles with his handkerchief-covered fingers, polished them one at a time, dropped them back into the purse. The telegram he held for a moment, then thrust it into his pocket. "Della," he said, "if she comes back, make her wait. I'm going out."

"How long will you be gone, chief?"

"I don't know. I'll give you a ring if I'm not back within an hour."

"Suppose she won't wait?"

"Make her wait. Tell her anything you want to. Go so far as to tell her I'm sorry for the way I treated her, if you want to. That girl's in trouble. She came to me for help. What I'm really afraid of is that she may *not* come back."

He stuck the purse into his side pocket, pulled his hat down on his forehead, strode to the door. His pounding steps echoed along the corridor. He speared the elevator signal with his forefinger, caught a down cage and signaled a cab at the sidewalk. "One twenty-eight East Pelton Avenue," he said.

Mason reclined in the cushions as the cab lurched forward, closed his eyes, folded his arms across his chest and remained in that position for the twenty-odd minutes that it took the cab to make the run to East Pelton Avenue. "Wait here," he told the driver as the cab swung in to the curb.

Mason walked rapidly up a cement walk, mounted three stairs to a stoop and held an insistent thumb against the bell button. There was the sound of steps approaching the door. Mason took the telegram from his pocket, folded the message so that the name and address were visible through the tissue-covered "window" in the envelope.

The door opened. A young woman with tired eyes regarded Perry Mason in expressionless appraisal. "Telegram for R. Montaine," said Perry Mason, holding the telegram in his hand. The young woman's eyes dropped to the address. She nodded her head. "You'll have to sign," Perry Mason told her.

The eyes regarded him with curiosity that, as yet, had not ripened into suspicion. "You're not a regular messenger," she observed, glancing past Mason to the cab that waited at the curb.

"I'm the branch manager," he told her. "I thought I could get the wire here quicker than by messenger. I was going this way on another matter."

He took a notebook from his pocket, whipped out a pencil, handed both pencil and notebook to the young woman. "Sign on the top line."

She wrote "R. Montaine," handed the book back to him. "Wait a minute," Mason said, "are *you* R. Montaine?"

She hesitated a moment, then answered, "I'm receiving messages for R. Montaine."

Perry Mason indicated the notebook. "Then you'll have to sign your own name below that of R. Montaine."

"I haven't had to before," she objected.

"I'm sorry," he told her. "Sometimes the messengers don't understand these things. I'm the branch manager."

She drew back the hand which contained the notebook, hesitated for an appreciable interval and then wrote, "Nell Brinley" under the "R. Montaine" she had previously signed.

"Now," said Perry Mason as she handed back the book and pencil, "I want to talk with you."

He slipped the telegram back into his side pocket before the snatching fingers could grab it from his hand.

Suspicion and panic filled the eyes of the woman who stood in the doorway. "I'm coming in," Mason told her.

She had no make-up on her face, was attired in a house dress and slippers. Her face went white to the lips.

Perry Mason moved past her, walked along the corridor, stepped into the living room with calm assurance, sat down in a chair and crossed his legs. Nell Brinley came to the doorway and stood staring at him, as though afraid either to enter the room or to leave him in sole possession. "Come in," Mason told her, "and sit down."

She stood still for a matter of seconds, then came toward him. "Just who do you think you are?" she asked in a voice that she strove to make vibrant with indignation, but which quavered with fear.

Mason's voice showed grim insistence. "I'm checking on the activities of R. Montaine. Tell me exactly what you know about her."

"I don't know anything."

"You were signing for telegrams."

"No. As a matter of fact, I thought the name R. Montaine was a mistake. I've been expecting a telegram. I thought that it must be mine. I was going to read it. If it hadn't been for me, I was going to give it back to you."

Mason's laugh was scornful. "Try again."

"I don't have to," she said. "I'm telling you the truth."

Mason took the telegram from his pocket,

spread it out on his knee. "This is the telegram," he pointed out, "that was received here at nine fifty-three this morning. You signed for it and delivered it to R. Montaine."

"I did no such thing."

"The records show that you signed for it."

"The signature," she said, "is that of R. Montaine."

"In the same handwriting," Mason insisted, "as that in this notebook, which I saw you sign and under which appears your signature — Nell Brinley. That's your name, isn't it?"

"Yes."

"Look here," Mason told her, "as a matter of fact, I'm friendly with R. Montaine."

"You don't even know whether it's a man or a woman," she challenged.

"It's a woman," he told her, watching her narrowly.

"If you're a friend of hers, why don't you get in touch with *her?*" Nell Brinley asked.

"That's what I'm trying to do."

"If you're a *friend* of hers, you'd know where to find her."

"I'm going to find her through you," Mason said doggedly.

"I don't know anything about her."

"You gave her this telegram?"

"No."

"Then," said Perry Mason, "it becomes necessary for me to disclose my real identity. I am a detective working for the telegraph company.

There have been complaints of unauthorized persons receiving and reading telegrams. You probably don't realize it, but it's a felony under our state law. I'm going to ask you to get your things on and come to the district attorney's office with me for questioning."

She gave a quick, gasping intake of breath. "No, no!" she said. "I'm acting for Rhoda. I gave her the telegram."

"And why," asked Perry Mason, "couldn't Rhoda receive telegrams at her own house?"

"She couldn't."

"Why not?"

"If you knew Rhoda, you'd know."

"You mean on account of her husband? Married women shouldn't have secrets from their husbands — especially brides."

"Oh, you know that, then!"

"What?"

"About her being a bride."

"Of course," Mason said, laughing.

Nell Brinley lowered her eyes, thinking. Mason said nothing, letting her think the matter over.

"You're *not* a detective from the telegraph company, are you?" she asked.

"No. I'm a friend of Rhoda's, but she doesn't know it."

Abruptly, she looked up and said, "I'm going to tell you the truth."

"It always helps," Mason commented dryly.

"I'm a nurse," she said. "I'm very friendly

with Rhoda. I've known her for years. Rhoda wanted to get some telegrams and some mail at this address. She lived with me here before her marriage. I told her it would be quite all right."

"Where does she live now?" Mason asked.

Nell Brinley shook her head and said, "She hasn't given me the address." Mason's laugh was scornful. "Oh, I'm telling you the truth," she said. "Rhoda is one of the most secretive women I have ever known in my life. I lived with her for more than a year. We kept this little house together, and yet I don't know the man she married or where she lives. I know that his name is Montaine. That's all that I know about him."

"Know his first name?" Mason asked.

"No."

"How do you know his name is Montaine?"

"Only because Rhoda had the telegrams come here addressed to that name."

"What was her maiden name?"

"Rhoda Lorton."

"How long's she been married?"

"Less than a week."

"How did you get this telegram to her?"

"She called up and asked if there was any mail. I told her about the telegram. She came out and got it."

"What's your telephone number?"

"Drenton nine-four-two-six-eight."

"You're a nurse?"

"Yes."

"A trained nurse?"

"Yes."

"You're called out on cases?"

"Yes."

"When was your last case?"

"I came in yesterday. I was special nurse on an operative case."

Mason got up, smiled. "Do you think Rhoda will call up again?" he asked.

"Probably, but I'm not sure. She's very queer, very secretive. There's something in her life that she's concealing. I don't know just what it is. She's never given me her full confidence."

"When she rings up," Mason said, "tell her that she must go back to the lawyer she called on to-day, that he has something of the greatest importance to tell her. Do you think you can remember that message?"

"Yes. How about that telegram?" she asked, her eyes on Mason's pocket. "It's addressed to Rhoda."

"It's the same telegram you delivered to her this morning," he said.

"I know that, but how did you get it?"

"That," Mason said, "is a professional secret."

"Who are you?"

Mason's smile was baffling. "I am the man who left you the message for Rhoda Montaine to go back to the attorney she called on earlier in the day." He walked through the corridor. She called some questions after him, but he banged the front door, moved rapidly down the steps, across the strip of cement sidewalk, and, as the cab driver pulled open the door of the cab, jumped inside. "Snappy!" he said. "Around the corner. Stop at the first place where there's a telephone." Nell Brinley came to the door and stood staring at the cab as it lurched into motion and swung around the corner.

The cab driver swung toward the curb in front of a candy store which exhibited a public telephone sign. "How will this do?" he asked.

"Fine," Mason said. The cab stopped. Mason strode into the candy store, dropped a coin into the telephone, held his mouth close to the transmitter and cupped his fingers over the hard rubber mouthpiece so as to muffle his voice. He gave the number of his office, and, when he heard Della Street's voice on the line, said, "Take a pencil and notebook, Della."

"Okay," she said.

"In about twenty minutes, ring up Nell Brinley at Drenton nine-four-two-six-eight. Tell her that when Rhoda Montaine comes in she is to call you at once. Give her a fake name. Tell her that it is a message from Gregory."

"Okay, chief, what do I do when she calls?"

"When she calls, tell her who you are. Tell her that she left her purse in my office. Tell her that I want to see her at once. Now, here's something else for you. Check over the marriage licenses. Find out if a marriage license was issued to a man by the name of Montaine, in which the name of the bride was Rhoda Lorton. Have Paul Drake send one of his men to the water, light and gas companies and see if they have made a service connection for a Montaine recently. When you get the right initials from the marriage license, check up with the telephone company and see if there's a telephone in his name. Have Drake put a man on addresses and see if he can run down the address of the bridegroom from the marriage license. Have him get in touch with the Colt arms people and see if he can trace the number on that gun. You've the number there in your notebook. Keep all of this stuff under cover. I want to get a line on that woman."

"Why," she asked, "has anything happened?"

"No," he told her, "but it's going to if I can't get in touch with her."

"You'll call me again to pick up what information I've received?" she asked.

"Yes," he said.

"Okay, chief."

Mason hung up, returned to the cab.

Chapter 4

The printer had a small stall between skyscrapers, adjacent to another stall which dispensed orange drinks. An oblong glass frame contained samples of the various types of printing. A placard announced that cards and stationery were printed while the customer waited. Perry Mason stared speculatively at the glass oblong, his manner that of one who is debating whether to buy or not to buy. The man behind the short counter leaned forward. "I can give you a quick drying ink," he said, "that will look like engraving. It will fool even an expert."

"How much?" asked Perry Mason. The man's ink-smeared forefinger indicated a schedule of samples and prices. Mason took a bill from his pocket, indicated one of the cards. "I like this one," he said. "Make it 'R. L. Montaine, one twenty-eight East Pelton Avenue.' Down in the left-hand corner put 'Insurance and Investments.' "

"It'll take me just a minute or two to get the type ready," the printer said, handing Mason his change. "Would you like to wait here or come back?"

"I'll be back," Mason said. He crossed to a drug store, telephoned his office, learned that Della had received no message as yet from Rhoda Montaine. He sat at the counter, sipped a chocolate malted milk meditatively, and let minutes slip by unnoticed. At length he crossed the street to the printer, and received the stack of freshly printed cards. He returned to the drug store, called his office again.

"Paul Drake has uncovered the marriage license," Della Street told him. "It's a Carl W. Montaine. The address was Chicago, Illinois; but there's a water and gas connection for a Carl W. Montaine at twenty-three hundred nine Hawthorne Avenue. It was made within the last week. — The license said she was a widow — Rhoda Lorton. Drake wants to know how strong you want him to go on expenses."

"Tell him," Mason instructed, "to go as strong as he has to in order to get results. I've apparently accepted a retainer to represent a client. I'm going to represent her."

"Don't you think," Della Street asked, "that you've done enough, chief? After all, it wasn't your fault. You didn't know about the retainer."

"No," Mason told her, "I *should* have known about the retainer. Anyhow, I'm going to see this thing through."

"But she knows where to come to get *you*."

"She won't come back."

"Not even when she knows she left her purse?"

"No," Mason said. "She must have recollected where she left it by this time; she's afraid to come back because of the gun."

"It's after four," Della Street pointed out. "The offices will be closing. Drake's got about all the official information he can get for tonight."

"Has he heard about the gun yet?"

"Not yet. He expects to hear before five."

"Okay," Mason said, "you stick around, Della, until I give you another buzz. If this girl calls in, be sure to hold her. Tell her we know her real name and address. That will bring her in."

"By the way," Della Street remarked, "there's something I thought you should know."

"What is it?"

"The number of Nell Brinley, that you told me to call, is Drenton nine-four-two-six-eight. The number that Rhoda Montaine left for us to call when she was in the office is Drenton six-eight-nine-four-two. She just took the last two numbers off of Nell Brinley's telephone number and put them on the front part of the number. That must mean that she's pretty familiar with that telephone number, because she rattled it off when I asked her. She must have lived at that address and used that telephone before she was married."

Perry Mason chuckled. "Good girl," he said. "Stick around until you hear from me again."

He hung up the receiver, mopped perspiration from his forehead, and walked briskly around the corner to the main office of the telegraph company. Approaching the counter, Perry Mason pulled a telegraph blank toward him, took a pencil from his pocket, spread the purloined telegram flat on the counter and frowned. He looked up and caught the eye of an attendant. She came to him, and Mason pulled one of the freshly printed cards from his pocket. "I would like," he said, "a little special service."

The young woman picked up the card, nodded and smiled. "Very well, Mr. Montaine, what can we do for you?"

"I received this telegram on an important business deal and I've lost the address. I understand your company requires the senders to leave their address on file in connection with any wire sent. There's some key number on this telegram. I am wondering if you can find the address of the sender by taking this key number and running down your records?"

"I think so," the young woman said, taking both his card and the message and walking toward the back of the room.

Perry Mason scrawled a telegram, addressing it only to "Gregory," leaving the address blank, "IMPORTANT DEVELOPMENTS NECESSITATE INDEFINITE POSTPONEMENT CALLING IN PERSON TO EXPLAIN." He signed the telegram "R. Montaine," and waited for the clerk to return.

She returned within less than five minutes with the name and address of the sender written on the message in a pencil notation. Mason studied the notation for a moment, nodded, and wrote the name "Moxley" after the word "Gregory," added below it "Colemont Apartments, 316 Norwalk Avenue." "Thank you very much," he said. "Please send this telegram."

"And now," smiled the attendant, "I'll have to ask *you* to fill in *your* address."

"Oh, certainly," he said, and wrote, "R. Montaine, 128 East Pelton Avenue."

He paid for the telegram, left the telegraph office and summoned a cab. "Three sixteen Norwalk Avenue," he said. He leaned back in the cushions, lit a cigarette and watched the passing scenery with thought-slitted eyes. By the time the cigarette was consumed, the cab pulled in at the curb.

The Colemont Apartments was a huge two-story building that had at one time been a residence. As the small numbered blocks of Norwalk Avenue had become choice apartment sites, the owners had remodeled the huge residence into four apartments. Perry Mason noticed that three of the apartments, apparently, were vacant. The influx of more modern apartment houses on either side had spelled disaster for the made-over private residence. In a short time it would be torn down to make way, in turn, for a larger apartment. Mason pressed the button on Apartment B, opposite the pasteboard slip on which appeared the words "Gregory Moxley."

Almost immediately there was the sound of an

electric buzzer releasing the door catch; the lawyer pushed open the door. A long flight of stairs loomed ahead of him. He climbed the stairs, heard the sound of motion in the corridor and then nodded to a man whose figure loomed at the head of the stairs. The man was some thirty-six years of age, with quick, watchful eyes, a ready smile, and a genial manner. Despite the heat of the day, his clothes were flawless and he wore them with distinction. He emanated an atmosphere of physical well-being and prosperity. "Good afternoon," he said. "I'm afraid I don't know you. I was expecting a visitor who had an appointment with me."

"You mean Rhoda?" asked Perry Mason.

For a swift instant the man stiffened as though bracing himself for a blow. Then the booming geniality was once more apparent in his voice. "Oh," he said, "then I was right after all. Come on up, come in and sit down. What's your name?"

"Mason."

"Glad to know you, Mr. Mason."

A hand shot out, gripped Perry Mason's hand in a firm, cordial clasp.

"You're Moxley?" Mason asked.

"Yes, Gregory Moxley. Come on in. Certainly is hot, isn't it?" He led the way to a library, indicated a chair.

The room was comfortably furnished, although the furniture was rather old-fashioned. The windows were open. Across fifteen feet of space loomed the side of a modern apartment house. Mason sat down, crossed his legs, reached mechanically for his cigarette case. "That other apartment house shuts out some of your ventilation, doesn't it?" he asked.

Moxley gave it a frowning glance of annoyance.

"It raises hell with both my privacy *and* my ventilation. On days like this it makes an oven out of my apartment."

Moxley grinned good-naturedly. It was the grin of one who has learned to take the world philosophically, accepting the bitter as well as the sweet.

"I presume," Mason said, "it won't be long before they tear this apartment down and put up one of those big apartments here."

"I suppose," Moxley agreed, his eyes studying Mason's face in thoughtful appraisal, "that it's inevitable. Personally, I don't like it. I like small apartment houses. I don't like these big places where there's a manager constantly snooping around, and an air of impersonal efficiency."

"You seem to be the only tenant in this place," the lawyer went on.

Moxley's laugh was quick and contagious. "Did you come here to discuss real estate?" he asked.

Mason joined in his laugh. "Hardly," he said.

"What did you come to discuss?"

Mason stared steadily at the man's watchful eyes.

"I came," he said, "as a friend of Rhoda."

Moxley nodded. "Yes," he said, "I presumed as much. I didn't suppose you had . . ."

The words were interrupted by the sound of a harshly strident bell which exploded the hot silence of the afternoon. Moxley frowned, looked at Perry Mason. "Was any one," he asked, "coming here to join you?" Mason shook his head.

Moxley seemed undecided. The smile faded from his face. The look of genial urbanity vanished. His eyes hardened into speculative appraisal. The lines of his face were grim. He got up from his chair without a word of excuse, walked on noiseless feet to the doorway, and stood where he could see both the corridor and Perry Mason.

The bell rang again. Moxley pressed a button, and stood waiting while an electric buzzer released the door catch. "Who is it?" he called in a voice that had entirely lost its booming cordiality.

"Telegram," said a man's voice. There were steps on the stairs, a rustle of paper, then steps going down the stairs and the slamming of the front door.

Moxley walked back to the room, tearing the envelope open. He unfolded the message, read it, then looked suspiciously at Perry Mason.

"This message," he said, "is from Rhoda."

"Uh huh," Perry Mason said, apparently without interest.

"She doesn't," said Moxley, "say anything about you."

"She wouldn't," Mason remarked casually.

"Why?"

"Because she didn't know I was coming."

Moxley had lost all of that veneer of quick friendliness. His eyes were hard and watchful. "Go on," he said, "tell me the rest of it."

"I'm a friend of hers," Mason said.

"You told me that before."

"I came here as a friend."

"That also is no news to me."

"I'm an attorney."

Moxley took a deep breath, walked with quick, purposeful steps across the room to a table, stood with his right hand resting on the knob of the drawer in that table.

"Now," he said, "you *are* telling me something."

"I thought I might be," Perry Mason said. "That's why I took pains to tell you that I came as a friend."

"I don't understand."

"I mean that I came here as a friend and not as a lawyer. Rhoda didn't retain me. Rhoda didn't know that I was coming."

"Then why did you come?"

"Simply as a matter of personal satisfaction."

"What do you want?"

"I want to know just what it is you're trying to get out of Rhoda."

"For a friend," Moxley said, his right hand remaining on the knob of the drawer, "you do a lot of talking."

"I'm ready to do a lot of listening," Mason told him.

Moxley's laugh was sneering. "What you're willing to do and what you're going to do," he remarked, "may not be the same." Moxley was no longer the genial host, no longer the hail-fellow-well-met. The ready friendliness of his manner had evaporated into a cold, watchful hostility.

"Suppose," Mason said, "I tell you my story?"

"Suppose you do."

"I'm an attorney. Something happened which caused me to interest myself in Rhoda. It doesn't make any difference what it was. Unfortunately, I can't get in touch with Rhoda. I knew you were in touch with her. Therefore, I decided to get in touch with you. I want you to tell me where I can find Rhoda."

"So you can help her?" asked Moxley.

"So I can help her."

Moxley's left hand drummed steadily on the top of the table. His right hand had left the knob of the drawer, but seemed to be held in poised readiness.

"For a lawyer," he said, "you talk like a damn fool."

Mason shrugged his shoulders. "Possibly I do."

After a moment, Moxley said, "So Rhoda spilled her guts to you, did she?"

"I have told you," Perry Mason said, "the exact truth."

"You're still not answering my question."

"I don't have to answer your question," Mason told him. "If you're not going to tell me anything then I'm going to tell you something."

"Go ahead and tell me," Moxley remarked.

"Rhoda Montaine," Mason said, "is a nice kid."

"Are *you*," inquired Moxley, "telling *me?*"

"I intended to help Rhoda Montaine."

"You told me that before."

"About a week ago Rhoda Montaine was married to Carl W. Montaine."

"That's no news to me."

"Rhoda's name before she was married was Lorton."

"Go on," Moxley said.

"Her application for license to marry says that she was a widow. The first name of the former husband was Gregory."

"Go on."

"I was just wondering," Perry Mason said, his face utterly without expression, "if perhaps Rhoda might have been mistaken."

"Mistaken about what?"

"About being a widow. If, for instance, the man she married hadn't really died, but had only disappeared for the statutory period of seven years. That makes a presumption of death. It's only a presumption. If the man showed up, alive and well, he'd still be her husband."

Moxley's eyes were glittering now with hostility.

"You seem to know a lot," he said, "for a friend."

Perry Mason's eyes were purposeful. "I'm learning more every minute," he commented.

"You've got a lot to learn yet."

"Such as?"

"Such as not butting into things that don't concern you."

A telephone began to ring with mechanical regularity, a steady insistence. Moxley wet his lips with the tip of his tongue, hesitated for several seconds, then walked warily around Mason to the telephone. He picked up the receiver with his left hand, clamped the last two fingers of the hand against the rubber mouthpiece, raised the receiver to his ear, the telephone to his lips. "What is it?" he asked.

The receiver made rasping, metallic noises. "Not now," Moxley said. "I've got visitors. . . . I tell you, not now. . . . You should know who the visitor is. . . . I say you *should*. I'm not mentioning any names, but you can draw your own conclusions. . . . He's a lawyer. His name is Mason."

Perry Mason jumped to his feet. "If that's Rhoda," he said, "I want to talk with her."

He strode toward the man at the telephone. Moxley's face twisted with rage. He doubled his right hand into a fist, shouted, "Get back!"

Mason continued to advance. Moxley

47

grabbed the telephone in his right hand, the receiver in his left, started to hang up. "Rhoda," called Perry Mason in a loud voice, "telephone my office!"

Moxley slammed the receiver back into position. His face twisted into a snarl of hatred. "Damn you!" he said. "You've got no business butting into this."

Mason shrugged his shoulders, said, "I've told you what I wanted to say," put on his hat, turned his back on Moxley and walked slowly down the long flight of stairs. Moxley came to the head of the stairs, stood staring with silent hostility at the broad shoulders of the departing attorney. Mason slammed the front door shut, stepped into his cab, drove three blocks to a drug store and telephoned Della Street. "Anything new?" he asked.

"Yes," she said, "we've chased back the records on Rhoda Montaine. She was Rhoda Lorton, wife of Gregory Lorton, and Gregory Lorton died in February of nineteen hundred and twenty-nine of pneumonia. The attending physician was Dr. Claude Millsap. He signed the death certificate."

"Where does Dr. Millsap live?"

"The Teresita Apartments — nineteen twenty-eight Beechwood Street."

"What else?" he asked.

"We've traced the gun that was in the purse."

"What did you find out?"

"The gun," she said, "was sold to Claude

Millsap, who gave the address as nineteen twenty-eight Beechwood Street."

Perry Mason gave a low whistle. "Anything else?" he asked.

"That's all so far. Drake wants to know how much work you want him to do."

"He can lay off on the other stuff," Mason said, "but I want him to find out all he can about a man named Gregory Moxley, who lives in the Colemont Apartments, three sixteen Norwalk Avenue."

"Want him to put a shadow on Moxley?"

"No," Mason said, "that won't be necessary. In fact, it would be very inadvisable, because Moxley has got a brittle disposition and I don't know just what his tie-up in the case is."

Della Street's voice showed she was worried. "Listen, chief," she cautioned, "aren't you getting in rather deep on this thing?"

Perry Mason's tone was once more good-natured and lighthearted. "I'm having the time of my life, Della," he said. "I'm earning my retainer."

"I'll say you are!" she exclaimed.

Chapter 5

Perry Mason left the telephone and approached the drug counter.

"What's 'Ipral?' " he asked.

The clerk studied him for a moment. "A hypnotic."

"What's a hypnotic?"

"A species of sedative. It induces sleep, not a drugged sleep, but a restful slumber. In proper doses there's no after effect."

"Would it act like knock-out drops?"

"Not at all — not in any proper dose. I told you, it induces a natural, restful and deep slumber. Can I? . . ."

Mason nodded, turned away from the counter. "Thanks," he said.

He emerged from the drug store whistling lightheartedly. The cab driver jumped to the sidewalk, opened the door of the cab. "Where to?" he asked.

Perry Mason frowned speculatively, as though weighing two possible plans of campaign in his mind. Three blocks down the street a car swung into Norwalk Avenue, the body swaying far over on the springs with the momentum of the turn.

Mason's eyes focused on it, and the eyes of the cab driver followed those of Mason. "Sure is coming," said the cab driver.

"A woman driving," Mason observed.

Abruptly, Mason stepped from the curb, held up his hand. The Chevrolet swerved toward the curb. Tires protested as brakes were applied. Rhoda Montaine's flushed face stared at Perry Mason. The car jerked to a dead stop.

The lawyer's first words were as casual as though he had been expecting her. "I've got your purse," he said.

"I know it," she told him. "I knew it before I'd gone half a block from your office. I started back after it, and then decided to let it go. I figured you'd open it and ask a lot of questions. I didn't want to answer them. What were you doing at Gregory's?"

Perry Mason turned to the cab driver. "That, buddy," he said, "is all."

He extended a bill, which the cab driver took, staring in puzzled speculation at the woman in the coupe. Mason jerked open the door of the car, climbed in beside Rhoda Montaine and grinned at her. "Sorry," he said. "I didn't know you'd left a retainer. When I found out about it I did what I could to help you."

Her eyes were glittering points of black indignation. "Did you call it helping me to bust in on Gregory?" He nodded. "Well," she said bitterly, "you've raised the devil. As soon as I knew you were there, I started to drive out as quickly as I

51

could. You've spilled the beans now."

"Why didn't you keep your five o'clock appointment?" he asked.

"Because I couldn't reach a decision. I telephoned him, to tell him that he'd have to wait until later."

"How much later?"

"A lot later."

"What," asked Perry Mason, "does he want?"

"That," she said, "is none of your business."

The lawyer stared at her speculatively, and said, "That is one of the things you were going to tell me when you called at my office. Why won't you tell me now?"

"I wasn't going to tell you."

"You would have if I hadn't hurt your pride."

"Well, you did!"

Mason laughed. "Look here," he said. "Let's not work at cross purposes. I've been trying to get in touch with you all day."

"I presume," she said, "you went through my purse."

"Every bit of it," he admitted. "What's more, I purloined your telegram, went to see Nell Brinley, started detectives to work getting all the dope I could."

"What did you find out?"

"Plenty," he said. "Who's Doctor Millsap?"

She caught her breath in quick consternation. "A friend," she explained vaguely.

"Does your husband know him?"

"No." Mason's shoulders gave an eloquent

shrug. "How did you find out about him?" she asked after a moment.

"Oh, I've been getting around," he told her. "I've been trying to put myself in a position to help you."

"You can't help me," she said, "except by telling me the one thing, and then leaving me alone."

"What one thing do you want to know?"

"Whether, after a man has disappeared for seven years, he's presumed to be dead."

"Under certain circumstances he is, yes. It's seven years in some cases, five in others."

There was vast relief on her countenance. "Then," she said, "a subsequent marriage would be legal."

Mason's face was lined with sympathy as he slowly shook his head. "I'm sorry, Mrs. Montaine," he said, "but that's only a presumption. If Gregory Moxley is really Gregory Lorton, your first husband, and he showed up alive and well, your marriage to Carl Montaine is voidable."

She looked at him with eyes that were dark with suffering. Slow tears welled up in them. Her lips quivered. "I love him so," she said simply.

Perry Mason's hand dropped to her shoulder, patted it reassuringly. It was the impersonal gesture of the protective male. "Tell me about him," he invited.

"Oh," she said, "you wouldn't understand.

No *man* would understand. I can't even understand, myself. I nursed him when he was sick. He had a drug habit and his folks would have died if they'd known. I'm a trained nurse, you know — that is, I was."

"Go on," Mason said. "Everything."

"I can't tell you about my marriage to Gregory," she said, her lips quivering. "That was ghastly. It happened when I was just a kid — young, innocent and impressionable. He was attractive — and nine years older than I was. People warned me against him, and I thought it was just jealousy and envy. He had that air of sophisticated deference that captivates a kid."

"Go on," Mason prompted as she paused.

"I had a little money saved up. Well, he took it and skipped out."

Mason's eyes narrowed. "Did you give him the money," he asked, "or did he steal it?"

"He stole it. I gave it to him to buy some stock. He told me about a wonderful bargain he could get by picking up some securities from a friend who was hard up. I gave him the money. He went out and never came back. I'll never forget the way he kissed me just before he beat it with all of my money."

"Did you tell the police?" Mason asked.

She shook her head, said, "Not about the money. I thought he had been in an accident of some kind, and I got the police to look over the records of accidents, and I telephoned all of the hospitals. It was a long time before I realized what had really happened. I was frantic."

"Why not have him arrested?" Mason asked.

"I don't dare to."

"Why?"

"I can't tell you."

"Why can't you tell me?"

"It's something I don't dare tell any one. It's something that has driven me to the verge of suicide."

"Was that what the gun was for?"

"No."

"You intended to kill Moxley?" She was silent. "Was that," Mason inquired, "why you wanted to know about the *corpus delicti?*"

Again she was silent. Mason pressed his finger into her shoulder. "Look here," he said, "you've got a lot on your mind. You need some one to confide in. I can help you. Suppose you tell me the truth and the whole truth?"

"I can't, it's terrible. I wouldn't dare to tell you the truth!"

"Does your husband know about any of this?" Mason asked.

"Good heavens, no! If you understood about his background you wouldn't ask."

"All right, what's his background?"

"Did you," she asked, "ever hear of C. Phillip Montaine of Chicago?"

"No, what about him?"

"He's a very wealthy man — one of those old fogies who traces his ancestry back to the Revolution, and all that sort of stuff. Carl is his son.

C. Phillip Montaine disapproved of me, very, very much. He's never seen me. But the idea of his son marrying a nurse came as a shock to the old man."

"You've met the father?" Mason asked. "After the marriage?"

"No, but I've seen his letters to Carl."

"Did he know Carl was going to marry you, before the wedding?"

"No. We ran away and were married."

"And Carl is very much under the influence of his father?" Mason queried.

She nodded vigorously. "You'd have to see Carl to understand. He's still weak — mentally and morally — because of the drug habit he had. That is, he hasn't a strong will power." She flushed, realizing what she was saying. "He'll be all right in time. You know what drugs do to a man." She went on nervously. "Now, he's still easily influenced. He's nervous. He's very impressionable."

"You see all of those defects in his character clearly," Mason said, in thoughtful speculation, "and yet you love him?"

"I love him," she said, "more than anything in the world. And I'm going to make a man of him. All he needs is time, and some one strong to help him. You'd have to understand what I went through, in order to realize how I love him and why I love him. I went through hell for years after my first marriage. I wanted desperately to commit suicide, and yet I didn't have the nerve.

56

That first marriage killed something in me. I could never love any man the way I could have loved my first husband. After that I didn't want that same kind of marriage. I suppose there's a lot of the maternal in my love now. My first love was that of illusion. I wanted a man to worship, a man to look up to — oh, you know." She broke off.

"Does your husband," asked Perry Mason, "appreciate that kind of love?"

"He will," she said. "He's been accustomed to knuckling under to his father. He's had it drilled into him that his family name and his family position are the two main things in life. He wants to go through life carried on the shoulders of his dead ancestors. He thinks family means everything. It's become a species of obsession."

"Now," Mason told her, "we're commencing to get somewhere. You're telling me the things that are on your mind, and you're feeling better already."

She shook her head in quick negation. "No," she said. "I can't tell you all. No matter how sympathetic you might be. After all, what I wanted to find out was about the legality of my marriage to Carl. I can stand anything if that marriage is only legal; but if he can walk away and leave me, or if his father can take him from me, it will break my heart."

"If," Mason said slowly, "he's the type who would walk away and leave you, don't you think you're wasting your affection on him?"

"That's just what I've been trying to make clear," she said. "It's because he is that type that he needs me and that makes me love him. He's weak, I love him and perhaps one reason is because he's weak. I've had enough of strong, purposeful, magnetic men who sweep me off my feet. I don't want to be swept off my feet. Perhaps it's a starved mother complex, perhaps it's just being goofy — I don't know. I can't explain it. It's the way I feel. You can't explain your feelings — you can only recognize them."

"What," asked Perry Mason, "is it you're keeping from me?"

"Something horrible," she told him.

"You're going to tell me?"

"No."

"Wouldn't you have told me if I'd been more sympathetic when you called at my office?"

"Good heavens, no!" she exclaimed. "I never intended to tell you *this* much. I thought you'd fall for that line about the friend who wanted the legal information. I'd rehearsed it in front of a mirror. I'd gone over it hundreds of times. I knew just what I was going to say and just what you were going to say. And then you saw that I was lying, and I was afraid. I was never so afraid in my life as I was when I left your office. I was so afraid, that I went down in the elevator and walked for half a block before I realized that I'd left my purse behind. That was a terrible shock. Then I didn't dare to go back after it. I started back, but I couldn't bear the thought of facing

58

you. I decided to let it wait until afterwards."

"Until after what?" Mason inquired.

"Until after I'd found some way out of the mess."

There was sympathy in the eyes of the lawyer. He said simply, "I wish you wouldn't look at me that way. — Your husband disappeared. You married in good faith, after you thought he was dead. You can't be blamed. You can go ahead and get a divorce from him and re-marry Carl Montaine."

She blinked tears from her eyes, but her lips were firm. "You don't understand Carl," she said. "If this marriage isn't good, I could never get a divorce and then re-marry Carl."

"Not even if you took a chance on a Mexican divorce?" Mason asked.

"Not even then." There was a moment of silence.

"Are you going to confide in me?" the lawyer asked. She shook her head. "Promise me one thing, then," he told her.

"What?"

"That you'll come to my office first thing in the morning. Sleep on it and see if you don't feel differently tomorrow."

"But," she said, "you don't understand. You don't . . ." A look of decision stamped itself upon her face. A cunning glint appeared in her eyes.

"Very well," she said, "I'll make you that promise."

"And now," Mason told her, "you can drive

me back to my office."

"No," she objected, "I can't. I've got to get back to my husband. He'll be expecting me. I was simply furious when I learned that you had gone to see Gregory. I didn't know what might happen. I came tearing out here to try and locate you. Now I've got to get back."

Mason nodded. His cab driver, hopeful of picking up a fare back to town, having learned from experience that merely because a man enters a car with a woman doesn't mean that he may not get out again, was waiting at the curb. Perry Mason snapped back the catch on the door. "To-morrow morning at nine o'clock?" he asked.

"Make it nine thirty," she suggested.

Mason nodded assent, smiled reassuringly at her. "To-morrow," he said, "you'll find that it isn't going to be hard to tell. You've told me enough now so that you can tell me the rest. I can almost figure it out for myself."

Her eyes regarded him wistfully, then hardened. "At nine thirty," she said, and laughed, a quick, nervous laugh. Mason closed the door. She snapped back the gearshift and the car growled into speed.

Mason nodded to the cab driver. "Well, buddy," he said, "you get to take me back after all."

The cabby turned away to hide his grin. "Okay, chief," he said.

Chapter 6

Perry Mason emerged from the garage where he kept his car, started to walk the half block to his office. A newsboy on the corner whipped a newspaper from under his arm, twisted it in a double fold. "Read all about it!" he screamed. "She hit him and he died! Read about it."

Mason purchased the newspaper, unfolded it, glanced at the headlines which streamed across the top of the page.

MIDNIGHT VISITOR KILLS CROOK
Woman May Have Clubbed Confidence Man

Mason folded the newspaper, pushed his way into the stream of pedestrians converging on the skyscraper entrance. As he entered a crowded elevator, a man touched his arm. "Good morning, Counselor," he said. "Have you read about it?"

Perry Mason shook his head. "I seldom read crime news. I see enough of it at first hand."

"Clever stunt you pulled in that last case of yours, Counselor."

Mason smiled his thanks mechanically. The man, having broken the conversational ice, was showing symptoms of that type of loquacity which is so well known to those who are in the public eye, a loquacity which is caused not so much by a desire to convey any particular idea, as to lay a foundation for repeating the conversation to friends, beginning in a carefully casual manner, "The other day when I was talking things over with Perry Mason, I suggested to him . . ."

"Nice of you," murmured Mason, as the elevator stopped at his floor.

"I tell you what I'd do, Counselor, if I were handling this case. The first thing I'd do would be to . . ."

Mason never knew when he might have that man sitting in a jury box as a juror, long after Mason himself had forgotten about the conversation, so his smile was cordial as the elevator door cut off the suggestion, but a look of relief flooded his features as he walked briskly down the corridor to his office and opened the door.

Della Street's eyes were dark with concern. "Have you seen it, chief?" she asked.

He raised his brows. She indicated the paper under his arm. "Just the headlines," he told her. "Some confidence man bumped off. Was it some one we know?"

Della Street's face was more eloquent than words.

Perry Mason pushed on to his private office, spread the newspaper out on the desk and read the account:

"While occupants of the Bellaire Apartments

62

at 308 Norwalk Avenue frantically telephoned for police at an early hour this morning, Gregory Moxley, thirty-six, residing at the Colemont Apartments, 316 Norwalk Avenue, lay dying from skull injuries inflicted by an unidentified assailant who may have been a woman.

"The police received a telephone call at 2:27 A.M. The call was relayed over the radio, and car 62, operated by Officers Harry Exter and Bob Milton, made a fast run to the Colemont Apartments, where they forced the door of Apartment B on the upper floor and found Gregory Moxley alive but unconscious. The occupant of the apartment was fully clothed, although the bed had been slept in. He was lying face downward on the floor, hands clutching at the carpet. An iron poker lying nearby, with blood stains on it, had evidently been used to strike at least one terrific blow. It had crushed the man's skull.

"The radio officers put in a hurried call for an ambulance, but Moxley died on the way to the hospital without regaining consciousness.

"At headquarters, police identified the body as being that of Gregory Carey, alias Gregory Lorton, a notorious confidence man whose activities were well known to the police. His method of operation was to fascinate an attractive but not too beautiful young woman of the working class who had saved some money. Using an assumed name, Moxley would court his victim. His suave manner, pleasing personality, well-tailored clothes and glib tongue made

63

women fall easy prey to the wiles of the swindler and usually resulted in money being turned over for 'investment.' When it became necessary to do so, the confidence man had no hesitancy about going through a marriage ceremony under one of many aliases. Police state that he may have married large numbers of young women, many of whom never made complaint when Moxley subsequently disappeared.

"That his assailant may well have been a woman is indicated by the statement of Benjamin Crandall, owner of a chain of service stations, who, with his wife, occupies Apartment 269 in the Bellaire Apartments. Between this apartment and the one occupied by the murdered man in the Colemont Apartments to the north there is an air line distance of less than twenty feet. The night was very warm and windows in both apartments were open.

"Some time during the night Crandall and his wife were awakened by the insistent ring of a telephone bell. They then heard Moxley's voice pleading with some one for 'a little more time.'

"Neither Crandall nor his wife can place the exact time of the conversation, although it must have been after midnight, because they did not retire until 11:50, and it was probably before two o'clock in the morning, because Moxley told the party at the other end of the telephone wire that he had an appointment with 'Rhoda' for two o'clock in the morning and that she would undoubtedly bring him more than sufficient funds to take care of his obligations.

"Both Crandall and his wife remember the name of 'Rhoda.' Crandall thinks the woman's surname was also mentioned, that it may have been a foreign name; that it ended in 'ayne' or 'ane.' The first part of the name was spoken very rapidly and he did not hear it distinctly.

"Following the telephone conversation, Crandall and his wife expressed annoyance at the disturbance and there was some talk of closing the window. Nothing, however, was done and, as Crandall stated to the police: 'I drifted off to sleep, was sort of half dozing when I heard conversations in Moxley's apartment. Then I heard a masculine voice that seemed to be raised in argument. There was a sound that may have been a blow, and then the sound of something falling with a jar.

" 'During this time, and at the very moment the blow was struck, the doorbell in Moxley's apartment was ringing as though some one was trying to get Moxley to open the street door. I drifted off to sleep once more and was awakened by my wife, who insisted that I should call the police. I went to the window, looked across to Moxley's apartment. I could see that the lights were on and in a wall mirror I could see the feet of a man who was apparently lying on the floor. I went to the telephone and called the police. The time was then approximately twenty-five minutes past two.'

"Mrs. Crandall says she did not go back to

65

sleep after she was awakened by the ringing of the telephone bell in Moxley's apartment; that she heard the conversation over the telephone concerning the woman named Rhoda; that thereafter she lay 'just dozing,' not fully awake and not asleep; that she heard the sound of low voices coming from Moxley's apartment and then the sound of a woman's voice, apparently that of a rather young woman, speaking rapidly; that she heard Moxley's voice raised in anger, then a sound that she feels certain was that of a blow, the noise of something thudding to the floor and then silence; that immediately preceding the sound of the blow, the doorbell in Moxley's apartment was ringing with steady, insistent rings, as though some one were holding his thumb against the bell, ringing steadily for long intervals, pausing for a moment and then ringing again. She says that the ringing continued for some minutes after the sound of the blow and that she thinks the party who was ringing secured admittance, because she heard whispers coming from the apartment, followed by a noise that may have been the gentle closing of the door and then silence. She lay for fifteen or twenty minutes, trying to go back to sleep, and then, feeling that the police should be notified, awakened her husband and suggested that he make an investigation.

"Police have a very definite clue as to the identity of the slayer. The woman who entered Moxley's apartment and who either inflicted the

66

blow which caused death or who was present when the blows were struck dropped from her gloved hands a leather key container containing the key to a padlock which police feel certain is used to lock the doors of a private garage, as well as keys to two closed cars. From the make of these keys, police have ascertained that one car is a Chevrolet and one is a Plymouth. They are, therefore, checking the automobile registrations to list all persons who own both Chevrolets and Plymouths, as well as taking steps to identify the garage key. Because of the fact that the woman evidently had access to two cars, police are inclined to think she is a married woman whose husband maintains two cars for the use of his family. Photographic reproductions of the keys appear on page 3.

"Because of the absence of fingerprints on the murder weapon, police feel that it was wielded by a woman who wore gloves. They are slightly puzzled by the fact that there are no fingerprints of any sort on either the murder weapon or the knob of the door. Police feel, however, that in this case fingerprints are secondary in importance to the positive identification of the mysterious visitor through the padlock-key which was left in the room.

"Moxley's police record shows that his real name is Gregory Carey, that on September 15, 1929, he was sentenced to San Quentin for the term of four years for . . . (Continued on page 2, column 1)."

Perry Mason was turning to page two when Della Street knocked perfunctorily and slipped quietly into the private office, closing the door carefully behind her. Perry Mason looked up with a frown.

"Her husband's in the office," she said.

"Montaine?" asked Perry Mason. She nodded. Perry Mason half closed his eyes in thought. "Could you get any statement from him about what he wanted, Della?"

"No. He said he'd have to talk with you; that it was a matter of life and death."

"Did he try to find out if his wife had been here yesterday?"

"No."

"How does he seem?"

"Nervous," Della Street said. "He's pale as a ghost. There are dark rings under his eyes. He hasn't shaved this morning, and his collar is wilted at the top, as though he'd been perspiring."

"What kind of a looking chap is he, Della?"

"He's short and small-boned. His clothes are expensive, but he doesn't wear them well. His mouth is weak. I have an idea he may be a year or two younger than she is. He's the sort of man who could be petulant if he wasn't frightened. He hasn't lived enough to be sure of himself or of any one else."

Perry Mason smiled. "Della," he said, "some day I'm going to let you sit beside me when I'm picking a jury. So far you've never failed to call the turn."

"You know about him?" she asked.

"Darn near *all* about him," the lawyer admitted. "Do you think we can keep him waiting while I finish this newspaper article?"

She shook her head swiftly. "That's why I came in to see you. He's frightfully impatient. I wouldn't be surprised if he left the office if you tried to keep him waiting."

Mason reluctantly folded the paper, thrust it in the drawer of his desk. "Send him in," he said.

Della Street held the door open. "Mr. Mason will see you, Mr. Montaine."

A man slightly below medium height entered the office with quick, restless steps, walked to the edge of Perry Mason's desk, and waited for Della Street to close the door before he spoke. Then he spilled words with the rattling speed of a child reciting poetry. "My name is Carl W. Montaine. I'm the son of C. Phillip Montaine, the Chicago multi-millionaire. You've probably heard of him."

The lawyer shook his head.

"You've seen the morning papers?" Montaine asked.

"I've looked at the headlines," Mason said. "I haven't had a chance to read the paper thoroughly. Sit down."

Montaine crossed to the big leather chair, sat on the extreme end of it, leaning forward. A mop of hair hung over his forehead. He brushed it back with an impatient gesture of his palm. "Did you read about the murder?"

Perry Mason wrinkled his brow, as though trying to focus some vague recollection in his memory. "Yes, I noticed it in the headlines. Why?"

Montaine came even closer to the edge of the chair, until he seemed almost ready to slide to the floor. "My wife," he said, "is going to be accused of that murder."

"Did she do it?"

"No." Mason studied the young man in silent appraisal. "She *couldn't* have done it," Montaine said forcefully. "She isn't capable of it. She's mixed up in it some way, though. She knows who did do it. If she doesn't know, she suspects. *I* think she knows, and she's shielding him. She's been his tool all along. Unless we can save her, this man will get her in such a position that no one can save her. Right now she's trying to shield him. He's hiding behind her skirts. She'll lie to protect him, and then he will gradually get her in deeper and deeper. You've got to save her."

"The murder," Mason reminded him, "was committed around two o'clock in the morning. Wasn't your wife home then?"

"No."

"How do you know?"

"It's a long story. I'd have to begin at the beginning."

Mason's tone was crisply definite. "Begin, then, at the beginning," he commanded. "Sit back in the chair and relax. Tell me the whole thing from the very beginning."

Montaine slid back into the recesses of the

70

leather chair, whipped his hand to his forehead with that quick, nervous gesture of brushing his hair back. His eyes were a reddish-brown. They were fastened on Perry Mason's face, as the eyes of a crippled dog might fasten themselves upon a veterinary.

"Go ahead," Mason said.

"My name is Carl Montaine. I'm the son of C. Phillip Montaine, the Chicago multi-millionaire."

"You told me that before," the lawyer said.

"I finished college," Montaine said. "My father wanted me to go into business. I wanted to see something of the world. I traveled for a year. Then I came here. I was very nervous. I had acute appendicitis. It was necessary for me to be operated on immediately. My father was tied up with a very involved financial matter. There were many thousands of dollars involved. He couldn't come here. I went to the Sunnyside Hospital and had the best medical attention that money could buy. My father saw to that. I had a special nurse night and day. The night nurse was named Lorton — Rhoda Lorton." Montaine stopped impressively, as though the words would convey some significance to Perry Mason.

"Go ahead," the lawyer said.

Montaine dug his elbows into the leather arms of the chair, hitched himself farther forward. "I married her," he blurted. His manner was that of a man who has confessed to some crime.

"I see," Mason remarked, as though marrying

71

nurses was the customary procedure of all con-valescents.

Montaine hitched forward to the edge of the chair once more and pushed back his hair. "You can imagine how that must have seemed to my father," he said. "I am an only child. The Montaine line must be carried on through me. I had married a nurse."

"What's wrong with marrying a nurse?" the lawyer asked.

"Nothing. You don't understand. I'm trying to explain this from my father's viewpoint."

"Why bother about your father's viewpoint?"

"Because it's important."

"All right, then, go ahead."

"Out of a clear sky, my father gets a telegram announcing that I have married Rhoda Lorton, the nurse who was employed on the case."

"You didn't tell him you intended to marry her?"

"No, I hardly knew, myself. It was one of those impulses."

"Why didn't you become engaged to her and notify him of that?"

"Because he would have objected. He would have made a great deal of trouble. I wanted to marry her more than I had ever wanted anything in the world. I knew that if I gave him any notice of my intentions, I could never carry them out. He would have discontinued my allowance, or-dered me to come home, done almost any-thing."

"Go ahead," Mason said.

"Well, I married her. I wired my father. He was very nice about it. He was still working on the business deal I spoke of and couldn't leave. He wanted us to come to Chicago to visit him. But Rhoda didn't want to go right away. She wanted to wait a little while."

"So you didn't go."

"No, we didn't go."

"Your father didn't like that?"

"I don't think he liked it."

"You wanted to tell me about a murder," Mason prompted.

"Have you a morning paper here in the office?" Mason opened the drawer of his desk, took out the newspaper he had been reading when Della Street had announced Carl Montaine. "Turn to page three, please," Montaine said.

Mason turned to the third page of the newspaper. The photograph of a key, reproduced in its exact size, appeared in the center of the third page. Below the picture appeared the words, "DID THE KILLER DROP THIS KEY?"

Montaine took a leather key container from his pocket, detached a key, handed it to Perry Mason. "Compare them," he said.

Mason held the key over the photograph, then placed the key on the other side of the paper, made a pencil tracing, slowly nodded his head. "How does it happen," he inquired, "that *you* have this key? I understood the police were holding it."

Montaine shook his head and said, "Not this key. This is *my* key. The one that's pictured there is my wife's key. We've got duplicate keys to the garage and to the two automobiles. She dropped her keys when she . . ." His voice trailed into silence.

He opened the leather key container, spread it on the desk and indicated the keys. "The door keys to the Chevrolet coupe and the Plymouth sedan. My wife usually drives the Chevrolet. I drive the sedan. But sometimes we change off, so, to simplify matters, we each have duplicate keys to the doors and then leave ignition keys right in the locks."

"You've talked with your wife before coming here? She knows you're consulting me?"

"No."

"Why?"

"I don't know just how to explain it so you'll understand."

"I don't know how I can understand unless you *do* explain it."

"I'd have to begin at the beginning and tell you the whole story."

"I thought that's what you were doing."

"I was trying to."

"Well, go ahead."

"She tried to drug me."

"Tried to what?"

"Tried to drug me."

"Look here," Mason said, "where is she now?"

"Home."

"Does she know that you know about this?"

Montaine shook his head.

"Well, let's hear the story," Mason said impatiently.

"It starts with when I came home from the hospital. That is, it really starts before that time. I had been very nervous. I started taking what I thought was a sedative. I didn't know it was habit-forming. It turned out it was habit-forming. My wife told me I must break it off. She got some Ipral to give me. She said that would help me cure myself."

"What's Ipral?"

"It's a hypnotic. That's what they call it."

"What's a hypnotic? Is it habit-forming?"

"It isn't habit-forming. It cures nervousness and insomnia. You can take two tablets and go to sleep and wake up in the morning without feeling dopey."

"Do you take it all the time?"

"No, of course not. That's the reason I took it, to quiet my nerves when I had one of those fits of nervous sleeplessness."

"You say your wife tried to drug you?"

"Yes. Last night my wife asked me if I would like some hot chocolate before I went to bed. She said she thought it would be good for me. I thought it would be fine. I was undressing in the bedroom. There was a mirror in the bathroom, and a door opened through to the kitchen. By looking in the bathroom mirror, I could see my wife fixing the chocolate. I noticed her fumbling with her purse. I thought that was strange, so I stood still, watching her in the mirror.

"I saw her take out the Ipral bottle and shake tablets into the chocolate. I don't know how many tablets she put in. It must have been more than the usual dose."

"You were watching her in the mirror?"

"Yes."

"Then what happened?"

"Then she brought the chocolate in to me."

"And you told her you'd seen her drugging the drink?"

"No."

"Why not?"

"I don't know. I wanted to find out why she was doing it."

"What did you do?"

"I slipped into the bathroom and poured the drink down the bowl. Then I washed out the cup with water, filled it with cold water and took it into the bedroom with me. We have twin beds. I sat on the edge of my bed and sipped the water as though it had been chocolate."

"She didn't see you were drinking water instead of chocolate?"

"No, I was sitting where she couldn't see into the cup, and I sipped it slowly, as though it had been chocolate."

"Then what did you do?"

"Then I pretended to be very sleepy. I lay perfectly motionless, waiting to see what happened."

"Well, what did happen?"

Montaine lowered his voice impressively. "At one thirty-five in the morning my wife slipped out of bed and dressed quietly in the dark."

Mason's eyes showed interest. "Then what did she do?"

"She left the house."

"Then what?"

"Then I heard her open the door of the garage and back her car out. Then she stopped the car and closed the garage door."

"What kind of a door?" Mason asked.

"A sliding door."

"A double garage?"

"Yes."

"And," Mason asked, "the only reason she stopped and closed that door was to keep any one from seeing her car was gone?"

Montaine nodded eagerly and said, "Now you've got the point. That's right!"

"Now then," Mason went on, "have you any reason to think any one was keeping a casual eye on the garage?"

"Why, no. Not that I know of."

"But your wife evidently thought some one might be looking at the garage — a night watchman perhaps."

"No. I think it was to keep me from looking out of the window and seeing the door was open."

"But you were supposed to have been drugged."

"Yes . . . I guess so."

"Then she must have been careful to close the door for another reason."

"I guess that's right. I hadn't thought of it in that way."

Mason asked thoughtfully, "How do the doors slide?"

"There are two tracks, one just outside of the other. Either door can slide all the way back and forth across the entire front of the garage. In that way, either car can be taken out. That is, you can take out the car on the left by sliding both doors to the right, or the car on the right by sliding both doors to the left. Then, when you close the garage, you simply leave one door on the left, slide the other back to the right and lock it with a padlock."

Perry Mason's fingers tapped the key which lay on his desk. "And this is your key to the padlock?"

"Yes."

Mason indicated the newspaper photograph. "And this is your wife's key?"

"Yes."

"How do you know?"

"Because there are only three keys. One of them I keep in the desk, one of them in my key container, and the other is in my wife's key container."

"And you have looked in the desk, to make sure that the third key isn't missing?"

"Yes."

"All right, go on. What happened after your wife closed the garage door?"

"She backed her car out, just as I've told you. Then she closed the garage door."

"Did she," asked Perry Mason, "lock the garage door?"

"Yes. . . . No, I guess she didn't . . . no, she couldn't have."

"The point I'm getting at," Mason said with slow emphasis, "is that if she dropped her keys while she was out, she couldn't have unlocked the garage door when she returned. I take it she did return, since you say she is home now."

"That's right. She couldn't have locked the garage door."

"What happened after she left?"

"I tried to dress," Montaine said, "so that I could follow her. I wanted to know where she was going. As soon as she left the room, I started getting into my clothes, but I couldn't make it. She had driven away before I had my shoes on."

"Did you make any effort to follow her?"

"No."

"Why not?"

"Because I knew I couldn't catch up with her."

"So you waited up until she came in?"

"No, I got back into bed."

"What time did she come back?"

"Some time after two thirty, and before three o'clock."

"Did she open the garage doors then?"

"Yes, she opened them and drove her car in."

"Then did she close them?"

"She tried to."

"But she didn't?"

"No."

"Why?"

"Well, sometimes when the doors are slid back, the brace on the inside of one of the doors catches on the bumper of the other car in the garage. When that happens you have to lift the doors back away from the bumper."

"The doors caught this time?"

"Yes."

"Why didn't she lift them away?"

"She wasn't strong enough."

"So she left the garage door open?"

"Yes."

"How did you know all this? You were lying in bed, weren't you?"

"But I could hear her tugging at the door. And then, when I went out to look this morning, I saw what had happened."

"All right, go on."

"I lay in bed, pretending to be asleep."

"When she came in?"

"Yes."

"Why didn't you confront her as she came in the room and ask her where the hell she'd been?"

"I don't know. I was afraid she'd tell me."

"Afraid she'd tell you what?"

"Afraid she'd tell me something that would — would —"

Perry Mason stared steadily at the reddish-brown eyes. "You'd better," he said slowly, "finish that sentence."

Montaine took a deep breath. "If," he said, "your wife went out at one thirty in the morning, and . . ."

"I'm a bachelor," Perry Mason said, "so leave me out of it. Tell me the facts."

Montaine fidgeted on the edge of the chair, pushed his hair back with his spread fingers. "My wife," he said, "is rather mysterious, rather secretive. I think she acquired that habit from the fact that she's been supporting herself and wasn't accountable to any one. She isn't the type to volunteer explanations."

"That still doesn't tell me anything."

"She was," Montaine said, "that is, she really is . . . What I mean to say is . . . well, she's very friendly with a doctor — a physician who does quite a bit of operative work at the Sunnyside Hospital."

"What's his name?"

"Doctor Millsap — Doctor Claude Millsap."

"And you thought she went to meet this Doctor Millsap?"

Montaine nodded, shook his head, then nodded again.

"And you were afraid to question her because you didn't want to have your suspicions confirmed?"

"I was afraid to ask her at the time, yes."

"Then what happened?"

"Then this morning I realized what *must* have happened."

"When did you realize what must have happened?"

"When I saw the paper."

"When did you see the paper?"

"About an hour ago."

"Where?"

"In a little all-night restaurant, where I stopped to get some breakfast."

"You hadn't had breakfast before that?"

"Yes, I got up early this morning. I didn't know just what time it was. I made some coffee and drank three or four cups of it. Then I went for a long walk, and stopped in at the restaurant on the way back. That was when I saw the newspaper."

"Did your wife know you had gone?"

"Yes, she got up when I was making the coffee."

"Did she say anything?"

"She asked me how I'd slept."

"What did you tell her?"

"I told her I'd slept so soundly I hadn't heard a thing all night; that I hadn't even rolled over in bed."

"Did she make any statements?"

"Yes, she said she'd slept very well, herself; that it must have been the chocolate that made us sleep so soundly. She said she went to bed and didn't know anything from the time her head hit the pillow until she woke up."

"And did your wife sleep well — after she came in?" Mason asked.

"No. She took something, a hypodermic I think it was. She's a nurse, you know. I heard her in the bathroom, moving around, opening the medicine chest. Even then she didn't sleep. She did a lot of twisting and turning."

"How did she look this morning?"

"She looked like the very devil."

"But she told you she'd slept well?"

"Yes."

"And you didn't question her statement?"

"No."

"Did you make any comment whatever?"

"No."

"And you made the coffee as soon as you got up?"

Montaine lowered his eyes. "It sounds bad when I tell it," he said, "but it was really the most natural thing in the world. I looked around, of course, when I got up, and I saw my wife's purse lying on the dressing-room table. She was lying quietly then, drugged, you know. I opened it and looked inside."

"Why?"

"I thought I might find some clue."

"Clue to what?"

"To where she'd been."

"But you didn't *ask* her because you were afraid she'd tell you," Mason said.

"By that time," Montaine blurted, "I was in an awful mental state. You don't know anything about the agonies I suffered during the still hours of the night. Remember that I had to pretend that I was drugged. I couldn't turn and twist in the bed. I just had to lie in the one position without moving. It was agony. I heard the clock strike every hour, and . . ."

"What did you find in her purse?" Mason asked.

"I found a telegram addressed to R. Montaine at one twenty-eight East Pelton Avenue. The telegram was signed 'Gregory' and said, 'Awaiting your final answer five o'clock to-day extreme limit.' "

"You didn't take the telegram?"

"No, I put it back in her purse. But I haven't told you all about it yet."

"Tell me all about it then. Get started. I don't want to have to drag it out of you a bit at a time."

"There was a name and address penciled on the telegram. It was Gregory Moxley, three sixteen Norwalk Avenue."

"The name and address of the man who was killed," Mason said thoughtfully. Montaine nodded his head in quick acquiescence. "Did you," Mason asked, "notice whether her keys were in her purse at the time?"

"No, I didn't. You see, at that time there was nothing to make me notice that particularly. I found the telegram, and, as soon as I read it, I thought that I understood why she'd gone out."

"Then it wasn't Doctor Millsap that she went to meet?"

"Yes, I think it *was* Millsap, but I didn't think so at the time."

"What makes you think it was Millsap?"

"I'm coming to that."

"For God's sake, go ahead and come to it, then."

"After my wife went out, I was in agony. I finally decided to call Doctor Millsap and let him know that I knew of his friendship with my wife."

"What good would that have done?"

"I don't know."

"Anyway, you called Doctor Millsap?"

"Yes."

"What happened?"

"I could hear the ringing noise of the telephone, and then, after a while, a Japanese servant answered the telephone. I told him I must speak with Doctor Millsap at once, that I was desperately ill."

"Did you give him your name?"

"No."

"What did the Jap say?"

"He said Doctor Millsap was out on a call."

"Did you leave word for the Doctor to call when he came back?"

"No, I hung up the telephone. I didn't want him to know who was calling."

Mason shook his head, took a deep breath. "Would you kindly tell me," he said, "why the devil you didn't have the matter out with your wife? Why you didn't confront her when she returned to the house? Why you didn't ask her what she meant when she handed you the drugged chocolate? Why you didn't . . ."

The young man drew himself up with dignity. "Because," he said, "I am a Montaine. We don't do things that way."

"What way?"

"We don't brawl. There are more dignified ways of settling those matters."

"Well," Mason said wearily, "you saw the newspaper this morning, and then what happened?"

"Then I realized what Rhoda . . . what my wife must have done."

"What?"

"She must have gone to meet Moxley. Doctor Millsap must have been there. There was a fight. Doctor Millsap murdered Moxley. My wife was mixed up in it in some way. She was in the room at the time. Her key container was left there. The police will trace it to her. She'll try to shield Millsap."

"What makes you think so?"

"I feel positive that she will."

"Did you say anything to your wife about the garage doors being open?"

"Yes," Montaine said; "from the kitchen window it's possible to look over to the garage. I called her attention to the garage doors when I was making the coffee."

"What did she say?"

"She said she didn't know anything about it at

first, and then, later on, she said she 'remembered' that she had left her purse in her car and had locked up the garage. She said that just before she went to bed she remembered it and went out to get the purse."

"How did she get in if she didn't have her keys?"

"That's what I asked her," Montaine said. "You see, she's rather forgetful about her purse. She's left it around two or three times. Once she lost over a hundred dollars. And she keeps her keys in her purse so I asked her how it happened she could have opened the door if her purse was locked in the car?"

"What did she say?"

"She said she got the extra key out of the desk."

"Did she seem to be lying?"

"No, she looked me straight in the eye and said it very convincingly."

Mason made drumming noises on the edge of his desk with the tips of his fingers. "Exactly what is it," he asked, "that you want me to do?"

"I want you to represent my wife," Montaine said. "I want you to promise me that you'll see to it she doesn't get herself into this thing trying to shield Doctor Millsap. That's first. The second thing I want is for you to protect my father."

"Your father?"

"Yes."

"How does he come into it?"

"It will kill him if our name is involved in a

murder case. I want you to keep the Montaine name out of it just as much as possible. I want you to keep him . . . er . . . in the background."

"That," Mason said, "is rather a large order. What else is it you want me to do?"

"I want you to assist in prosecuting Millsap if it should turn out that he's guilty."

"Suppose the prosecution of Millsap should involve your wife?"

"Then, of course, you'd have to see that he wasn't prosecuted."

Mason stared steadily at Carl Montaine. "There's a pretty good chance," he said, with slow emphasis, "that the police may not know anything about this garage key. They'll check down the list of persons owning Plymouth and Chevrolet cars. But if they should find your name, go to your garage and find that there wasn't any padlock on it or find a different padlock, they might not even question you or your wife."

Montaine drew himself up once more. "The police," he said, "are going to know about it."

"What makes you so positive?" Mason inquired.

"Because," Montaine said, "I am going to tell them. It is my duty. I don't care if she is my wife, I can't conceal facts. I can't stand between her and the law."

"Suppose she's innocent?"

"Of course, she's innocent," Montaine flared. "That's what I'm telling you. It's this man, Millsap, that's guilty. You can put two and two together. She was out. He was out. Moxley was murdered. She'll try to protect him. He'll sell her out. The police must be notified and . . ."

"Look here, Montaine," Mason interrupted, "you're jealous. That makes your mental perspective cockeyed. You'd better forget Millsap. Go to your wife. Get her explanation. Don't say a word to the police until . . ."

Montaine got to his feet, stood very dignified and very reserved, his heroic manner marred somewhat by the mop of hair which was slumped down over his forehead. "The very thing Millsap would want," he said. "He has primed my wife with a lot of lies. She'd try to keep me from notifying the police. Then when the police *did* discover about the keys, where would I be? No, Counselor, my mind is made up. I must maintain my integrity. I will be firm with my wife, firm but sympathetic. To Millsap I shall be an avenging fury."

"For God's sake," Mason exploded, "quit that damned posing and come down to earth. You've sympathized with yourself so much that you've gone goofy and built up a mock heroic attitude . . ."

Montaine interrupted, his face flushed. "That will do," he said with the forceful dignity of one who is saturated with self-righteousness. "My mind is made up, Counselor. I am going to notify the police. I feel it is for the best interests of all concerned that I do so. Millsap can dominate my wife. He can't dominate the police."

"You'd better go easy on that Millsap business," Mason warned. "You haven't a thing against him."

"He was out — at the very time the murder was being committed."

"He *may* have been out on a call. If you insist on telling the police about your wife, that's one thing. But you start spilling stuff about Millsap and you'll find yourself in a jam."

"Very well," Montaine agreed, "I will think over what you say. In the meantime you will represent my wife. You may send me a bill for your services. And please don't forget about my father. I want you to protect him in every way you can."

"I can't divide my allegiance," Mason said grimly. "I'll represent your wife first. If Millsap gets in the way, he'll be smashed. I don't see where your father needs any protection. But if I'm going to represent your wife I'm not going to have my hands tied. What's more, I'm going to make your father come across with some coin. This business about 'sending a bill' doesn't sound good to me."

Montaine said slowly, "Of course, I can see how you feel. . . . My wife must come first . . . that's the way I want it."

"Before your father?" asked Mason.

Montaine lowered his eyes, said very faintly, "If it comes to that, yes."

"Well, it won't come to that. Your father isn't mixed up in it. But he *does* control the purse strings. I'm going to make him pay me for what I do."

"He won't. He hates Rhoda. I'll get the money somewhere, somehow. He won't pay a cent."

"When are you going to notify the police?" Mason asked, changing the subject abruptly.

"Now."

"Over the telephone?"

"No. I'm going to see them personally."

Montaine turned toward the door, then, suddenly remembering something, spun about and approached Mason's desk with outstretched palm. "My key, Counselor," he said. "I almost forgot that."

Perry Mason heaved a sigh, picked up the key from the desk and reluctantly dropped it into Montaine's palm. "I wish," he said, "you'd hold off doing anything until . . ." But Montaine marched to the corridor door, his manner oozing self-righteous determination.

Chapter 7

Perry Mason frowningly consulted his wristwatch, jabbed an impatient thumb against the bell button. After the third ring he turned away from the door and looked at the houses on either side. He saw the surreptitious motion of lace curtains in the adjoining house. Mason gave the bell one more try, then, when he heard no response, crossed directly to the house where he had detected the flicker of interest back of the curtain.

His ring was followed almost immediately by the sound of clumping steps. The door opened and a fleshy woman stared at him with glittering eyes. "You ain't a peddler?" she asked. Mason shook his head. "And if you were one of those college boys getting magazine subscriptions, you wouldn't wear a hat."

The lawyer let his smile become a grin.

"Well," she said in a voice that trickled effortlessly from the end of a glib tongue, "*what* is it?"

"I'm looking," said Perry Mason, "for Mrs. Montaine."

"She lives next door." Mason nodded, waiting. "Did you try over there?"

"You know I did. You were staring out at me

from behind the curtain."

"Well, what if I was? I've got a right to look out of my own window, haven't I? Look here, my man, this is my house, bought and paid for. . . ."

Perry Mason laughed. "No offense," he said. "I'm trying to save time, that's all. You're a woman with an observing disposition. You saw me over at Montaine's. I'm wondering if, perhaps, you didn't see Mrs. Montaine when she left?"

"What's it to you if I did?"

"I'm very anxious to get in touch with her."

"You're a friend of hers?"

"Yes."

"Ain't her husband home?"

Perry Mason shook his head.

"Hmm," said the woman. "Must have gone out this morning a lot earlier than usual. I didn't see him, so I thought he was still in bed. They've got money, so he doesn't have to do anything he doesn't want to."

"Mrs. Montaine?" asked Perry Mason. "How about her?"

"She was his nurse. She married him for his money. She went away in a taxicab about half an hour ago, maybe a little less."

"How much baggage?" Perry Mason asked.

"Just a light bag," she said, "but there was an expressman came about an hour ago and got a trunk."

"You mean a transfer man?" asked Perry Mason.

"No, it was the express company."

"You don't know when she'll be back?"

"No. They don't confide their plans to me. The way they look at me, I'm just poor folks. You see, my son bought this house and didn't have it all paid for. That was when times were good. He had some kind of a life insurance loan that paid off the house when he died. That was the way Charles was, always kind and thoughtful. Most boys wouldn't have thought of their pa and ma and taken out insurance . . . ."

Perry Mason bowed. "Thank you," he said, "very much. I think you've given me just the information that I want."

"If she comes back, who should I say called?" asked the woman.

"She won't be back," Perry Mason said.

The woman followed him to the edge of the porch. "You mean won't ever be back?" she asked. Perry Mason said nothing but strode rapidly to the sidewalk. "They say his folks don't approve of the match. What's her husband going to do if his father cuts him off without a cent?" the woman called after him.

Mason lengthened his strides, turned, smiled, raised his hat and rounded the corner. He caught a cab at the boulevard. "Municipal Airport," he said. The driver snapped the car into motion. "If," said the lawyer, "there are any fines, I'll pay them." The cab driver grinned, nursed his car into speed, slipped in and out of traffic along the boulevard with deft skill.

"This is as fast as the bus goes?" asked Perry Mason.

"When I'm driving it, it is."

"There's a good tip if you get me there in a rush, buddy."

"I'll get you there just as fast as it's safe to drive," the cab driver rejoined. "I've got a wife and kids and a job. . . ."

He broke off as he slammed his foot on the brake pedal, twisted the steering wheel sharply, as a light sedan whizzed around a corner. "There you are," he called back over his shoulder, "that's what happens when you try to make time, and they don't give us any breaks in the home office. The cab driver is always wrong. We've got to drive our car, and we've got to drive the other fellow's car for him, too. When we get in a smash, we're laid off, and . . . Say, buddy, do you know you've got a tail?"

Perry Mason straightened to rigid attention. "Don't look around," warned the cab driver. "He's commencing to crowd up on us. It's a Ford coupe. I noticed it a ways back, just after you got in, and I didn't think anything of it, but he's been sticking pretty close to us all through the traffic."

Perry Mason raised his eyes and tried to see the road behind him in the rear-view mirror. "Wait a minute," the cab driver said, "and I'll give you a break."

He took advantage of a clear stretch in the traffic to raise his hand and adjust his mirror so that Perry Mason could watch the stream of traffic in the road behind him.

"You watch the rear. I'll keep an eye on the front," the driver told him.

Perry Mason's eyes narrowed thoughtfully. "Boy," he said, "you need a quick eye to spot that fellow."

"Oh, shucks," the cab driver protested, "that's nothing. I have to see what's going on in this racket, or the wife and kids would starve to death. You've got to have eyes in the back of your head. That's all I'm good for, driving a cab, but that's one thing I *am* good for."

Perry Mason said slowly, "A Ford coupe with a dented fender on the right. Two men in it. . . . Tell you what you do, you swing to the left at the next corner and figure-eight around a couple of blocks. Let's just make it sure."

"They'll figure we've spotted them if you figure-eight," the driver said.

"I don't care what they figure," Perry Mason rejoined. "I want to smoke them out in the open. If they *don't* follow us, they're going to lose us. If they *do* follow us, we'll stop and ask them what it's all about."

"Nobody that's likely to start throwing lead around, is it?" the driver inquired apprehensively.

"Nothing like that," Mason said. "They might be private dicks, that's all."

"Trouble with the wife?" the driver inquired.

"As you so aptly remarked," Perry Mason

said, "you're an excellent cab driver. That is one of the things that you are good at. In fact, I believe you said that was the *one* thing you were good at."

The driver grinned. "Okay, chief," he said, "I'll mind my own business. I was just being sociable. Hang on. Here we go to the left."

The cab lurched into a fast turn, slid down a side street. "Hold everything, buddy, we're making another turn to the left." Once more the cab screamed into a wide turn.

"They went by," Perry Mason said. "Pull in close to the curb and stop for a minute. Let's see if they circle down the other street. I was watching them in the mirror. They slowed down at the intersection. They got there just as we made the second turn to the left. They acted for a minute as though they were going to make the turn, and then they passed it up."

The cab driver turned in his seat, chewed gum with rhythmic monotony as he peered through the window in the rear of the cab. "All the time we stand here, we're losing time," he said. "You going to take a plane?"

"I don't know," Perry Mason said, "I want to get some information."

"Uh huh. . . . They ain't coming down any of these side streets."

"Suppose we run down to another boulevard and try for the airport along it. You could run down to Belvedere, couldn't you?"

"Sure, we could. You're the boss."

"Let's go," Mason said.

The driver straightened back in the seat and readjusted the rear-view mirror. "You won't want this any more, buddy," he told Perry Mason.

The cab once more clashed through its gears and rattled into speed. The lawyer sank back in the cushions. From time to time, he turned to look thoughtfully back at the road behind him. There was no sign of pursuit.

"Any particular place?" asked the cab driver, as the car turned in to the airport.

"The ticket office," Mason told him.

The cab driver nodded his head in a gesture of indication and said, "There's your boy friends."

A Ford coupe with a dented fender was parked beside the curb at the place where signs painted in red announced there was, "No Parking."

"Police, eh?" asked the cab driver.

Mason stared curiously. "I don't know, I'm sure."

"They're dicks or they wouldn't park there," the cab driver remarked positively. "You want me to wait, buddy?"

"Yes," Mason said.

"I'll have to drive down there for a parking place."

"Okay. Go down and park. Wait for me."

Perry Mason walked through the door to the lobby of the airport ticket office, took half a dozen quick strides toward the ticket window, then abruptly halted as he caught sight of a

98

brown coat with a brown fur collar. The coat was catching sunlight in a small enclosed space next to a swinging gate. Beyond this gate was a big tri-motored plane glistening in the sunlight. The propellers were clicking over at slow speed. Perry Mason pushed his way through the door. A uniformed official strode toward the gate. A stewardess climbed down from the plane and stood by the steps leading to the fuselage. Perry Mason moved up behind the coated figure. "Don't show any surprise, Rhoda," he said in a low voice.

She seemed to stiffen perceptibly, then slowly turned. Her eyes, dark with apprehension, flashed up at him. There was a quick intake of breath, then she turned away. "You," she said in a voice that would have been inaudible for more than ten feet.

"There are a couple of dicks looking for you," Mason went on in a low voice. "They probably haven't a photograph — just a description. They're watching the people getting aboard the plane. After the plane leaves, they'll search the airport. Go over to that telephone booth. I'll follow you in just a minute."

She slipped unobtrusively from the crowd at the gate, walked with rapidly nervous steps to the telephone booth, entered, and closed the door.

The uniformed attendant slid back the gate. Passengers started to board the plane. Two broad-shouldered men appeared from behind the fuselage, scanned each of the passengers with shrewd appraisal. Perry Mason took advantage of their preoccupation to walk with swift strides to the telephone booth. He jerked open the door. "Drop down to the floor, Rhoda," he said.

"I can't. There isn't room."

"You've got to make room. Turn around facing me. Get your back flat against the wall under the shelf that the telephone's on. . . . That's it. . . . Now double up your knees. . . . That's fine."

Perry Mason managed to pull the door closed, stood at the telephone, his eyes making a swift survey of the lobby of the building. "Now listen," he said, "and get this straight. Those dicks either had a tip that you're taking this plane, or else they're covering all exits out of town — airports, railway stations, bus depots and all of that. I don't know them, but they know me, because they recognized me when I left your house and picked up a taxicab. They figured I was going to join you. They tried to tail me for a while, but I shook them, and they came out here. When they see me here, they'll figure that I was to meet you and give you some last minute instructions before you got on the plane, that you missed the plane and I'm telephoning, trying to locate you. I'll let them know after a while that I've seen them and keep in the telephone booth as though I was trying to hide. Do you get the sketch?"

"Yes," she said, her voice drifting up from the

floor in mumbling acquiescence.

"All right, they're starting to look around now," Mason said. "I'll be talking over the telephone."

He removed the receiver from the hook but did not deposit a coin. He held his mouth against the mouthpiece of the telephone and talked rapidly, ostensibly to some party on the other end of the wire, in reality, giving swift instructions to Rhoda Montaine. "You were a little fool to try to get away on a plane," he said. "Flight is an indication of guilt. If they'd caught you boarding that plane with a ticket to some other city, they'd have strengthened the case against you. Now you've got to work things in such a way that they can't prove you were guilty of flight."

"How did you know I was here?" she asked.

"The same way they did," he said. "You left your house with some light articles of baggage. You shipped a trunk by express. If you'd been going on a train, you'd have checked the trunk.

"Now you're going to surrender, but not to the police. You're going to surrender to some newspaper that will get an exclusive story."

"You mean you want me to tell them my story?"

"No," Mason said. "We'll simply let them *think* you're going to tell them your story. You'll never have a chance."

"Why?"

"Because the detectives will grab you just as

101

soon as you put in an appearance and before you have a chance to talk."

"Then what?"

"Then," he said, "keep silent. Don't tell any one anything. Tell them that you won't talk unless your attorney is present. Do you understand?"

"Yes."

"All right," he told her, "I'm going to telephone the *Chronicle*. These birds have got me spotted now, but they don't know that I've seen them. I'm going to telephone the *Chronicle*, and then I'm going to let them know that I've seen them and turn my back pretending to hide. That'll make them think I'm expecting you here, and waiting for them to leave before I go out of the booth. They'll get some place where they can watch me and stick around waiting for me to come out, or for you to join me."

He dropped a coin in the telephone, gave the number of the *Chronicle* and, after a moment, asked for Bostwick, the city editor. There was the sound of a man's voice on the wire, and Mason said, "How would you fellows like to have the exclusive story of Rhoda Montaine, the woman who had the two o'clock appointment with Gregory Moxley this morning? . . . You could also have the credit for taking her into custody. . . . Yes, she would surrender to *Chronicle* reporters. Sure, this is Perry Mason. Of course I'm going to represent her. All right, now get this straight. I'm here at the Municipal Airport. Naturally, I don't want any one to know

102

that I'm here or that Mrs. Montaine is here. I'm in a telephone booth. You have a couple of reporters come to the telephone booth and I'll see that Rhoda Montaine surrenders herself to them. . . . I can't guarantee what's going to happen after that. That's up to you, but, at least, your paper can get on the street with the news that Rhoda Montaine surrendered to the *Chronicle*. But get this straight. You can't have it appear that the *Chronicle* ran her to earth as she was trying to get away. It's got to be a surrender. . . . That's right, she's going to play it that way. *She* surrenders to the *Chronicle*. You can be the first on the street with it.

"No, I can't put her on the telephone and I can't give you her story. I can't even guarantee that you'll *get* a story. How much more do you want for nothing? You can get an extra ready and have it on the street as soon as your men telephone a release. Frankly, Bostwick, I'm afraid the detectives are going to grab her before your men get a chance to interview her, and she isn't going to say very much to detectives right now. . . . Okay, get your extra ready. Start your boys out here and I'll give you some of the highlights on the situation. Now, mind you, *I* don't want to be quoted in this. I'll simply give you bits of information that you can get for yourself. Rhoda Montaine married a chap named Gregory Lorton some years ago. You'll find the marriage license in the Bureau of Vital Statistics. Gregory Lorton was none other than Gregory Moxley, otherwise known as Gregory Carey, the man who was murdered.

"A week or so ago, Rhoda Lorton married Carl W. Montaine. Montaine is the son of C. Phillip Montaine, a multi-millionaire of Chicago. The family's not only respectable but high hat. In the application for a marriage license, Rhoda Lorton described herself as a widow. Gregory Moxley showed up and started to make trouble. Rhoda had been living with a Nell Brinley at one twenty-eight East Pelton Avenue. Moxley sent telegrams to Rhoda at that address, telling her certain things. If you can get those telegrams either from the police files or from the files of the telegraph company, you can use them. Otherwise you can't. Nell Brinley will admit that she received telegrams. . . . That's all I can tell you, Bostwick. You'll have to make up a story from that. You can start running down those angles so that you can have something to put in the special edition you throw on the streets. . . . Yes, she'll surrender herself at the airport. The reason she came to the airport is because I told her to meet me here. . . . No, that's all I can tell you. I've given you all the dope I can. Good-by."

The receiver was still squawking protests as Perry Mason slammed it back on the hook. He turned around as though to leave the telephone booth, looked through the glass, caught sight of one of the detectives, paused, turned his shoulder so that it concealed as much of his face as possible, lowered his head, picked up the telephone receiver and pretended once more to be telephoning.

"They've spotted me, Rhoda," he said, "and know that I've spotted them. They're going to give me a chance to walk into the trap now. They'll get under cover somewhere."

"Aren't they likely to come in here?" she asked in a muffled voice.

"No," he said, "it's you they want. They've got nothing on me. They figure it's a cinch you're going to meet me here and that I'm waiting for you, that I'm trying to keep under cover until they leave. They'll stick around in plain sight for a while and then pretend to leave, figuring that will draw me out in the open."

"How did you know about me?" she asked.

"Your husband," he said.

She gave a quick gasp. "But my husband doesn't know anything!" she said. "He was asleep."

"No, he wasn't," Mason told her. "You slipped some Ipral tablets into his chocolate, but he was too foxy for you and didn't drink the chocolate. He pretended to be asleep and heard you go out and heard you come back. Now go ahead and tell me what happened."

Her voice sounded indistinct as it drifted up from the lower part of the telephone booth. Perry Mason, with the receiver pressed against his ear, cocked his head slightly so that he could hear her words.

"I had done something awful," she said. "Gregory knew about it. It was something that would put me in jail. Not that I was so frightened about going to jail, but it was on account of Carl. His parents thought Carl had married beneath him — a woman who was little better than a street walker. I didn't want to have anything happen that would give Carl's father a chance to say, 'I told you so,' and I didn't want to have my marriage to Carl annulled."

"You aren't telling me very much," Mason said, ostensibly into the telephone.

"I'm trying to tell you the best I can," she wailed, her voice sounding as though she were about ready to start sobbing.

"You haven't got any too much time," Mason warned her, "so don't waste any of it feeling sorry for yourself and crying."

"I'm not feeling sorry for myself and I'm not going to waste time crying," she snapped back at him.

"Your voice sounded like it."

"Well, you try sitting down here, with your head pushed up against a metal telephone box and your knees pushed up against your chin, with a man's feet tramping all over your dress, and you'd talk like that too."

Perry Mason indulged in a chuckle. "Go on," he told her.

"Gregory was in trouble. I don't know just what kind of trouble. He's always in a jam of some sort. I think he'd been in prison. That's why I hadn't heard anything from him. He'd disappeared. I'd tried to trace him. I couldn't find out anything about him, except that he'd been killed in an airplane wreck. I don't know yet why he wasn't. He had a ticket to go on the plane, but, for some reason, he didn't take the plane. I guess he was afraid officers were watching for him. The passenger list showed that he had been on the airship. I thought he was dead. I'd have wagered anything he was dead, but his body wasn't found. And then . . . well, then I just acted on the assumption that he *was* dead."

The lawyer started to say something, checked himself just as the words were on his lips.

"Were you going to say something?" she asked.

"No. Go on."

"Well, Gregory came back. He insisted that I could get money from Carl. He said that Carl would pay to keep from having his name dragged into a lawsuit. He was going to sue Carl for alienation of affection. He said that I was still his wife and that Carl had come between us."

Mason's laugh was sardonic. "Notwithstanding the fact that Gregory had taken your money, skipped out, and you hadn't heard from him for years," he said.

"You don't understand. It wasn't a question of whether he could *win* the lawsuit; it was a question of whether he had the legal right to bring it. Carl would have died before he would have let his name get dragged into the courts."

"But," Mason protested, "I thought you promised me you weren't going to do anything until you'd told me the whole story."

"I went back to see Nell Brinley," she said. "There was another telegram there. It was from Gregory. He was furious. He told me to telephone him. I telephoned him, and he told me I would have to give him a final answer that night. I told him I could give him my final answer right then. He said no, he wanted to talk with me. He said he'd give me a break if I'd come to talk to him. I knew that I couldn't get away while my husband was awake, so I made an appointment for two o'clock in the morning with Gregory and then slipped a double dose of Ipral into Carl's chocolate, so that he'd be asleep."

"Then what?" Mason asked, shifting his position slightly so that he could steal a hasty glance through the glass door of the telephone booth into the lobby of the airport building.

"Then," she said, "I got up shortly after one, dressed and sneaked out of the house. I unlocked the garage door, backed out my Chevrolet coupe, closed the garage door, and evidently forgot to lock it. I started to drive away from the house, and then realized I had a flat tire. There was a service station that was open a few blocks from the house. I drove on the flat to that service station. A man there changed the tire for me, and then we found that the spare tire had a nail in it. It was almost flat. There was enough air in it so the puncture didn't show until he'd changed the tires. So he had to take that tire off, pull out the nail and put in a new tube. I told him I couldn't wait for him to repair the other, so he gave me a claim check for it and I was to pick it up later on."

"You mean the tube that had the nail in it?"

"Yes. He was going to put that in the other tire and put it back on the spare. The tube that had been in there was ruined. I'd driven on it when it was flat."

"Then what?"

"Then I went to Gregory's apartment."

"Did you ring the bell?"

"Yes."

"What time was it?"

"I don't know. It was after two o'clock. I was late. It must have been ten or fifteen minutes after two."

"What happened?"

"Gregory was in an awful temper. He told me I had to get him some money, that I must deposit at least two thousand dollars to his credit in the bank by the time the bank opened in the morning, that I had to get another ten thousand dollars from my husband, that if I didn't get it, he was going to sue my husband and have me arrested."

"What did you do?"

"I told him I wasn't going to pay him a cent."

"Then what happened?"

"Then he got abusive, and I tried to telephone you."

"What happened next?"

"I ran to the telephone and reached for the receiver."

"Just a moment," Mason said. "Were you wearing gloves?"

"Yes."

"All right, go on."

"I tried to pick up the receiver. He grabbed me."

"What did you do?"

"I struggled with him and pushed him away."

"What happened after that?"

"I broke loose from him. He came toward me again. There was a stand by the fireplace, with a poker, a shovel and a brush on it. I dropped my hand and grabbed the first thing I came to. It was the poker. I swung it. It hit him somewhere on the head, I guess."

"Then did you run away?"

"No, I didn't. You see, the lights went out."

"The lights went out?" Mason exclaimed.

She squirmed about, vainly trying to find relief from her cramped position. "Yes, every light in the place went out all at once. The power must have been turned off."

"Was that before you hit him, or afterwards?" Perry Mason asked.

"It was *just* as I hit him. I remember swinging the poker and then everything got dark."

"Perhaps you didn't hit him, Rhoda."

"Yes, I did, Mr. Mason. I know I hit him, and he staggered back and I think he fell down.

There was some one else in the apartment — a man who was striking matches."

"So then what happened?"

"Then I ran out of the room, into the bedroom and stumbled over a chair and fell flat."

"Go on," Mason said.

"I heard a match striking — you know, the sound made by a match scraping over sandpaper, and the sound of a man trying to follow me into the bedroom. It all happened in just a second or two. I ran through the bedroom, out into the corridor, and started to go downstairs, and some one was following me."

"Did you go down the stairs?" the lawyer asked.

"No, I was afraid to. You see, the bell had been ringing."

"What bell?"

"The doorbell had been ringing."

"The doorbell. Some one was trying to get in?"

"Yes."

"When did it start ringing?"

"I don't know exactly. It was sometime during the time we were struggling."

"How long did it continue to ring?"

"Quite a while."

"How did it sound?"

"As though some one were trying to waken Gregory. I don't think the person at the door could have heard the sounds of the struggle, because he rang the bell in a funny way. He rang it

111

for several seconds at a time, then stopped for several seconds, and then rang again. He did that several times."

"You don't know who it was?"

"No."

"But you didn't go down until the bell stopped ringing?"

"That's right."

"How soon after the bell stopped ringing?"

"Just a minute or two. I was afraid to stay in there."

"You don't know whether Gregory was dead or not?"

"No. He dropped to the floor when I hit him and lay motionless. Anyway I heard him fall. I guess I killed him. I didn't mean to. I just hit out blindly."

"So, shortly after the bell stopped ringing, you went downstairs, is that right?"

"Yes."

"Did you see anyone?"

"No."

"Where was your car parked?"

"Around the corner on the side street."

"You went to it?"

"Yes."

"Now, then, you'd dropped your keys in Gregory's apartment. Apparently you dropped them when you picked up the poker."

"I must have."

"Did you know they were missing?"

"Not then."

"When did you find it out?"

"Not until I read the newspaper."

"How did you get in the car?"

"The car door wasn't locked. The ignition key was in the lock. I drove the car back to the garage, and . . ."

"Just a minute," Mason interrupted. "You had closed the door of the garage when you left, but hadn't locked it?"

"Yes, I thought I locked it, but I didn't. It was unlocked."

"And it was still closed?"

"Yes."

"Just as you had left it?"

"Yes."

"So what did you do?"

"So I opened the door."

"And in order to do that, you had to slide it back along the runway?"

"Yes."

"All the way back?"

"Yes."

"And you did that and then drove your car into the garage, is that right?"

"Yes."

"And you left the garage door open?"

"Yes. I tried to close it, but when I'd pushed it back, I'd shoved it over the bumper of the other car. It caught there, and I couldn't get it loose."

"And you went upstairs to bed?"

"Yes. I was nervous. I took a powerful sedative."

"You had a talk with your husband this morning?"

"Yes, he was up making coffee. I thought it was rather strange, because I'd given him enough hypnotic to keep him sleeping until late."

"You asked him for some coffee?"

"Yes."

"He asked you if you'd been out?"

"No, not that way. He asked me how I'd slept."

"And you lied to him?"

"Yes."

"Then he went out?"

"Yes."

"And what did you do?"

"I went back to bed, dozed a bit, got up, took a bath, dressed, opened the door, brought in the milk and the newspaper. I thought Carl had gone for a walk. I opened the newspaper and then realized I was trapped. The photograph of the garage key was staring me in the face. I knew Carl would recognize it as soon as he saw it. What's more, I knew the police could trace me sooner or later."

"So then what?"

"So I telephoned the express company, had them express my trunk to a fictitious name and address, packed up my things, had a cab come, and rushed out here to take a plane."

"You knew there was a plane that left about this time?"

"Yes."

114

Perry Mason pursed his lips thoughtfully.

"Have you any idea," he asked, "who the person could have been that was ringing the door-bell?"

"No."

"Did you leave the doors open or closed when you left?"

"What doors?"

"The door into the hallway from Gregory's apartment, and the door at the foot of the stairs, that leads to the street."

"I can't remember," she said. "I was frightfully excited. I was quivering all over and drenched with perspiration. . . . How did *you* know about the garage door?"

"Your husband told me."

"I thought you said he told the police?"

"He did. He came to call on me first."

"What did he say?"

"He said he'd recognized the key that was photographed in the newspaper, that he knew you had tried to drug him; that you'd gone out, that he'd heard you come in, that you got the garage door stuck and lied to him when he asked you about it being open."

"I didn't think he was that clever," she wailed, "and that lie about the garage door is going to trap me, isn't it?"

"It won't do you any good," Mason said grimly.

"And Carl told you he was going to tell the police?"

"Yes. I couldn't do anything with him on that. He had ideas of what his duty was."

"You mustn't judge him by that," she said. "He's really nice. . . . Did he say anything about . . . about any one else?"

"He told me he thought you might try to shield some one."

"Who?"

"Doctor Millsap."

Mason could hear her gasp. Then she said in startled tones, "What does *he* know about Doctor Millsap?"

"I don't know. What do *you* know about him?"

"He's a friend."

"Was he there at Moxley's house last night?"

"Good heavens, no!"

"You're sure?"

"Yes."

Perry Mason dropped another nickel into the telephone, gave the number of Paul Drake's office. "Perry Mason talking, Paul," he said when he heard the voice of the detective on the wire. "You've read the papers, of course."

The receiver made a succession of metallic sounds. Rhoda Montaine, crouched in the cramped position on the floor of the telephone booth, moved a few inches to one side, shifted her knees slightly. "Okay," Mason said. "You know the general situation then. I'm representing Rhoda Montaine. You probably know by this time that she's the woman you saw come out

116

of my office yesterday. I want you to start a general investigation. The police must have taken photographs of the room where Moxley was found. I want to get some of those photographs. Some of the newspaper men should be able to give you a break. I want you to investigate every angle you can uncover. And here's something funny. There were no fingerprints on that doorknob. I want to know why. . . . What if she was wearing gloves? . . . That would have concealed her fingerprints, but others must have been using that door. Moxley must have opened and closed it a dozen times during the day. I was there earlier in the day. It was a hot day, and my hands were perspiring. There must have been *some* fingerprints on that doorknob.

"Yes, keep on with Moxley. Find out everything you can about him and about his record. Interview the witnesses. Get all the dope you can. The district attorney will probably sew up the witnesses who are going to testify for him. I'm going to beat him to it if I can. Never mind that now. I'll see you later. . . . No. I can't tell you. You get started. There'll be some developments within a few minutes. G'by." Mason slammed the receiver back on the hook.

"Now," he said to Rhoda Montaine, "we've got to work fast. The men from the *Chronicle* will be here any minute. Those fellows drive like the devil. The police are going to question you. They're going to do everything they can to make you talk. They're going to give you all kinds of opportunities to bust into conversation. You've got to promise me that you'll keep quiet. Can you do that?"

"Yes."

"No matter what happens you're going to keep quiet?"

"Yes."

"Insist on calling me. Tell them you want me there whenever they get you on the carpet. Will you do that?"

"Of course. I've told you I would half a dozen times. How many more times do I have to tell you?"

"Dozens," he told her, "and that probably wouldn't be enough. They'll . . ." There was a gentle tap on the door of the telephone booth. Mason broke off and looked through the glass. A young man held a card against the glass. The card showed that he was a reporter from the *Chronicle*. Perry Mason twisted the knob of the door. "Okay, Rhoda," he said, "let's go."

The door opened. "Where's the girl?" asked the newspaperman.

Another reporter slipped around from behind the corner of the telephone booth. "Hello, Mason," he said.

Rhoda Montaine reached for Perry Mason's hand, got to her feet. The newspaper men stared at her in surprise. "She was in there all the time?" asked one of the reporters.

"Yes," Mason said. "Where's your car? You've got to rush her. . . ."

The second reporter rasped out an oath. "The cops," he said.

Two men emerged from behind the low, glass-enclosed partition which separated the ticket office from the lobby. They came up on the run. "This," said Perry Mason, speaking rapidly, "is Rhoda Montaine. She surrenders to you gentlemen as representatives of the *Chronicle*, knowing that the *Chronicle* will give her a square deal. She has recognized the garage key which was published in the paper as the key to her garage. She . . ."

The two detectives swooped down on the group. One of them grabbed Rhoda Montaine by the arm. The other pushed a face that was livid with rage up close to Mason's face. "So that's the kind of a dirty damn shyster you are, is it?" he said.

Mason's jaw jutted forward. His eyes became steely. "Pipe down, gumshoe," he said, "or I'll button your lip with a set of knuckles."

The other detective muttered a warning. "Take it easy, Joe. He's dynamite. We've got the girl. That's the break we need."

"*You've* got hell!" one of the reporters said. "This is Rhoda Montaine, and she surrendered to the *Chronicle* before you ever saw her."

"Like hell she did. She's our prisoner. We tracked her here and made the arrest. We get the credit."

One of the reporters moved toward the telephone booth. He grinned as he dropped a nickel and gave the number of the *Chronicle*. "In just about fifteen minutes," he said, "you boys can buy a paper on the street and read all about who gets the credit."

Chapter 8

Perry Mason paced his office with the restlessness of a caged tiger. Gone was the patient air of philosophical contemplation which characterized many of his meditative indoor perambulations. He was now a grim fighter, and his restless walking furnished an outlet for excess physical energy, rather than a means of concentration. Paul Drake, the detective, a leather-backed notebook poised on his knee, took notes from time to time of the points of information Mason wanted uncovered. Della Street was seated at a corner of the desk, her stenographer's notebook under the tip of a poised pencil. She watched the lawyer with eyes bright with concentrated admiration. "They've buried her," Mason said, frowning at the silent telephone. "Damn them! They *would* work that trick on me."

Paul Drake looked at his wristwatch. "Perhaps," he volunteered, "they . . ."

"I tell you, they've buried her," Mason interrupted, his tongue savage. "I've arranged to be notified whenever she enters either headquarters or the district attorney's office. She's showed up at neither place. They've taken her to some outlying precinct." He flung about and snapped an order at Della Street. "Della," he said, "get to the files. Dig out the application for a writ of *habeas corpus* in the case of Ben Yee. Follow the allegations of that petition. I'll sign it as an attorney acting on behalf of the prisoner. Get one of the typists to rush it out. I'll slap them in the face with a *habeas corpus.* That'll smoke them into the open before they've got a chance to do *too* much damage."

Della Street, swiftly efficient, vanished from the office. Perry Mason whirled toward the detective. "Another thing, Paul," he said. "The district attorney is going to sew up the husband."

"As a material witness?" Drake asked.

"Either as a material witness or as an accomplice. Anyway, he'll sew him up so we can't get at him. We've got to figure some way of getting at him. I've got to reach that man." He paced the floor in savage silence.

The detective volunteered a suggestion. "We could," he said, "fake a message that his father was ill in Chicago. They'd let him go to see his father if they thought you didn't know about it. It's a cinch he'd go by plane. We could watch the plane and stick one of my men on as a passenger. The operative could contact Carl and pump him dry en route."

Perry Mason paused in his restless pacing to frown thoughtfully. The door from the outer office opened, and Della Street returned to her seat at the desk. Slowly, the lawyer shook his head. "No," he said, "that won't do. It's too risky. We'd have to forge a signature to a telegram. They'd raise hell. It won't work."

"Why won't it work?" Drake demanded. "It's a good scheme. He'll . . ."

"The father," Mason said, "is the type that will come on here to have a hand in things. In fact, I'm sort of planning on bringing him here if he doesn't come of his own accord."

"Why?"

"Because I want to get some money out of him."

"You mean you want him to pay for defending Rhoda?"

"Yes."

"He won't do it."

"He will when I get done with him," Mason said, resuming once more the savage pounding of his heels as he strode up and down the office. Abruptly he whirled. "Here's one more thing. They've got to use the testimony of Carl Montaine to build up the case against Rhoda. Now, Carl Montaine is her husband. As such, he can't be called as a witness in a criminal case, to testify against his wife, unless the wife consents."

"That's the law in this state?" asked Paul Drake.

"That's the law."

"Well," asked Drake, "isn't that a break for you?"

"No," Perry Mason said, "because that means they'll start an action to annul the marriage between Rhoda and Carl Montaine."

"Not a divorce?" Drake asked.

"No, a divorce wouldn't do any good. They'd still have been husband and wife when the murder took place. What they'll do is start an action for annulment, on the ground that the marriage was void from the beginning."

"Can they do that?"

"Sure. If they can prove Rhoda Montaine had another husband living at the time she married Carl that second marriage would be void from its inception."

"Then the husband can testify?" Drake asked.

"Yes. Now, I want you to start digging out a lot of stuff about Gregory Moxley. I want to know all about his past life. It's a cinch the district attorney will have some of this. I want to get a lot more. I want to get everything about him, from soup to nuts. Dig into his past and find out, if you can, every one that he's victimized."

"You mean women?"

"Yes, particularly those that he went through a marriage ceremony with. This wasn't a first time with him. It was his mode of operation. Crooks don't usually change their modes of operation." Paul Drake scribbled in his notebook. "Now, there was a telephone call," Mason went on. "That's the telephone call that woke Moxley up. It must have come in some time before two o'clock. He had an appointment with Rhoda at

124

two o'clock, and he mentioned over the telephone that he was going to meet Rhoda at two o'clock and that she was going to give him money. See if you can find out anything about that telephone call. It may be you can trace it."

"You think it came before two o'clock?" Drake asked.

"Yes, I think so. I think you'll find it was the telephone call that woke Moxley up. He was waiting for this two o'clock appointment. He lay down to get a few hours' sleep. Then the telephone rang and woke him up. He got up out of bed and answered it."

Drake's pencil traveled over the page of his notebook. "All right," he said, "what else?"

"There's the business of that shadow — the one who was tailing Rhoda Montaine when she came to this office. We haven't found out about him yet. He may have been a professional detective. If he was, some one hired him. You've got to find out who was willing to pay out good money to find out what Rhoda was doing."

Drake nodded. Mason swung to Della Street. "Della," he said, "I want to set the stage for some publicity. We've got a delicate job on our hands. If the first newspaper accounts sketch this woman as a nurse who drugged her husband, it's going to be bad for us. We've got to center the attention on the wrong that was done her *by* her husband, rather than the wrong that she did *to* her husband. One of the morning papers has a readers' column in which they publish letters from readers. Take a letter to that newspaper, to the attention of the editor of the readers' column. Be sure that it isn't on stationery that can be traced to this office."

Della Street nodded, poised her pencil. Perry Mason started to dictate quick, explosive words:

"I'm just an old-fashioned husband. Perhaps I have lived past my time. I don't know what the world is coming to, with those new ideas that make it seem that a person who has lived frugally and saved a part of his income is an economic leper, that motion picture actors can't be popular unless they punch women in the nose, but I do know that I swore to love, honor and cherish my wife, and I certainly shall try to do so to the best of my ability. The current press contains the account of a 'law-abiding' husband who read in the papers some stuff that made it appear his wife had been in contact with a man who was murdered, shortly be- fore his death. In place of trying to shield his wife, in place of going to her for an explanation, this 'law-abiding' husband rushes to the police and gets them to arrest his wife, and pledges his cooperation to help the police make out a case. Perhaps this is just the trend of modern times. Perhaps I have lived too long. Personally, I don't think so. Personally, I think the world is going through another one of those periods of hysteria.

"We look back on our spending orgy that culminated in 1929, and shake our heads sadly that we could have been swept off our feet by such contagious financial fallacies.

"Isn't it equally possible that some sweet spring morning we will wake up with a terrific headache and wonder if we weren't just as hysterical in our anxiety to sweep aside all of our old standards, to embark upon an orgy of governmental spending, when we should have tried governmental economy, to have penalized those who had weathered the economic storm with savings in the bank, and, last but not least, to have given the sanctions of our prosecuting officers to a husband who would rush frantically to the nearest police station to snitch on his wife.

"Personally I think so, but then, I am just an

"OLD-FASHIONED HUSBAND."

Paul Drake looked up at Perry Mason and said in his drawling voice, "What good's that going to do, Perry?"

"A lot of good," Mason said. "It's going to start a discussion."

"You mean about the husband?"

"Sure."

"Then why put all the political stuff in it?"

"Because I want to be sure that it starts a discussion. Lots of people wouldn't care enough one way or the other to write in and take sides with Rhoda or with her husband, but, by putting in this other stuff, there will be enough sentiment, pro and con, to bring in a flood of correspondence that will make the newspaper sit up and take notice, and it will assign a sob sister to play up the angle of the betraying husband."

Drake nodded slowly. "I guess," he said, "you're right at that."

"How about that photograph?" asked Perry Mason. "Did you get photographs of the room where the murder was committed?"

Paul Drake picked up a brief case which he had propped against the foot of his chair, pulled out a manila envelope and extracted four photographs printed on glossy paper. Mason took the photographs, spread them on his desk, studied them carefully for several minutes. Then he opened the drawer of his desk, took out a magnifying glass and studied one of the photographs through it. "Take a look at this, Paul," he said.

The detective pushed over to the desk. Perry Mason indicated a portion of the photograph. "Yes," Drake said, "that's the alarm clock. It was on a stand by the bed."

"And, as I understand it, Paul, the bed had been slept in but Moxley was fully dressed at the time he was killed."

"Yes."

"Then," Mason went on, "the importance of that alarm clock becomes doubly significant."

"Why?"

"Take a glass and look at it."

The detective nodded. "Yes," he said, "the alarm clock is pictured plainly enough to show the hands distinctly. The hands point to three seventeen. The figures in the right-hand corner of the photograph, where the police photographer made a note of the location of the camera, the time of exposure, and so forth, shows the picture was taken at three eighteen. That puts the alarm clock only a minute off, as compared with police time."

"That's only part of it," Perry Mason told him. "Take another look."

"What are you getting at?"

"By looking closely," Mason said, "you can see the dial in the upper part of the alarm clock, the dial that regulates the alarm."

"What about it?"

"It shows that the hand was set just a little before two o'clock."

"Sure," Drake said. "He had an appointment for two o'clock with Rhoda Montaine. He wanted to be awake when she called."

"Didn't leave much time to dress," Mason remarked. "That hand looks to me as though it was set for perhaps five or ten minutes before two o'clock."

"Remember, he'd been her husband once. She probably had seen him in pajamas before."

"You still don't get my point," Mason said, drumming with his fingers on the edge of the photograph. "That telephone call woke Moxley up. Therefore, he didn't need the alarm. He was all dressed by the time the alarm went off."

Paul Drake's glassy eyes surveyed Perry Mason steadily. "There's *lots* of your points I don't get," he said. "Why the devil don't you go in and plead self-defense? I'm not asking you to violate any of your client's confidences, but if she told you the truth, she's undoubtedly told you there was a struggle and she struck Moxley with the poker. It doesn't seem to me it would be a hard job to make the jury believe that was what happened. That's self-defense."

Perry Mason shook his head slowly. "That," he said, "is the danger of formulating a defense before you know *all* the facts."

"What's wrong with that as a defense?" asked the detective.

"In the first place," the lawyer replied, "there's that business of drugging her husband. You've got to understand something of the psychology of jurors in order to figure what they'll do in any given case, and it's not always easy to look at the thing just the way they're going to figure it. But one of the bad things in this case is that Ipral bottle. The fact that Carl Montaine's wife was a nurse, and that she placed a drugged drink in his hand, is going to do more to prejudice an American jury against her than anything that could possibly be uncovered in connection with the murder. Moreover, if she's going to plead self-defense, she's got to admit that she did the killing. I'm not certain that the prosecu-

130

tion can show she did the killing."

"They can show she was in the room at the time of the death," Drake said. "The killing certainly must have taken place right around two o'clock, between two and two twenty, when the neighbors decided to notify the police. It's a foregone conclusion that Rhoda Montaine had left her house in the dead of night to go to Moxley's apartment. The fact that she was there is shown by the fact that her garage keys were there. She had to have the garage keys in order to open the garage doors when she started. She left them there. If she didn't kill him herself, the jury certainly is going to believe that she was there when the killing took place, and must know who did it."

"That's just the point," Perry Mason said slowly. "I'm not certain but what she may be trying to shield somebody."

"What makes you think that?"

"The fact that there are no fingerprints on the doorknob," Mason said.

"Rhoda wore gloves," the detective reminded him.

"Well, what if she did? If she had worn gloves, she wouldn't have left fingerprints on anything, would she?"

"That's right. And the police didn't find any of *her* fingerprints."

"Then," Mason insisted, "if she hadn't left fingerprints because she wore gloves, she wouldn't need to worry about fingerprints."

"What do you mean?"

"I mean that a woman wearing gloves wouldn't leave any of her fingerprints, but when there were *no fingerprints* on the knob of the door or on the murder weapon it means that some one took a rag and carefully obliterated *all of the fingerprints*. The only reason a person would do that would be to obliterate certain tell-tale fingerprints. A person who was wearing gloves wouldn't have left behind any fingerprints to worry about — nothing she would need to obliterate."

Drake's frown was thoughtful. "So *that's* what you were getting at when you phoned me," he said.

Perry Mason resumed his pacing of the office. Abruptly, he jerked open the door of a coat closet, pulled out a hat, clapped it firmly into position on his head, glanced meaningly at Della Street. "Take a look at that *habeas corpus* petition," he said. "It should be ready for my signature."

She nodded, moved with the swiftly silent efficiency of a nurse making things ready for a major operation. A few moments, and she returned, bearing a piece of paper in her hand. "This is the last page," she said, "ready for your signature."

Perry Mason scrawled his signature. "Send it up," he said. "Get a judge to issue the writ. See that it's served. I'm going out."

"Going to be long?" asked Paul Drake.

Perry Mason's smile was ominous. "Just long enough," he said, "to give Doctor Claude Millsap the works."

Chapter 9

Doctor Millsap's nurse bristled with indignation. "You can't go in there," she said, "that's Doctor Millsap's private office. He doesn't see people without an appointment. You'll have to make an appointment at his convenience."

Perry Mason stared steadily at her. "I don't like to fight with women," he said. "I've told you that I was an attorney and that I was going to see Doctor Millsap on a matter of great importance to him. Now you get through that door and tell Doctor Millsap that Perry Mason wants to see him about a .32 caliber Colt automatic that was registered in his name. You tell him that I'm going to wait just exactly thirty seconds, then I'm coming in."

A hint of panic showed in the nurse's eyes. She hesitated, turned, opened the door of Doctor Millsap's private office and slammed it shut behind her with emphasis. Perry Mason consulted his wristwatch. Precisely at the end of thirty seconds he strode to the door, twisted the knob and pushed it open.

Doctor Millsap wore a white robe. A concave mirror was fastened about his forehead with a leather strap, giving him a decidedly professional appearance. The office smelled of antiseptics. Surgical instruments glittered in glass cases. A row of bookcases was visible through an open doorway. On the other side could be glimpsed a tiled operating room.

The nurse had one hand on Doctor Millsap's shoulder. Her eyes were wide. She had been leaning toward the physician. At the sound of the opening door she whirled, with panic in her eyes. Doctor Millsap's face was a sickly gray. Perry Mason shut the door behind him with silent finality. "It happens," he said slowly, "that time's valuable. I didn't have any to waste in preliminaries, and I didn't want you to take time to think up a bunch of lies and make me waste more time proving that they *were* lies."

Doctor Millsap squared his shoulders. "I don't know who you are," he said, "and I certainly don't understand the meaning of this unwarranted intrusion. You can either get out, or I'll call the police and have you put out."

Perry Mason's feet were planted wide apart, his chin belligerent, his eyes cold and steady. He was like a solid block of granite — foursquare, cold, unyielding. "When you get the police on the telephone, Doctor," he said, "explain to them just how it happened that you made a false burial certificate for Gregory Lorton in February, 1929. You can also explain to them how it happened that you gave Rhoda Montaine a .32 caliber automatic, with instruc-

134

tions to shoot Gregory Moxley."

Doctor Millsap ran his tongue along the line of his dry lips, looked over to the nurse with desperate eyes. "Get out, Mabel," he said.

She hesitated for a moment, stared venomously at Perry Mason, then walked past him through the door. "See that we're not disturbed," Mason told her. The slamming of the door of the outer office constituted his answer.

Mason held Doctor Millsap's eyes. "Who are you?" asked Doctor Millsap.

"I'm Rhoda Montaine's attorney."

Momentary relief became apparent in Doctor Millsap's expression. "She sent you here?"

"No."

"Where is she?"

"Under arrest," Perry Mason said slowly, "for murder."

"How did you happen to come here?"

"Because I wanted to find out about that death certificate and the gun."

"Sit down," said Doctor Millsap, and dropped into a chair as he spoke, as though his knees had lost their strength. "Let's see," he said, "a man by the name of Lorton. . . . Of course, I have a great number of cases and I can't remember, offhand, the facts connected with each one. I could, perhaps, look it up in my records. You say it was in 1929? . . . If you could recall some of the particular circumstances . . ."

Mason's face flushed with anger. "To hell with that line of stuff!" he said. "You're friendly with Rhoda Montaine, I don't know how friendly. You knew she'd married Gregory Lorton and that Lorton had skipped out. For some reason she didn't want to get a divorce. On February twentieth, 1929, a patient was admitted to the Sunnyside Hospital with pneumonia. The name under which he was booked was that of Gregory Lorton. You were the attending physician. The patient died on February twenty-third. You signed the death certificate."

Doctor Millsap licked his lips once more. His eyes were sick with panic. Perry Mason shot out his left arm, doubled it smartly at the elbow so he could consult the dial of his wristwatch. "You've got ten seconds," he said, "to start talking."

Doctor Millsap took a deep breath. Quick, panic-stricken words poured from his lips like water from a hose. "You don't understand. You wouldn't adopt that attitude if you did. You're Rhoda Montaine's lawyer. I'm her best friend. I'm in love with her. I care more for her than anything in the world. I've loved her ever since I've known her."

"Why did you sign the death certificate?"

"So she could collect the life insurance."

"What was wrong with the life insurance?"

"We couldn't prove that Gregory Lorton had died. There was a rumor that he had been in an airplane wreck. The records of the transportation company showed that he'd purchased a ticket to go on that plane, but we couldn't prove conclusively that he had been on that plane. No bodies were recovered, except the body of one man. The life insurance company wouldn't take that as proof. Some lawyers told Rhoda she would have to wait for seven years and then bring an action to have it established on the records that her husband was dead. She didn't want to remain married to him. If she had secured a divorce, that would have been an admission that he was alive. She didn't know what to do. She felt she was a widow. She felt, beyond any doubt, that he was dead.

"Then I got an idea. There were a lot of charity patients applying for hospitalization. Many of them couldn't be accommodated, many of them suffering from fatal maladies. A man of about the size, build and age of Gregory Lorton was trying to get admission to the hospital. I saw that he was suffering from pneumonia and knew that the case would be almost certain to terminate fatally. I told him that if he would consent to use the name of Gregory Lorton, and answer questions as to his father's and his mother's name and address in a certain way, I could get him into the hospital, because Gregory Lorton had an unused credit on the books of the hospital.

"The man did it. He answered all the questions so that the records of the hospital showed just the same as they did on the application for a marriage license. We did everything we could for the man. I'll swear to that. I didn't try to hasten the end, in fact, I tried my best to save his life, because I thought that if he lived I could do the same thing over again with some other unfortunate, until one of them *did* die. But, despite everything I could do, this man died. I made a death certificate, and then Rhoda had her attorney stumble on the fact of death a few weeks later by writing to the Bureau of Vital Statistics. The attorney acted in good faith. He put the matter up to the insurance company and they paid the policies."

"How much were the policies?"

"Not very much, otherwise we couldn't have worked it as easily as we did. I think they were around fifteen hundred dollars in all."

"Were they policies that Lorton took out in favor of his wife?"

"Yes. He persuaded Rhoda that they should each take out some insurance in favor of the other. He told her that he was negotiating for a fifty thousand dollar insurance policy in her favor, but that there was some hitch in it and the company would only write fifteen hundred dollars temporarily, until an investigation had been completed. He got her to take out a policy in his favor for ten thousand dollars. Undoubtedly, he intended to kill her and collect the insurance if he hadn't been able to get what money she had and skip out with it."

"Of course, he quit paying the premiums on the policies just as soon as he left her?" Perry Mason said.

"Yes," Doctor Millsap said. "That fifteen hundred policy was just a blind. The probabilities are he'd forgotten about it. He just paid one premium on it and then left. Rhoda went on paying for the fifteen hundred policy. The airplane accident took place within a few months of the time the first premium was paid. The death certificate was filed within a year. If Rhoda had gone about it right in the first place, I don't think she'd have had any trouble getting the payment made on the strength of the airplane disaster. As it was, she got up against some officious clerk in the insurance company who tried to make things difficult for her."

"Then what happened?"

"Then, there was that period of waiting, and Rhoda collected the policy from my death certificate."

"You've known Rhoda some little time?"

"Yes."

"Tried to get her to marry you?"

Doctor Millsap's face flushed. "Is all this necessary?" he asked.

"Yes," said Mason.

"Yes," Doctor Millsap admitted with defiance in his voice, "I've asked her to marry me."

"Why didn't she?"

"She swore that she'd never marry again. She had lost her faith in men. She'd been a simple, unspoiled girl when Gregory Lorton tricked her into going through a marriage ceremony, and his perfidy had numbed her emotional nature. She dedicated her life to nursing the sick. She had no room for love."

"Then out of a clear sky she married this millionaire's son?" asked Perry Mason.

"I don't like the way you say that."

"What don't you like and why?"

"The way you describe him as a millionaire's son."

"He is, isn't he?"

"Yes, but that isn't the reason Rhoda married him."

"How do you know?"

"Because I know her and I know her motives."

"Why did she marry him?"

"It was a starved maternal complex. She wanted something to mother. She found just what she was looking for in this weak son of rich parents, a young man whose character was commencing to disintegrate. He looked up to Rhoda as a pupil looks up to his teacher, as a child to his mother. He thought it was love. She didn't know what it was. She only knew that all of a sudden she wanted something she could hold tightly to her and care for."

"Naturally you objected to the match?"

Doctor Millsap's face was white. "Naturally," he said in a voice that was edged with suffering.

"Why?"

"Because I love her."

"You don't think she's going to be happy?"

Doctor Millsap shook his head.

"She can't be happy," he said. "She isn't fair with herself. She isn't recognizing the psychological significance of her feelings. What she really wants is a man she can love and respect. Having a child would give her the natural outlet for her maternal affections. What she's done is to suppress her natural sex feelings over a period of years, until, finally, the starved mother complex has given her the irresistible desire to pick up some man who is weak and unfit, and try to protect that man from the world, gradually nursing him back to a normal place in life."

"Did you tell her that?"

"I tried to."

"Get any place with that line of argument?"

"No."

"What did she say?"

"That I could never be more than a friend to her, and that I was jealous."

"What did you do?"

Doctor Millsap took a deep breath. "I don't like to discuss these matters with a stranger," he said.

"Never mind what you like," Perry Mason told him, without taking his eyes from the man's face, "go ahead and spill it, and make it snappy."

"I care more for Rhoda than I do for life itself," Doctor Millsap said slowly, with obvious reluctance. "Anything that will make her happy is the thing I want. I love her so much that it's an unselfish love. I'm not going to confuse her happiness with mine. If she could be more happy with me than with any one else that would be the most wonderful thing that could happen to me. If, on the other hand, she could be more happy with some one else, than with me, I want her to have that some one else, because her happiness comes first."

"So you stepped out of the picture?" Mason inquired.

"So I stepped out of the picture."

"Then what?"

"Then she married Carl Montaine."

"Did it interfere with your friendship with Rhoda?"

"Not in the least."

"And then Lorton showed up."

"Yes. Lorton, or Moxley, whichever you want to call him."

"What did he want?"

"Money."

"Why?"

"Because some one was threatening to send him to jail for a swindle he'd worked."

"Do you know what the swindle was?"

"No."

"Do you know who the person was who threatened to send him to jail?"

"No."

"Do you know how much money he wanted?"

"Two thousand dollars at once and ten thousand dollars later."

"He demanded it of Rhoda?"

"Yes."

"What did she do?"

"Poor child, she didn't know what to do."

"Why not?"

"She was a bride. The suppressed emotional nature of years was commencing to re-assert itself. She thought that she was in love with her husband. She thought that her life was entirely wrapped up in his. Then, suddenly this detestable cad appeared on the scene. He demanded money. It was money that she didn't have to give him. He insisted that if she didn't get it for him he would have her arrested for working a fraud on the life insurance company; also for bigamy. She knew that before he did any of those things, he'd appeal directly to Carl Montaine and try and get money from him. Montaine had a horror of having his name dragged through the newspapers. Moxley was very clever. He knew something about Montaine's absurd complex about family and the snobbish attitude of Montaine's father."

"So what happened?" Mason demanded.

"So she faced Moxley, told him that if he didn't clear out she'd have him arrested for the embezzlement of her money."

"You suggested that she do that?"

"Yes."

"And you gave her a gun with which to kill Moxley if the opportunity presented itself?"

Doctor Millsap's shake of the head was vehement. "I gave her a gun," he said, "because I wanted her to have something to protect herself with if it became necessary. I knew that this man Lorton, or Moxley, was utterly without scruple. I knew that he would lie, steal, or kill in order to accomplish his purpose. I knew that he was in a jam and needed money. I was afraid to have Rhoda go and see him alone, yet Moxley stipulated that she couldn't have any one with her."

"So you gave her the gun?"

"Yes."

"You knew that she was going to see Moxley?"

"Of course."

"Did you know she was going to see him last night?" Doctor Millsap's eyes shifted uneasily. He fidgeted in his chair. "Yes or no?" asked Mason.

"No," said Millsap.

Mason snorted. "If," he said, without rancor, "you can't lie better than that on the witness stand, you're not going to make Rhoda a very good witness."

"The witness stand!" exclaimed Millsap in dismay. Mason nodded. "Good God, I can't go on the witness stand! You mean to testify for Rhoda?"

"No, the district attorney will call you to testify *against* Rhoda. He's going to try to build up just as much adverse sentiment against Rhoda Montaine as he can. He'll try to show a motive for the murder — that motive will be an attempt on the part of Rhoda to conceal the fraud she perpetrated on the insurance company. Therefore, he'll show the fictitious death certificate and the conspiracy to defraud the insurance company. You know where that's going to leave you."

Doctor Millsap's mouth sagged slowly open. Perry Mason stared steadily at him. "You knew that Rhoda was going to meet Gregory Moxley at two o'clock in the morning, Doctor?"

Doctor Millsap seemed to wilt. "Yes," he said.

Perry Mason nodded slowly. "That," he said, "is better. Now tell me, Doctor, where were *you* at two o'clock in the morning?"

"Asleep, of course."

Perry Mason said tonelessly, "Can you prove it?"

"I can prove it the same way any ordinary individual can. I went to bed and slept through until morning. A man doesn't ordinarily take an alibi to bed with him. Under the circumstances, I would think my statement would be sufficient."

"It would, Doctor," Mason said slowly and impressively, "if it weren't for the fact that the district attorney will question you and your Japanese servant about a telephone call that came in at two o'clock in the morning, and the state-ment that your Japanese man servant made that . . ." The expression on Doctor Millsap's face stopped Perry Mason in mid-sentence. "Well," he asked, "what about it?"

"Good God!" Millsap said. "How could the district attorney have found out about that telephone call? I didn't figure there was one chance in a million that telephone call would ever enter into the thing at all. My Japanese servant told me it was a man who seemed to be drunk, calling from a public pay station."

"How did he know the man was drunk?"

"I don't know. I guess he sounded drunk. All I know is what he told me when I came back . . . I mean. . . ."

"Suppose," the lawyer suggested, "you tell me the facts."

Words spilled from the doctor's mouth. "I was there. Not at two o'clock, but later. I woke up and couldn't sleep. I knew Rhoda must have gone to keep her appointment. I looked at my wristwatch. I wondered what Rhoda was doing. I wondered if she was all right. I got up and dressed, drove to Norwalk Avenue. Rhoda's car was parked on a side street. I looked up at Moxley's apartment. The windows were all dark. I rang the bell of Moxley's apartment. No one answered. I kept ringing, minute after minute. I became alarmed when no one answered. If Rhoda's car hadn't been there I'd have thought Moxley was asleep. I decided to prowl around the back of the house and see if there was any way I could get in. But I didn't want to leave my car in front of the house, so I drove around the block, left my car, came through the alley, walking rather slowly, and then saw the lights were on in Moxley's apartment. I figured my ringing the doorbell had awakened him, so I walked around past the side street to go to the front of the house and ring the bell again, and then saw that Rhoda's car was gone."

"When you were ringing the doorbell," Mason

said, "you were standing on the little porch near the street, is that right?"

"Yes."

"Could you hear the ringing of the bell in the upper apartment?"

"No, I couldn't hear the bell."

"Could you hear the sound of any struggle?"

"No, I couldn't hear anything."

Perry Mason frowned thoughtfully. "I wouldn't want to be quoted in what I am about to say," he said.

"What is it?" Doctor Millsap asked.

"You don't look well," Perry Mason said.

"Good God!" Millsap rejoined. "How did you think I'd look? This thing has been on my mind for days, ever since Rhoda told me Lorton was alive and in the city. I haven't been able to sleep. I haven't been able to eat. I can't concentrate. I can't handle my practice. I can't . . ."

"I said," Perry Mason interrupted, "that you didn't look well."

"Of course I don't look well, I don't feel well. I'm almost crazy!"

"What," asked Perry Mason, "would you advise a patient to do if he came to you in the mental state that you are now in — and if he didn't look well?"

"What are you driving at?"

"Would you advise, perhaps, a long ocean voyage?"

"I'd certainly advise a change of scenery. I wouldn't want . . ." Millsap stopped speaking abruptly in the middle of the sentence, his jaw sagging.

"As I remarked," said Perry Mason, getting to his feet, "I wouldn't want to be quoted in the matter, and I'm not a physician. In order to make it appear perfectly regular, you might consult some friendly physician. You don't need to tell him what's worrying you, but you can tell him that you're worrying yourself sick. You might even go so far as to ask him about an ocean voyage."

"You mean," Doctor Millsap asked slowly, "that I'm to get out where they can't reach me? Wouldn't that be running away and leaving Rhoda to stand the brunt of the whole thing alone?"

"As far as Rhoda is concerned," Mason said, "your presence here would do her more harm than good. My suggestion, however, has nothing to do with Rhoda. I'm merely interested in your health. You don't look well. There are circles under your eyes. Your manner is decidedly jumpy. By all means call on some reputable physician. Let him diagnose your case. In the meantime, here's one of my cards. If there should be any developments call on me at once."

Mason dropped his business card on Doctor Millsap's desk. Millsap jumped to his feet, grabbed Mason's hand and pumped it up and down. "Thanks, Counselor. It's an idea I hadn't thought of. It's swell. It's the best yet."

Mason started to say something, but stopped

as the sounds of muffled commotion came from the outer office. The men heard the protesting voice of Doctor Millsap's office nurse. Perry Mason jerked open the door. The two detectives of the homicide squad who had arrested Rhoda Montaine at the airport stared at the lawyer with incredulous surprise, then their eyes shifted to Doctor Millsap. "Well, well," said one of the detectives, "you certainly do get around."

Perry Mason jerked his head toward Doctor Millsap. "Thank you, Doctor," he said, "for your diagnosis. If you ever need a lawyer, don't hesitate to call on me. In the meantime, I see these two men want to talk with you. For your information, they are detectives from the Homicide Bureau. I won't delay you any longer. Incidentally, as an attorney, I might tell you that you don't have to answer any questions you don't want to, and . . ."

"That's enough," one of the detectives said, advancing belligerently.

Perry Mason held his ground, his shoulders squared, his chin thrust forward, granite-steady eyes holding the detective in scornful appraisal. "And," continued Perry Mason, "if you *should* need an attorney, you've got my telephone number on that card on your desk. I don't know what these men want, but if I were in your place I wouldn't answer *any* questions."

Mason pushed past the detectives, without looking back. They glowered at him for a moment, then strode into the private office and slammed the door shut. Outside, in the entrance room, Doctor Millsap's office nurse dropped her head to the crook of her elbow, pillowed it on her desk and sobbed. Perry Mason stared at her for several seconds, his forehead furrowed in thoughtful appraisal. Then he slipped through the outer door and silently closed it behind him.

Chapter 10

Morning sun streamed through the windows of Perry Mason's office. The telephone rang. A long, thin shadow blotched against the frosted glass of the corridor door, then the knob turned, and Paul Drake entered the room as Della Street's busy fingers snapped the keys on the telephone board. Perry Mason opened the door from his inner office. "For you, chief," Della Street said, indicating the telephone.

Mason grinned at the detective. "See if it's important, Della," he told her.

Paul Drake held out a couple of newspapers. "See what's happened?" he asked. Mason raised his eyebrows in mute interrogation. Drake made a gesture of utter weariness, and said, "She's spilled her guts."

The lawyer stared steadily at the detective, his feet planted wide apart. Slowly he smiled. Della Street slammed the telephone back into place, looked up at Perry Mason, her face white with rage. "What's *your* trouble, sister?" Mason asked.

"That," she said, "was some smart aleck at headquarters who wanted to tell you — in a voice that fairly oozed gloating triumph — that your client, Rhoda Montaine, had just finished signing a statement in the district attorney's office, and that you could see her at any time. He said you wouldn't need a writ of *habeas corpus;* that she was being charged with murder in the first degree and that the authorities at the jail would be only *too* glad to let you see her at any time you wanted — and he put just the right amount of nasty sarcastic emphasis upon the *'too.'* "

Perry Mason stared down at her without changing a muscle of his facial expression. "Why," he asked, "didn't you let me talk with him?"

"Because he was just trying to goad you," she said.

Mason said slowly, "Hereafter, when any one wants to do that, put me on the line. Remember this, Della, I can dish it out, and I can take it." He turned to Paul Drake. "Come in, Paul," he said.

The men entered Mason's inner office, closed the door. Paul Drake whipped over a newspaper. "Details?" asked Perry Mason.

"Lots of them. They don't give the signed statement, but the paper was evidently held for release until the statement *had* been signed."

"What does she say?" Mason asked.

"She says that Moxley was trying to blackmail her; that he insisted on her coming to see him at two o'clock in the morning; that she got up while

152

her husband was asleep, left the house and went to see Moxley; that she rang the doorbell for several minutes and couldn't get in, so she turned around, got in the car and went home."

"Does she say anything about how she rang the bell?"

"Yes, pushing her finger against the button and holding it there for several seconds at a time because she thought perhaps Moxley was asleep."

"And then," Perry Mason said, "I suppose they flashed the fact of the garage key on her, and asked her to explain how it got in Moxley's apartment, if she hadn't been able to get him to answer the door."

"Exactly," Drake said. "And the way she answered it was that she'd been there earlier in the afternoon and had dropped the keys; that she hadn't realized it until quite a bit later."

Mason smiled, a wry smile which held no mirth. It was like the grimace of a man who has bit into a lemon. "And all of this time," he said, "Carl Montaine is insisting that he locked the door of the garage when he put his car in, and that Rhoda must have had her keys in order to get the garage open; that she, herself, told him she had left her purse in the car and that she went out and unlocked the door in order to get the purse just before she went to bed."

"Oh, well," Drake said, reassuringly, "*some one* on the jury will believe her."

"Not after the district attorney's office gets

done with the facts," Perry Mason said slowly. "You see they've trapped her into making the most damaging admission she could make."

"I don't see it," Drake said, his protruding eyes staring steadily at Mason.

"Don't you see?" Mason pointed out. "The strongest claim she could have made would have been self-defense. It would have been her word against the sealed lips of a dead man. There was nothing the district attorney's office could have done to have contradicted her story. If she'd sprung it at the proper time and in the proper way, she'd have been almost certain to have won the sympathy and belief of the jury.

"Now, the newspaper accounts show that the people who lived next door heard the doorbell ringing during the time the murder was being committed. Rhoda kept thinking about that, and realized that there was an opportunity for her to claim *she* was the one who had been ringing the doorbell. At first blush, it looked like an easy out for her. If she could put herself in the position of having been on the porch, ringing that doorbell, she'd have an air-tight alibi. It was a trap and she walked right into it.

"Now, the district attorney has got three shots at her. First, he can show, from the time element, that it couldn't have been she. Second, he can show from the keys that were found in the room that she *must* have been in the room with Moxley *after* she had unlocked the door of the garage. Third, and most dangerous of all, he can

154

uncover the person who really was ringing that doorbell and put him on the witness stand to rebut Rhoda's testimony.

"By that time, the door to a plea of self-defense has been closed. She's either got to establish the fact that she wasn't there at all, or she's got to be caught in so many falsehoods that she's guilty of first degree murder."

Drake nodded his head slowly. "I hadn't thought of it in just that light," he said, "but I can see where it fits in."

Della Street twisted the knob of the door, opened it just wide enough to slip through into Perry Mason's private office. "The father," she said, "is out there."

"Who?" asked Perry Mason.

"C. Phillip Montaine, of Chicago."

"How does he look, Della?"

"He's one of those men who are hard to figure. He's past sixty, but there isn't any film on his eyes. They're as bright as the eyes of a bird. He's got a close-cropped white mustache, thin, straight lips and a poker face. He's well-tailored and distinguished looking. He knows his way around."

Mason glanced from Della Street to Paul Drake, said slowly, "This man has got to be handled just right. In many ways, he represents the key to the situation. He controls the purse strings. I want to put him in such a position that he'll pay for Rhoda's defense. My idea of what he would be like doesn't check with that description, Della. I figured him for a pompous, egotistical man who has been accustomed to dominating people through his financial position. I figured that I'd make him mad and frighten him a little bit by letting him think he had to give Rhoda a break to keep the newspapers from ridiculing the Montaine name that he's so touchy about."

Mason stared thoughtfully at the silent Della Street. "Well," he said, "say something." She shook her head and smiled. "Go on," the lawyer said, "you can read character pretty well. I want to find out how this man impresses you."

"You can't handle him that way, chief," she said.

"Why not?"

"Because," she said, staring steadily at him, "he's got poise and intelligence. He's got something all planned out — a campaign of his own. I don't know what it is he wants, but I'll bet he's figured out how he's going to handle you, just the way you've figured out how you were going to handle him."

Mason's eyes glinted. "Okay," he said, "I can handle him that way, too." He turned to Paul Drake. "You'd better go out through the outer office, Paul, so you can get a look at him. We may have to shadow him later on, and I want you to know what he looks like."

Drake nodded. A grin emphasized the droll humor of his face. He sauntered to the door, opened it and paused in the doorway. "Thank you very much, Counselor," he said, "for the advice. I'll let you know if I have any more trouble." He closed the door.

Mason faced Della Street. "Della," he said, "I may have to get rough with this guy. He'll probably try coming in here with a lot of talk about what an important man he is. I want to beat him to it, and . . ."

The door to the outer office pushed open. Paul Drake, speaking hastily, said, "There was one matter I forgot to ask you about, Counselor. I know you'll pardon me." He strode through the door, pushing it shut, extended his long legs and covered the distance to Perry Mason's desk in four swift steps. "Pin this bird down as to the time he came to town," he said, speaking rapidly.

"You mean the father?" Mason asked, his eyes showing surprise.

"Yes."

"Presumably after he read about the murder," Mason said. "His son tells me that the father was working on a financial deal of major importance, and . . ."

"If that man in your outer office," Paul Drake interrupted, "is C. Phillip Montaine, he came here *before* Moxley was murdered — not afterwards." Mason pursed his lips and gave a low whistle. Drake leaned across the lawyer's desk and said, "You remember that when I saw Rhoda Montaine coming out of this office, I noticed she was being shadowed, and I trailed along for awhile?"

157

"Are you trying to tell me," Mason asked, "that this man was the shadow?"

"No, he wasn't the shadow, but he was sitting in an automobile parked close to the curb. He's got the type of eyes that don't miss much. He saw Rhoda Montaine, he saw the man who was following her, and he saw me. I don't know whether he figured there was any connection or not."

"You can't be mistaken, Paul?"

"Not a chance."

"But his son told me that his father was in Chicago."

"The son might have been lying or the father might have been lying."

"Perhaps the old man's lying," Mason said. "The son isn't. If Carl had known his father was here in the city he'd have brought the old man along to give him moral support when he first came here. Carl's the type who needs some one to back his play. He's relied on his dad all his life. The old man may have been here without letting the son know he was here."

"Why would he do that?" Drake asked.

"I don't know, but maybe I can find out. Did he see you, Paul?"

"Sure he saw me. What's more I think he remembered me. But I pulled a dead-pan on him and he doesn't know I've spotted him. He thinks I'm just a client. I'll duck out now. I wanted you to have the low-down before you saw him."

Mason said slowly, "There's one other explanation, Paul. This guy may not be Montaine at all."

The detective nodded slow agreement.

"But why," demanded Della Street, "would an impostor call on you, chief?"

Mason's laugh was grim and mirthless. "Because the district attorney might figure I was going to try and put the screws on the old man," he said, "So the D.A. figured he'd run in a ringer and see what I did about it."

"Oh, please," Della pleaded, "do be careful, chief!"

"That would mean," the detective remarked thoughtfully, "that the man's out of the D.A.'s office; and *that* would mean the D.A. was having Rhoda shadowed *before* the murder. Perry, you'd better find out *all* about this guy before you open up on him."

Mason indicated the door. "Okay, Paul. Make an artistic getaway."

The detective once more opened the door, said as though he had opened the door in the middle of a sentence, ". . . glad I thought of it now. It's a complication I was afraid of, but I see you have the matter in mind. Thank you very much, Counselor." The door slammed.

Della Street's eyes pleaded with Perry Mason. The lawyer motioned her toward the door. "We can't have any delay now, Della," he said, "or he'll be suspicious. He probably remembered Paul Drake. He'll naturally wonder whether Paul came back to tip me off. So open the door and bring him in."

Della Street opened the door. "Mr. Mason will see you, Mr. Montaine," she said.

Montaine entered the room, bowed, smiled, and did not offer to shake hands. "Good morning, Counselor," he said.

Perry Mason, on his feet, indicated a chair. Montaine dropped into the chair. Mason sat down, and Della Street closed the door to the outer office. "Doubtless," Montaine said, "you know why I am here."

Mason spoke with disarming frankness. "I'm glad you are here, Mr. Montaine. I wanted to talk with you. I understood from your son, however, that you were involved in a very important financial deal. I presume you dropped everything when you heard about the murder."

"Yes, I chartered a private plane and arrived late last night."

"You've seen Carl?" Mason inquired.

There was a frosty twinkle in Montaine's eyes. "Perhaps, Counselor," he said, "it would be better if I stated my errand first and then you questioned me afterwards."

"Go ahead," Mason said bluntly.

"Let's start out by being fair and frank with each other," Montaine said. "I am a financier. The attorneys I contact are lawyers who have specialized in corporation law. They are usually men who have made fortunate investments through the judicious use of influential connections. You are the first criminal attorney I have

160

ever met professionally.

"I know, generally, that you men are in many ways sharper than the attorneys I have done business with. You have a reputation for being less scrupulous. Whenever the respectable element wants to find a goat for the ever increasing 'crime waves' it blames the criminal attorney.

"My son consulted you. He's anxious to have his wife cleared of the charges against her. Yet, because he is a Montaine, he won't lie." Montaine paused impressively. "He is going to tell nothing more nor less than the exact truth, regardless of what the cost may be."

"You haven't told me anything yet," Mason said.

"I'm laying a foundation."

"Forget the foundation. You don't need it. Get to the point."

"Very well. My son retained you to represent his wife. I know that you expect pay for your services. I know that you know my son has virtually nothing in his own name. I realize, therefore, that in the back of your mind you have fixed upon me as the source of your fee. I am not a fool, and I assume that you are not.

"I am not questioning my son's judgment. I think he selected an excellent attorney for the purpose. However, I don't want you to underestimate *me*. Under certain circumstances I'm willing to pay for the defense of Rhoda Montaine and to pay handsomely. Unless these conditions

161

are met, I shall refuse to pay a red cent."

"Go on," Mason said, "you're doing the talking."

"Unfortunately," Montaine remarked, after biting at the end of his stubby white mustache for a moment, "there are some things I cannot say. The district attorney's office has advised me of certain steps they contemplate taking. I can't reveal those steps to you without violating a confidence. On the other hand, I know that you are a very shrewd individual, Mr. Mason."

"So what?" Perry Mason asked.

"So," Montaine said, "while *I* can't tell *you* what those steps are, if *you* should tell *me* that you have anticipated those steps, we might then discuss the matter frankly."

Perry Mason made drumming gestures with his fingertips. "I presume," he said, "you're referring to the fact that as long as your son and Rhoda are husband and wife, the district attorney's office can't use Carl as a witness. They will, therefore, try to get an annulment of the marriage."

A smile lit Montaine's face. "Thank you, Counselor," he said. "Thank you very much, indeed. I had hoped you might make a statement of that nature. You will understand my position in relation to that annulment action."

"You," Mason said, "feel that your son married beneath him, is that right?"

"Certainly."

"Why?"

"He married a woman who was after him only for his money; a woman whose previous life had certainly not been above reproach; a woman who continued to make clandestine appointments with the man who had been her former husband, and also with a doctor who had been intimately associated with her."

"You think that association was improper?"

"I am not saying that."

"You are implying it."

"After all, Counselor, isn't this rather beside the point? You asked me a question and I answered it fairly and frankly. Perhaps you do not agree with my feelings. Nevertheless, your question concerned my feelings, rather than facts."

"The reason I asked the question," Mason said, "was because I want to get your attitude clarified in my own mind. I take it you're anxious to have the marriage declared null and void. What you want me to do is to promise you that while I'll put up the best defense I can for Rhoda Montaine, I'll not fight the annulment action. Moreover, when it comes to the cross-examining of your son, you'll expect me to lay off making him appear too ridiculous. If I'll promise to coöperate on these things you're willing to pay me a nice fee. If I don't coöperate, you're not going to give me a dime. Is that right?"

Montaine seemed uncomfortable. "You have expressed the idea," he said cautiously, "far more bluntly than I would have dared to."

"But accurately?" Mason asked.

Montaine met his eyes. "Yes," he said, "quite accurately. You do not, of course, know the amount of the fee I am prepared to pay. It is, I think, much larger than would be considered customary. Do you understand me?"

Perry Mason clenched his fist tight, pounded it slowly upon the desk, giving emphasis to his words. "I get you now. I'm even way ahead of you. You want to get rid of Rhoda Montaine. If she'll let the district attorney annul the marriage to Carl, you'll be willing to give her a break on the murder case. If she insists on the legality of the marriage, you'll try to get rid of her by having her convicted of murder. Carl's a weak sister. You know it, and I know it. If Rhoda is acquitted and still remains Carl's wife she might prove troublesome. If she's willing to give Carl up, you'll give her money to defend the charges against her. If she insists on sticking to Carl, you'll throw in with the district attorney and try to get her convicted of murder. You're so damned cold-blooded you don't care about anything except getting your way."

"Isn't that," Montaine asked coldly, "being rather unfair to me?"

"No," Mason said, "I think not."

"I think so."

"Perhaps," Mason said, "because you haven't been fair with yourself. Perhaps you haven't gone so far as to analyze your motives and to determine just how far you are ready to go."

"Is it necessary, Counselor, that we should

discuss my motives in order to get your answer to my proposition?"

"Yes."

"I don't see why."

"Because," Mason said, "your motives, for reasons which I shall presently discuss, may be of controlling importance."

"You still haven't given me an answer to my proposition."

"My answer," Mason said, "is an emphatic negative. I am called upon to defend Rhoda Montaine. I think it will be very much to her advantage to seal the lips of your son by insisting upon the legality of the marriage. Therefore, I shall contest any annulment suit."

"Perhaps you *can't* contest it."

"Perhaps."

"The district attorney feels certain that you can't. He says the matter is legally dead open-and-shut. I only came to you because I have a great respect for your mental agility."

Mason permitted himself to grin. "Do you mean ability or agility?" he asked.

"I mean agility," Montaine said.

Mason nodded slowly. "Perhaps," he said, "I can convince you that there is some ability, as well as some agility. For instance, let us now return to an analysis of your motives. You are proud of your family name. If Rhoda Montaine was legally married to your son and was executed for murder, it would be a black spot upon that family name. Therefore, ordinarily, you would reserve the proposition. If Rhoda Montaine was *not* your daughter-in-law, you wouldn't care whether she was convicted of murder or not. If the marriage was legal, you'd move heaven and earth to get her acquitted.

"Your proposition shows you'd do *anything* to get Rhoda out of the family. Offhand, I'd say this was because you recognize Rhoda's influence over your son. You wouldn't know of this casually. You must have acquired the information at first hand. I should, therefore, surmise that you didn't leave Chicago last night as you say you did, but that you have been here in this city for several days, keeping your presence a secret from both your son and Rhoda Montaine. I might even go farther and surmise that you employed detectives to shadow Rhoda, in order to find out just what sort of a woman she was, just what she was doing, and just how much Carl was actually under her influence.

"I might surmise, further, that you have some other marriage in view for Carl, a marriage which is, perhaps, of the greatest importance to you financially; that you want to have Carl legally free to enter into such a marriage."

Montaine got to his feet. His face was entirely without expression. "You are deducing these matters," he said, "*merely* from an analysis of my motives, Counselor?"

"Perhaps," Mason said, "I am thinking out loud."

Montaine said softly, "Perhaps you are, and

166

then, again, it may have been rather a peculiar coincidence that the detective who left your office as I was waiting in the outer room found it necessary to return for a final word with you. I'll admit he did it rather cleverly. He looked at me casually, walked past me to the door and then suddenly 'remembered' that it was necessary for him to return to your private office."

"Then," Mason said, "you *were* here, spying upon Rhoda Montaine."

"You might say," Montaine said, "that I was gathering certain data."

"Does your son know this?"

"No."

"And you employed detectives to shadow Rhoda Montaine?"

"I think," Montaine said, "I have answered enough of your questions, Counselor. I have only one more statement to make — that is that you may feel you can make a valid legal claim against Carl for your services in defending Rhoda. Therefore, you feel you have nothing to lose by refusing to accept my offer. I want to assure you, however, that Carl has nothing in his own name and unless you do accept my offer, the chances that you will receive any remuneration for your work in behalf of Rhoda are exceedingly slim."

"Aren't you," Mason asked, "rather hard?"

"I am inflexible, if that is what you mean."

"That isn't what I meant."

Montaine bowed. "Well, Counselor," he said,

"I think we understand each other perfectly. Think it over. Don't give me a final answer now. Despite your mental *ability* I might prove a dangerous adversary."

Mason held open the door to the corridor. "You've got my final answer," he said. "If you want war you can have it."

Montaine paused in the hallway. "Sleep on it," he suggested.

Mason said nothing, banged the door shut. He stood for a moment in thoughtful contemplation, then strode to the telephone, picked up the receiver, and, when he heard Della Street's voice on the wire, said, "Get me Paul Drake, Della."

A moment later the telephone rang. Mason spoke swiftly. "Paul," he said, "we've got to work fast. Here's something I want you to get busy on right away: Moxley was a swindler. He specialized in swindling women. We know that some one telephoned Moxley a short time before he was murdered. We know that this someone was demanding money. That person is very likely to have been a woman. We know that on at least one occasion Moxley went through a marriage ceremony in order to get possession of some money he wanted. You're checking back on Moxley's life. As fast as you get an alias that he used, have your men cover the hotel registers and the public utility offices to see if a woman using one of those aliases as a married name has recently arrived in the city. We might locate the person who was putting the screws on Moxley

168

before the police get the information."

"Good idea," Drake said. "How about Montaine? Do you think we should try to put a shadow on him?"

"No," Mason said. "It wouldn't do any good. He didn't come to my office until he was ready to. From now on, his life is going to be out in the open. We could shadow him until Doomsday, and wouldn't find anything. Whatever mischief *he's* been up to, he's been up to before he came here."

"I was right then," the detective inquired, "and he'd been here for several days?"

"Yes."

"Did he admit it?"

"Not until after I put the screws on him. He spotted you, and he knew you were a detective."

"What was he doing here?" Drake asked.

"That," Mason said, "is something we can only surmise. He wasn't talkative. There's more to this than we figure, Paul."

"He must have been following Rhoda," Drake said. "He must have shadowed her to your office."

"Yes, I think he did."

"Then, when Carl called on you," Drake said, "Carl must have known through his father that his wife had called on you."

"Yes, I think he did."

"Then the father and the son must be working together."

"That's an inference," the lawyer agreed, "but

we've got to feel our way, Paul. We're going up against a tough combination."

Drake's voice betrayed a trace of excitement. "Look here, Perry," he said, "if Montaine was following Rhoda around, he must have known about Moxley."

"He did."

"Then he must have known about the appointment for two o'clock in the morning."

"He didn't admit that."

"Did you ask him about it?" Drake inquired.

Perry Mason laughed. "No," he said, "but I will."

"When?"

"At an opportune moment," the lawyer replied, "and I think you'd better forget about Montaine, Paul. He's an intelligent man and a ruthless man. For all of his vaunted family pride, he thought nothing whatever of sacrificing the life of Rhoda Montaine in order to further his own interests."

"Well, don't let him crawl out of the picture," Drake cautioned.

"Hell!" Mason exclaimed. "I'd no more let him crawl out of the picture than a kid would let Santa Claus crawl out of the picture around Christmas time."

Chuckling, he hung up the telephone. Della Street opened the door from the outer office. "A messenger," she said, "has just brought papers that were served on Rhoda in the case of Carl Montaine against Rhoda Montaine. It's an action for an annulment of the marriage.

"And Doctor Millsap rang up and told me to tell you they sweated him at headquarters all night, without getting anything out of him. He seemed real proud of himself."

Mason's tone was grim. "They're not done with *him* yet," he said, reaching for the papers Della Street held out to him.

Chapter 11

Perry Mason moved cautiously through the night shadows. In the doorway of the Colemont Apartments he paused to listen. Along Norwalk Avenue lay the silence of staid respectability. From the main boulevard came the noise of an occasional horn, the whining sound of cars rushing through the night. The midnight carousers, turning from gay revelry to a contemplation of the morrow's work, sought to atone for wasted hours by crowding automobiles to greater speed.

The entrance to the Colemont Apartments was dark and silent. A short distance down the street, the Bellaire Apartments glowed with illumination from an indirect lighting fixture which shed a soft radiance over the foyer, the mail boxes, call bells and speaking tubes. Some of this brilliance radiated to the sidewalk, filtered into the entrance of the all but obsolete apartment house where Moxley had met his death. Perry Mason stood for some five minutes in the shadows, making certain that no patrolling steps were beating down the sidewalk, that no police radio car was cruising in the vicinity.

Earlier in the day Perry Mason, working

through a real estate agent, had rented the entire building. Three of the apartments had been vacant for several months. The fourth had been rented by the week, furnished, by Gregory Moxley. The march of progress had doomed the old frame building to eventual destruction. Tenants demanded more modern apartments. The owners of the building had been only too glad to accept the rental offer made by the lawyer's representative, without inquiring too minutely as to the purpose for which the building was to be used, or the identity of the tenant.

Mason took from his pocket the four keys which had been delivered to him. Shielding the beam of a flashlight under his coat, he selected one of the keys, inserted it quietly in the lock and paused once more to listen. A car turned off the main boulevard and whined past the street intersection. Mason waited until it had reached the next corner before turning the key. The lock clicked, the door swung open and Perry Mason stepped into the darkness, pausing to close and lock the door behind him. He groped his way up the stairs upon cautious feet that kept crowding the side of the stair treads, lest they should make unnecessary noise.

The apartment that had been occupied by the murdered man covered the entire south side of the upper floor. Street lights, sending beams through the windows, furnished sufficient illumination to disclose the outlines of the furniture.

What had, at one period of the history of the house, been a front bedroom was now remodeled into a living room. Back of it, a room had been fitted as a dining room, and back of the dining room was a kitchen and a corridor. The corridor led to a bedroom in the back of the kitchen. A bathroom opened from the bedroom. Perry Mason moved quietly through the room, checking the articles of furniture against the copies of the police photographs which he carried in his hand and which he illuminated with his small flashlight. He moved to the window which looked out toward the Bellaire Apartments. That window was now closed and locked. Perry Mason made no effort to raise it. He stood by the window, staring at the dark apartment directly opposite, an apartment which was, he knew, occupied by Benjamin Crandall and wife.

Perry Mason moved back across the room, out into the corridor and entered the kitchen. Over a gas stove he found what he was looking for.

The lawyer tip-toed to the window, carefully pulled down the curtain, making certain that it was fixed in an even position at the bottom, so that no light would trickle through. He snapped on his flashlight, took from his pocket a screwdriver and a pair of pliers, a roll of adhesive tape and some wire. He picked up a chair, carried it across to a point of vantage, stood on the chair, and let the circle of illumination from his flashlight rest upon the electric bell which had been screwed into the wall. Working with painstaking caution, Perry Mason unfastened the screws, disconnected the wires, removed the bell from the wall. When he had it in his hand, he carefully studied it, then stepped down from the chair. Using the beam of the flashlight to guide him, he walked to the head of the stairs. Here he had placed a package which had been under his arm when he entered the apartment.

He untied a heavy cord, opened the package and disclosed four buzzers, similar in appearance in every way to the bell which he had taken from the wall above the gas stove. The only difference was that the one he had removed was a bell which rang by agitating a clapper between two hollow hemispheres of metal; while the others were buzzers which gave forth an explosive buzzing sound when the current went through the coils.

Mason carried one of the buzzers back to the kitchen, climbed on the chair, screwed the buzzer into position and saw that the wires were connected. Then he replaced the chair and raised the curtain. He paused to listen, picked up his package and tip-toed down the stairs. He waited for several seconds before he unlocked the door and slipped out into the cool night air.

Hearing no sound, he locked the door behind him, took another key from his pocket and opened the door of the lower apartment. This apartment exuded a smell of musty closeness — a smell that assailed the nostrils with a message of untenanted neglect. Perry Mason found the call bell in the kitchen, and replaced it with a buzzer. Then he raised the curtain and slipped silently into the night.

He next opened the door which led to the upper apartment, opposite the one in which Moxley had been killed. Working swiftly and silently, he again disconnected the call bell and installed one of the buzzers. He was on the point of leaving the apartment when the beam of his flashlight picked up the stub of a burnt match in the corridor. The match was one of those waxed paper affairs which had been torn from a pocket package. Mason slid the beam of his flashlight along the boards of the corridor, soon picked up another match stub, and then another. He followed those stubs to the back porch, where the light fuse boxes for the apartment were kept. Here was also a place for the delivery of groceries and garbage.

Mason noticed that a similar porch-like platform projected from the apartment on the south which Moxley had occupied. An agile man could easily slip across the intervening space, climb a railing and find himself in the back of Moxley's apartment, with access through corridor and kitchen to the bedroom where Moxley was murdered.

Mason stepped across to the adjoining porch. Here he found one more match, and then, over in the corner where it apparently had been discarded, the empty container from which the matches had been torn. It was of waxed pasteboard with a flap which folded over the matches. On the back of this folder was printed a cut of a five story building, below which appeared the printed words "Compliments of the Palace Hotel, the best in Centerville."

Perry Mason wrapped the bit of pasteboard in a handkerchief, slipped it in his pocket. He retraced his steps, left the upper apartment and made a brief visit to the remaining lower apartment. When he left the house, there was not a single electric doorbell in the building. Each one of the four apartments was equipped with buzzers.

Mason wrapped the bells carefully in the heavy, brown paper, tied up the package into a compact bundle, listened to make sure no one was about, and then stepped out from the shadows of the foyer to the sidewalk.

Chapter 12

Perry Mason flung back his shoulders and inhaled the fresh air of the morning. He consulted a small memorandum book, looked at the street numbers, paused as his eyes caught a sign on the glass window of a small storeroom. The sign read, "OTIS ELECTRIC COMPANY." Mason pushed open the door, heard a bell ringing in the back of the store. He stood in a narrow space between counters that were loaded down with electric light globes, brackets, switches, and wires. Overhead, the ceiling was clustered with various chandeliers and indirect lighting fixtures.

A door from the rear opened. A young woman smiled ingratiatingly. "I want to see Sidney Otis," said Perry Mason.

"You got something to sell?" she asked, the smile fading from her face.

"Tell him," Mason said, "that Perry Mason, the lawyer, wants to see him."

There was the sound of commotion from the back room, the noise of something being dropped to the floor. Quick steps pounded the floor. A burly figure in overalls pushed the young woman to one side and stood staring at Perry

Mason, a wide grin twisting his lips away from tobacco-stained teeth. Sidney Otis weighed well over two hundred. His weight was evenly distributed. He radiated a genial booming honesty. His arms were bare to the elbow, and smeared with grease. His overalls had, very apparently, never seen the interior of a wash tub, but there was wholehearted cordiality in his welcome. "Perry Mason!" he said. "This *is* an honor! I didn't think you'd remember me."

Mason laughed. "I always remember people who sit on my juries, Otis," he said. "How are you?" He extended his hand.

The big man hesitated for a moment, then wiped his paw up and down on the leg of his overalls, and folded his fingers about Mason's hand. "Tickled to death, Counselor," he said, suddenly self-conscious.

"There's something you can do for me," Mason told him.

"Tell me what it is and I'll do it." Perry Mason glanced significantly at the young woman.

The big electrician jerked his head toward the rear. "Beat it, Bertie," he said. "I've got some business to talk over with Mr. Mason."

"Aw gee, dad, I never get to . . ."

"You heard me," Otis boomed, his big voice filling the shop, but his face twisted in a grin. "Beat it."

The girl pouted, moved toward the rear of the store on reluctant feet. When the spiteful bang of the door announced that she had moved out of earshot, Otis turned an inquiring face to the lawyer.

"Where are you living now, Otis?"

The man lowered his eyes apologetically. "I used to keep an apartment upstairs," he said, "but sledding has been tough lately. I've got a room where I keep the missus and the little girl, the other one stays down here with me and helps run the shop. I've got a bed in the back that I sleep on, and . . ."

"I have taken a lease on an apartment for six months," Perry Mason said, "and it happens that I can't live in the apartment. I'd like to have you move in."

"In an apartment!" said Otis, the grin fading from his face. "Oh, shucks, Counselor, I couldn't afford anything like that. . . ."

"The rent," Perry Mason said, "is all paid for six months. It's rather a nice apartment."

Otis frowned. "How come?" he asked.

"It is," said Perry Mason, "the apartment where a man was murdered. You probably read about it in the paper. It's Apartment B of the Colemont Apartments at 316 Norwalk Avenue. A man by the name of Carey was murdered there. That was his real name. He was going under the name of Moxley at the time of the murder."

"Yeah, I read about it," Otis said. "They got some woman for it, didn't they? The wife of a wealthy guy from Chicago."

Mason nodded. There was a moment of silence and then the lawyer went on in a low voice, "Of course, Otis, your family wouldn't need to know that a murder had been committed there. They might recognize the place, or some of the neighbors might tell them, but by that time they'd be moved in. It's a very comfortable little apartment. It would be a nice place for the folks. It's on the south side of the house and catches the sunshine."

"Gee, that'd be swell," Otis said, "but why do that for me, Counselor?"

"Because," Perry Mason said, "I want you to do something for me."

"What is it?"

"When you move into the apartment," Perry Mason said impressively, "and I'd like to have you move in today, I want you to take off the doorbell that's in the apartment and put on one of your own."

The electrician frowned and said, "Take off the doorbell?"

"It may be a bell, or it may be a buzzer," Mason said. "Whichever one it is, I want you to take it off and put on another one. The doorbell that you put on must be one that you've taken from stock. I want it to have your price mark on it, and I want you to have at least two witnesses who see you take off the one that's there now and put the new one on. Those two witnesses can be two members of your family if you want, but I want to be certain they see you do it, and I don't want any one to know *why* you're doing it. You can make some objection to the bell or buzzer that's there now. Say that you don't like the sound of it, or something of that sort."

"You don't want me to put on a buzzer?" asked Otis, puzzled. "If there's a buzzer on there now, do you want me to put on a buzzer?"

"No. Put on a doorbell, and put on one that you've taken from stock. Be sure it's a bell and not a buzzer."

The electrician nodded.

"One more thing," Mason said, "the bell or buzzer that's on there now must be kept, and when you take it off, you can put some mark of identification on it so you'll know it if you see it again. For instance, you can let your screwdriver slip and make a long scratch across the enamel, something that will look like an accident, and yet will furnish means of identification. Do you understand?"

Otis nodded. "I think I do," he said. "Tell me, is it on the up and up?"

"Absolutely. I've paid the rent to the landlord for six months in advance. If any one should ask you how you happened to rent that apartment, you can say that you wanted an apartment where you could put your family, a place where there was some sunlight; that you didn't want to pay a high rental; that as soon as you saw in the paper that a murder had been committed in this apartment, you knew that it could be rented cheap.

"Here's the key to the apartment and here's fifty dollars which will cover the expenses of moving in. It's furnished, but there's room for anything you've got."

The big electrician made a brushing motion with his hand, pushing back the folded fifty dollar bill.

Mason insisted. "It's a matter of business all around, Otis," he said. "You're doing me a favor and it gives me a chance to do you a favor."

Otis was undecided for a moment; suddenly his forehead puckered to a frown. "Wasn't there something in that case," he said, "about people next door hearing a doorbell ring when the murder was being committed?"

Perry Mason stared steadily at him. "Yes," he said.

Otis grinned, reached out and took the fifty dollars. "Thanks, Counselor," he said, "we'll move in today."

Chapter 13

Paul Drake was seated in Perry Mason's outer office chatting with Della Street when Mason pushed open the door, removed his hat and grinned greeting. The detective elevated a bony forefinger toward the morning paper which was folded under the lawyer's arm. "Have you read it?" he asked.

Mason shook his head. "I usually buy it from the boy at the corner," he said, "and read it before I start the daily grind. Why? Is there anything important in it?"

The detective nodded lugubriously. Della Street's face was serious. Perry Mason looked from one to the other.

"Go ahead," he said, "spill it."

"The district attorney," Drake said, "has evidently got a regular professional publicity man on the job."

"Why?"

"Because every morning he keeps releasing something dramatic against your client."

Mason said tonelessly, "He'll run out of facts one of these mornings. What is it this time?"

"He's going to exhume the body of the man who was buried under the name of Gregory Lorton. He intimated he expects to find poison. He keeps harping back to the fact that Rhoda Montaine was a nurse; that she put Ipral in her husband's chocolate when she wanted him to sleep soundly; that if she wanted him to sleep just a little more soundly, it would have been an easy matter for her to have put in a deadly poison."

The lines of Mason's face became harsh. "They're afraid they won't be able to use the testimony of the husband in court, so they're spreading this Ipral business all over the newspapers.

"There's no question they're using a deliberate campaign of adverse newspaper publicity. They're trying to slap me in the face with the front page of a newspaper every morning."

"Anything you can do about it?" asked Paul Drake.

Mason narrowed his lips and said, "A lot I can do about it. If he wants to give that girl a fair trial, that's one thing. If he wants to try the case in the newspapers and try to prejudice the public against her, that's another thing."

"Watch your step, chief," Della Street warned; "the district attorney may be trying to get you to do something desperate."

Perry Mason's slow grin held grim portent. "I've fought the devil with fire before this, and haven't had my fingers burnt."

"You've had your hair singed a couple of times," Drake pointed out. "When you start pulling fast ones, you can take more chances than any one I ever knew."

A twinkle came to the lawyer's eyes. "Well," he said, "I'll promise you both something."

"What is it?"

"You haven't seen anything yet."

"You mean you're going to pull a fast one in this case?" Della Street asked, her eyes dark with concern.

"So fast," Mason said, "that it's going to whiz over the home plate before any one knows whether it's a strike or a ball."

"What good's it going to do if the umpire can't call it?" Drake inquired, the droll humor of his face more emphasized than ever.

"Perhaps," said Perry Mason softly, "it's not anything that I want called by the umpire. I may be aiming at the man who's doing the batting. . . . Come on in, Paul."

The two men seated themselves in Mason's private office. Drake pulled a notebook from his pocket.

"Got something, Paul?"

"I think so."

"What is it?"

"You told me to check back on Moxley and find out everything he'd been doing, as nearly as I could."

"Yes."

"It wasn't easy. Moxley did time. He got out

of jail broke. He needed money pretty badly. He was a lone wolf, so it's pretty hard to tell *all* that he did, but I've got a line on something that he did, that is, I *think* he did it."

"Go ahead," the lawyer said.

"We found out Moxley put through a long distance call to Centerville. We also discovered his trunk had a label from the Palace Hotel in Centerville. We checked the records of the Palace Hotel and couldn't find where Moxley had ever been registered there. However, there's one peculiar thing about his record. He'd keep changing his last name, but he'd nearly always keep his first name as Gregory. He probably did that so when people called him by his first name, he didn't have to watch his step to remember an alias. Anyhow, we went back over the records of the Palace Hotel, and found that a Gregory Freeman had been registered there for something over two months. So we took a look through the marriage licenses and found out that a man named Gregory Freeman had married a girl by the name of Doris Pender.

"We looked up the Pender woman and found that she'd been employed as a stenographer and bookkeeper in a creamery, there at Centerville. She was a steady, industrious worker and had saved up a little money that she'd put in stocks and bonds. Then she got married, gave up her job and moved away with her husband. Apparently, she didn't have any relatives there in Centerville, although the people at the creamery thought she had a brother some place in the northern part of the state."

Mason's eyes glittered with concentration. He nodded his head thoughtfully. "Good work, Paul," he said.

"So," the detective went on, "we checked through the meter connections of the electric light company, just on a chance that Gregory Moxley and this Pender woman might have lived under the name of Gregory Freeman. We didn't find any connections under that name, but we did find a meter connection about two weeks ago under the name of Doris Freeman at the Balboa Apartments, at seven twenty-one West Ordway. She's got apartment 609. She's living there by herself. No one seems to know a thing about her."

"Perhaps," said the lawyer, "we can trace some telephone calls through the apartment switchboard, and . . ."

The detective grinned. "Listen," he said, "what do you think us guys do to earn our money?"

"Oh," Mason said pointedly, "*do* you earn it?"

"Wait until I finish and you'll say we do," Drake said. "I haven't told you anything yet."

"Go ahead then and tell me something."

"We found there was a switchboard in the lobby. There's some one on duty in the lobby all the time. The switchboard isn't particularly busy. They keep a record of calls that are made and the number of the apartment from which the calls come.

"We were afraid to try and pump the person who had the records, so we arranged to decoy him away from the desk for a few minutes, and one of my operatives slipped in and took a look in the book that lists the telephone records.

"These records aren't kept on an hourly basis — just by the date on which the calls are put through — but we found that this apartment was charged with a call to South nine-four-three-six-two on the sixteenth day of June, and that call was the first call in the book under date of June 16th, so it must have been made shortly after midnight."

"Where's the book?" asked the lawyer.

"Out there. But we got a photograph of the page that shows the call. That will keep them from doctoring the book, in case we want to bring it into court."

Mason nodded thoughtfully. "Good work," he said. "We may want to bring that book into court — and then, again, we may not. Have you got a good man that we can put on the job? One who's dependable, Paul?"

"Sure. I've got Danny Spear. He's the one who took the photograph."

"Is he good?"

"I'll say he is, one of the best in the business. You should remember him, Perry. We used him in that hatchet murder case."

Mason nodded. "Let's get him," he said,

"and go on out there."

"To the Balboa Apartments?"

"Yes."

Drake picked up his hat. "Let's go," he said.

Chapter 14

Paul Drake slowed his light car and swung in close to the curb. Danny Spear, a nondescript individual, with a flat-crowned brown hat tilted back to show rusty brown locks straggling out from under the sweat band, glanced inquiringly at Perry Mason.

Spear would never have been taken for a detective. There was something wide-eyed and innocent about him that made him appear to be a typical "rube" pausing in front of a shell game at a country fair. His face habitually wore the pleased grin of a yokel who is seeing the world for the first time. "What do I do?" he asked.

"You trail us into the apartment house," Mason told him. "We'll go in the jane's apartment and buzz the door. If she opens the door to let us in, you walk on past as though you were going to some apartment down at the end of the corridor. But you time things so that you get a look at her face as you walk past the door. It'll only be a quick glimpse, but you can get a flash of her face so you can spot her later on. Now, it's important that you get her fixed in your mind. If you don't get enough of a look to recognize her, you'd better wait until we get in and then come and knock at the door and put up some kind of a stall about knowing the jane that used to live in the apartment, or something of that sort. If you do get a good look at her, take a divorce from us and tail her if she goes out. We'll leave you with the car. When Drake and I leave the place, we'll call a cab. You can be sitting in the car. Do you get that straight?"

Danny Spear nodded. "I gotcha," he said.

"The probabilities are she'll watch us when we leave," Mason said. "She'll be worried, because that's what we're going there for. We're going to worry her. I don't know whether she pulled this stuff alone, or whether she didn't, but that's one of those things I want to find out."

"Suppose she telephones?" asked Spear.

Mason said slowly, "She won't telephone. We're going to make her think her line has been tapped."

"You're just going to make her suspicious, is that right?"

"Yes."

"She'll be *looking* for a shadow," Danny Spear protested.

"That's something we can't help. That's where you've got to play it carefully, and that's why I want you to get a divorce from us as soon as we leave the place. She'll see you walking past us in the corridor and won't figure that you're with us at all."

"Okay," Danny Spear said. "You birds had

better drive around the block and let me off at the corner. I'll walk up behind you and time things so we go in the apartment house together. There's just a chance some of her friends might be watching out of a window. If they saw the three of us get out of the same car, it might not be so hot."

Drake nodded, shifted the car into gear, ran around the block, dropped Danny at the corner, swung once more into a parking place in front of the apartment house, got out leisurely, and pulled down his vest, gave his coat collar a jerk and adjusted his tie. With well-simulated carelessness, the two men entered the apartment house, walking slowly. Behind them came Danny Spear, walking rapidly.

A fat man was seated in a rocking chair in the lobby. He was the only occupant.

Still walking slowly toward the elevator, Paul Drake and the lawyer swung slightly to one side as Danny Spear bustled past them. To the fat man in the chair it seemed purely a fortuitous combination of circumstances which placed all three men in the elevator at the same time.

In the upper corridor, Danny Spear held back, while the other two found the door of the apartment they wanted and tapped on the panels. There was the sound of motion, the click of a lock. The door opened, and a rather plain woman of about twenty-five years of age, with large brown eyes and thin, firm lips, stared in mute interrogation.

"Are you," asked Perry Mason in rather a loud voice, "Doris Freeman?"

"Yes," she said. "What do you want?"

Perry Mason turned slightly to one side, so that Danny Spear, walking rapidly down the corridor, could see the young woman's face.

"My business," said Perry Mason, "can hardly be stated in the corridor."

"Book agent?"

"No."

"Life insurance?"

"No."

"Selling anything?"

"No."

"What do you want?"

"To ask you a few questions."

The thin lips clamped more firmly together. The eyes widened. There was a flicker of fear in their depths. "Who are you?"

"We're collecting some data for the Bureau of Vital Statistics."

"I'm sure I don't know what you're talking about."

By this time, Danny Spear had gone well past them toward the end of the corridor, where he was pounding on a door with imperative knuckles. The door swung open, and a man's voice gruffed a greeting and the operative said, "I've got an express package down stairs for C. Finley Dodge. Where do you want it delivered? . . ."

Perry Mason boldly pushed his way past the woman, into the apartment. Drake followed and kicked the door shut. She remained standing, clad in a print housedress, and, as the light from the windows struck her face, it brought out incipient caliper lines which were stretching from her nostrils toward the ends of her thin lips. There was no make-up on her face, and her shoulders were slightly rounded. There could be no mistaking the fear in her eyes as her glance shifted from Mason to Drake, then back to Mason again. "What is it?" she asked.

The lawyer, who had been sizing her up carefully, nodded imperceptibly to Paul Drake. "It's important," he said, in a harsh, aggressive voice, "that you answer all of our questions truthfully. If you start lying to us, you're going to get into trouble, do you understand that?"

"What do you mean?" she countered.

"Are you married or single?" asked Perry Mason.

"I don't know what business it is of yours."

Mason raised his voice. "Never mind that, sister. You just answer my questions and keep your comments until later. Are you married or single?"

"I'm married."

"Where did you live before you came here?"

"I'm not going to tell you."

Mason looked over at Paul Drake and said significantly, "This is the best proof of guilt we can have."

As Doris Freeman turned to stare apprehensively at Paul Drake, Perry Mason lowered his right eyelid in a significant wink. "That isn't a sign of guilt, in itself," said Paul Drake, pursing his lips thoughtfully.

Mason whirled toward the young woman. Once more, his voice became the voice of a lawyer browbeating a witness. "You lived in Centerville, didn't you? Don't deny it. You might as well admit it now as later."

"Is it," she asked, "a crime to live in Centerville?"

Mason turned buck to Drake. His lips twisted in a sneer. "How much more do you want?" he asked. "If she isn't in on it she wouldn't stall like that."

Doris Freeman's hands crept to her throat. She walked unsteadily toward an overstuffed chair, sat down suddenly, as though her knees had lost their strength. "What," she said, "what . . ."

"Your husband's name," said Perry Mason.

"Freeman."

"What's his first name?"

"Sam."

Perry Mason's laugh was scornful. He flung his arm out in rigidly pointing accusation. An extended forefinger was leveled at her face as though it had been a loaded revolver. "Why do you tell us that," he said, "when you know his name was Gregory?"

She wilted, as though the life force had oozed from her pores. "Who . . . who are you?"

"If you really want to know," Perry Mason said, "the telephone company is investigating a charge that your phone has been used for black-mail."

She straightened slightly and said, "Not for blackmail. You can't call that blackmail."

"You were trying to collect money."

"Of course I was trying to collect money. I was trying to collect money that was due me."

"Who was helping you?" asked Perry Mason.

"That's none of your business."

"Don't you know that you can't use the tele-phone for that purpose?"

"I don't know why not."

"Haven't you ever heard that it's against the law to demand money on a postal card?"

"Yes, I've heard of that."

"And yet you have the nerve to sit there and claim that you don't know it's against the law to ring up a man and demand that he pay you money?"

"We didn't do that," she said.

"Didn't do what?"

"Didn't ring him up and demand that he give us money — not in so many words."

"Who's the 'we?' " asked Paul Drake.

Mason frowned at him, but the detective caught the significance of the signal too late to check the question.

"Just me," said Doris Freeman.

Perry Mason's voice showed exasperation. "And you didn't know that it was against the law to ask for money over the telephone?"

"I tell you we . . . I didn't ask for money."

"It was a man's voice," Perry Mason chanced, staring steadily at the young woman. "Our operator says it was a man's voice that did the talking." Doris Freeman was silent. "What have you to say to that?"

"Nothing . . . that is, it may have been a mistake. I had a cold. I talked rather gruffly."

Mason strode abruptly across the room, jerked the telephone receiver from its hook, placed it to his ear. At the same time, his right hand, resting carelessly across the top of the telephone, surreptitiously pushed down the telephone hook so there was no connection over the line. "Give me the investigations department, official six-two," he demanded.

He waited a few moments, then said, "This is Number Thirteen talking. We're out at this place where the threatening telephone call came through on the morning of June sixteenth. The apartment is in the name of Doris Freeman, but she's shielding some male accomplice. She claims she didn't know it was against the law to make a demand like that over the telephone."

He waited for a few more moments, then laughed sarcastically. "Well," he said, "that's what she *claims.* You can believe it or not. She came here from Centerville. Maybe they *haven't* got a city ordinance against that in Centerville. You never can tell. . . . Well, what do you want me to do with her, bring her in? . . . What?" screamed Perry Mason. "You mean that call that went through was to Moxley, the man that was murdered! . . . Gee, chief, that puts a different aspect on the situation. This is out of our hands. You'd better notify the district attorney. And watch the calls that come in over this line. . . . Well, you know how I feel about it. . . . Okay. G'by."

Mason hung up the telephone, turned to Paul Drake. His eyes were wide with well-simulated, startled surprise. He lowered his voice, as though awed by the grim portent of that which he had discovered. "Do you know who that call was to?" he asked.

Paul Drake also lowered his own voice. "I heard what you said to the chief," he remarked. "Was that right?"

"That's right. That call went through to Gregory Moxley, the man that was murdered, and the call went through just about half an hour before his death."

"What's the chief going to do?"

"There's only one thing he can do — turn it over to the district attorney. Gosh, I thought it was just a routine investigation, and here it has run into a murder rap."

Doris Freeman spoke with hysterical rapidity.

"Look here," she said, "I didn't know anything about any law that we couldn't use the telephone to collect money. That was money that was due to me. It was money that man had stolen from me. It was money he'd swindled me out of. He was a devil. He deserved to die. I'm glad he's dead! But the telephone call didn't

199

have anything to do with his murder. It was Rhoda Montaine that killed him! Don't you fellows ever read the papers?"

Mason stared at her with scornful appraisal. "The woman that was in the room when he was killed may have been Rhoda Montaine," Mason said, "but it wasn't a woman that struck that blow, and the district attorney's office knows it. That blow was struck by a powerful man. And you folks certainly had a motive for murder. It's a perfect case. You rang up less than half an hour before the death and told him he had to kick through. . . ." Mason abruptly shrugged his shoulder, lapsed into silence.

Paul Drake took up the conversation. "Well," he said, "you'd better come clean and . . ."

"Let's just forget it, Paul," Perry Mason said. "The chief is going to turn it over to the district attorney. The D.A. won't like the idea of having us mixed in on it. It's entirely outside of our province. Let's quit talking about it."

Drake nodded. The two men started for the door. Doris Freeman jumped to her feet. "But let me explain!" she said. "It isn't what you think it is at all. We didn't . . ."

"Save it for the D.A.," Perry Mason told her, and pulled the door open, motioning to Paul Drake to precede him into the corridor.

"But you don't understand," she said, "It's just a question of . . ."

Mason literally pushed the detective into the corridor, jumped out after him and slammed the door shut. Before they had gone five steps, Doris Freeman had the door open. "But won't you let me explain?" she said. "Can't I tell you . . ."

"We're not mixing in that kind of a mess," the lawyer declared. "That's outside of our jurisdiction. The chief has taken it up with the D.A. It's up to him."

The men almost ran to the elevator, as though the woman who stood in the doorway might be afflicted with some sort of plague. When the elevator door had closed on them and the cage was rattling downward, Paul Drake glanced inquiringly at Perry Mason. "She was ready to spill her story," he said ruefully.

"No, she wasn't. She was going to pull a line to get our sympathy, a long tale of woe about how Moxley tricked her. She'd never have told us about the man. He's the one we want. She'll go to him now. There's nothing that gets a person's goat like not letting them talk when they are trying to make a play for sympathy."

"Do you suppose it's some one living there with her?" Drake asked.

"It's hard to tell who it is. The thing that I'm figuring on is that it may be a detective or a lawyer."

The dectective gave an exclamation. "Boy, some lawyer is going to be plenty mad when she comes to him with a story about a couple of dicks who were going to arrest her for using the telephone to demand money. Do you suppose she'll call him on the telephone to tell him?"

201

"Not after the line we handed her about the calls being watched. She'll be afraid to use the telephone. She'll get in touch with him personally, whoever he is."

"You think she smelled a rat?" asked Drake.

"I doubt it," Mason answered. "Remember, she's awed by the city — and, if she does smell a rat, she'll think we're police detectives laying a trap for him."

The men piled out of the elevator, strode across the lobby and were careful not to even glance in the direction of the car, where Danny Spear sat slumped behind the wheel. They turned to the right, crossed the street, so that they would be in full view of the apartment house, and signaled a cruising cab.

Chapter 15

Back in his office, Perry Mason paced the floor, his thumbs thrust in the arm-holes of his vest. Della Street, seated at the corner of the big desk, the sliding leaf pulled out to hold her notebook, took down the words which Perry Mason flung over his shoulder as he paced up and down the room.

". . . wherefore, plaintiff prays that the bonds of matrimony existing between her, the said Rhoda Montaine, and the defendant, the said Carl W. Montaine, be dissolved by an order of this court; that the said plaintiff do have and recover of and from the said defendant, and that the said defendant pay to the said plaintiff by way of alimony, and as a fair and equitable division of the property rights of the said parties herein, the sum of fifty thousand dollars, twenty thousand of which to be paid in cash, the remaining thirty thousand to be paid in monthly installments of five hundred dollars each, until the whole of the same is paid, such deferred payments to bear interest at the rate of seven percent per annum; that the said plaintiff prays for such other and further relief as to this court may seem meet and equitable. . . ."

"That's all, Della. Put a blank on there for the signature of the attorney for the plaintiff and an affidavit of verification for Rhoda Montaine to sign."

Della Street finished making pothooks across the page of the notebook, raised her eyes to Perry Mason and asked, "Is she really going to file this suit for divorce, chief?"

"She is when I get done with her."

"That puts you in a position of fighting the annulment action, yet filing an action for divorce?" Della Street asked.

"Yes. If they got the annulment there wouldn't be any alimony. That's one of the things that C. Phillip Montaine is figuring. He wants to save his pocketbook. The district attorney wants Carl to testify in the murder trial."

"And if you can beat the annulment action, he can't testify?"

"That's right."

"Will he be able to testify if he gets a divorce, chief?"

"No. If they can annul the marriage Carl can give his testimony. In the eyes of the law a void marriage is no marriage at all. If there was a valid marriage, even if it was subsequently dissolved by divorce, he can't testify against his wife without her consent."

"But," Della objected, "you can't keep them from getting an annulment. The law plainly says that a subsequent marriage contracted by any person during the life of a former spouse is void from the beginning."

"I'm glad it does," Mason answered, grinning.

"But, when Rhoda married Carl Montaine, her former husband was still living."

Mason resumed his savage pacing of the office. "I can lick them on that with my eyes shut," he said. "It's the other things that are worrying me. . . . Stick around, Della, and give me a chance to think. I want to think out loud. I may have something for you to write out. Is some one watching the telephone board?"

"Yes."

"I'm expecting an important call," Mason said, "from Danny Spear. I think we're going to find the persons who were putting the screws on Moxley for the money."

"Do you *want* to find them, chief?"

"I don't want the district attorney to subpoena them," he said. "I want to get them out of the country."

"Won't that be dangerous, compounding a felony, or something of that sort?"

He grinned at her, and the grin, in itself, was an eloquent answer. After a moment, he said softly, "And are *you* telling *me?*"

She looked worried and made aimless designs on the pages of her notebook. At length she glanced up at him, followed his pacing with anxious eyes and said, "Don't you think it would have been better if you'd relied on self-defense?"

He whirled on her savagely. "Sure, it would,"

he said. "We could have worked up a case of self-defense that would have stuck. We might not have secured an acquittal, but it's a cinch the prosecution could never have secured a conviction. But she walked into the D.A.'s trap. She can't claim self-defense now. She's placed herself in front of the door, ringing the doorbell, when the murder was committed."

Della Street pursed her lips and asked thoughtfully, "You mean she didn't tell the police the truth?"

"Of course, she didn't tell them the truth. They gave her a nicely baited hook, and she grabbed at it, hook, line and sinker. She doesn't know that she's hooked yet, because it hasn't suited the district attorney to jerk the line and set the hook."

"But why *didn't* she tell them the truth, chief?"

"Because she couldn't. It's one of those cases where the truth sounds more unreasonable than any lie you can think up. That happens sometimes in a criminal case. When a person is guilty, a clever attorney makes up a story for him to tell the jury. Therefore, the defendant's story usually sounds pretty convincing. When a defendant is innocent, the facts don't sound nearly so plausible as they do when they're fabricated. When a person makes up a story, the first thing he tries to bear in mind is to make up a story that's plausible. When he relates events just as they happened, the story doesn't sound as plausible."

"I can't exactly see that," Della Street objected.

"You've heard the old adage," he asked, "that truth is stranger than fiction?" She nodded.

"This is simply a concrete example of that same principle. There are millions of facts that may fall from the wheel of chance in any possible combination. Ninety-nine times out of a hundred those combinations of facts are plausible and convincing, but once out of a hundred the actual truth challenges credulity. When a defendant is caught in that kind of a trap, it's one of the worst cases a lawyer can get hold of."

"What are you going to do?" she asked.

"Under the circumstances," he said, "I'm going to try to make the stories of the prosecuting witnesses sound improbable. What's more, I'm going to try and prove an alibi."

"But you *can't* prove an alibi," she said. "You, yourself, have just admitted that the witnesses for the prosecution will prove that Rhoda Montaine was out keeping an appointment with Gregory Moxley."

He nodded and chuckled. "Why the chuckle?" she asked.

"I've thrown some bread out on the water," he said. "I'm waiting to see what comes back."

There was a knock at the door. One of the typists who watched the switchboard when Della Street was in Perry Mason's private office said in a thin, frightened voice, "A man named Danny Spear just rang up. He said that he was one of

207

Paul Drake's detectives, and that he couldn't wait for me to get you on the line. He said for you to come to forty-six twenty Maple Avenue just as fast as you could get there, that he'd be waiting for you in front of the entrance. He said that he'd already tried to get Paul Drake, and that Drake wasn't in his office, and that you should come at once."

Perry Mason jerked open the door of the coat closet, pulled out his hat, jammed it down on his head. "Did he sound as though he was in trouble?" he asked.

The girl nodded her head.

"Type out the divorce complaint, Della," Perry Mason said as he shot through the door. He sprinted down the corridor, caught an elevator, flagged a cab at the entrance to the office building, and said, "Forty-six twenty Maple Avenue, and keep a heavy foot on the throttle."

Danny Spear was standing at the curb as the cab pulled in to the sidewalk. "There you are, boss," said the cab driver. "It's the dump over there on the right — the Greenwood Hotel."

Mason fumbled in his pocket for change. "I'll say it's a dump," he said.

The cab driver grinned. "Want me to wait?"

Mason shook his head, waited until the cab had rounded the corner before he turned to Danny Spear.

Danny was a dejected and bedraggled looking individual. The collar of his shirt had been ripped open, and was now held in place with a

208

safety pin. His necktie had been torn. His left eye was discolored, and his lower lip was puffed out and red. "What happened, Danny?" asked Perry Mason.

"I walked into something," Danny Spear said.

Mason surveyed the battered countenance, nodded, waited for further information. Spear pulled the hat lower on his forehead, depressed the brim so that it shaded his bad eye, tilted his head forward and turned toward the Greenwood Hotel. "Let's go in," he said. "Barge right past the bench warmers in the lobby. I know the way."

They pushed their way through the swinging doors. Half a dozen men were sprawled about the narrow lobby of the third-rate hotel. They stared curiously. Danny Spear led the way past the long row of chairs and thick-bellied, brass cuspidors, to a narrow, dark stairway. Over on the left was an elevator shaft screened with heavy iron wire. The cage seemed hardly as large as the average telephone booth. "We can make time using the stairs," Danny Spear called back over his shoulder.

They reached the corridor on the second floor, and Spear led the way to a door which he flung open. The room was dark and smelly. There was a white enameled bed with a thin, lumpy mattress, a bedspread with several holes in it. A pair of socks, one of them with a large hole in the toe, had been thrown over the iron rail of the bed. A shaving brush with dried lather on it was standing on the bureau. A wrinkled necktie hung to the side of the mirror. A piece of brown paper, large enough to wrap a bundle of laundry in, lay on the floor. A laundry ticket was beside it. Half a dozen rusted safety razor blades were on the top of the scarred bureau. To the left of the bureau was a half open door which led to a closet. Chips of wood lay all over the floor. The lower part of the door had been whittled away and broken out. Danny Spear closed the door to the corridor, swept his arm about the room in an inclusive gesture. "Well," he said, "I stepped on my tonsil."

"What happened?" asked Perry Mason.

"You and Paul crossed over to the other corner and took the taxicab after you came out of the Balboa Apartments. I guess the jane was watching you from a window, because you hadn't any more than rounded the corner before she came out in a rush and ran over to the curb, looking for a cab to flag. It took her three or four minutes to get a cab, and she was almost wringing her hands with impatience.

"A yellow finally pulled in to the curb for her. Evidently she never figured on being followed. She didn't even bother to look out of the rear window as the cab pulled away. I started the crate and jogged along behind, nice and easy, not taking any chances on losing her. She came to this place and paid off the cab. She was wide open.

"When she started to go in the hotel, however,

she seemed to get a little bit suspicious. It didn't look so much as though she suspected she'd been followed, as though she was doing something she shouldn't. She looked up and down the street, hesitated and then ducked into the hotel.

"I was afraid to crowd her too closely, and by the time I hit the lobby, she'd gone on up. The elevator was at the second floor. I figured she'd left it there. There were just the usual bunch of barflies hanging around the lobby, so I took the stairs to the second floor, went over there in the shadows by the fire escape and sat tight, watching the corridor. I guess it was ten minutes later that she opened the door of his room, stood in the corridor for a minute, pulling the old business of looking up and down, and then started for the stairs. She didn't take the elevator.

"I marked the room, let her get a good start, and then went on down after her. She didn't take a cab this time, and I had a little trouble picking her up. She'd rounded the corner before I found her. She was walking down to the car-line. She took a surface car that would take her to within a block of the Balboa Apartments at seven twenty-one West Ordway. So I figured it was a safe bet she was just economizing on cab fare and that I could come back and spot the bird she'd been talking with. That was where I pulled the prize bonehead play of the day."

"Why?" asked Mason. "Did he recognize you?"

"Naw, he didn't recognize me. I was sitting on

top of the heap, if I hadn't tried to get *too smart*."

"Well, go on," Mason prompted impatiently. "Let's have it."

"Well, I came back to the hotel, climbed the stairs and knocked on the door of the room. A big guy came to the door. He was in his shirt sleeves. There was a suitcase on the bed that he'd been packing. It was one of those cheap, big-bellied suitcases that the country merchandise stores feature, and it was pretty well sunbleached, as though it had been in a show window on display or had been left out in the sun somewhere. The guy was about thirty years old, with heavy-muscled shoulders, as though he'd been pitching hay all of his life. Somehow, though, I didn't figure him so much for a ranch hand, as for a garage mechanic. Maybe it was just a hunch, but there was grime worked into his hands, and something about the way he kept his sleeves rolled up that spelled garage to me.

"He looked pretty hostile and just a little bit scared, so I smirked at him and said, 'When your partner comes in, tell him that I've got some stuff that's way ahead of this blended caramel water the drug stores are passing out; and the price is right.' He wanted to know what I was talking about, and I pulled the old stall about being a bootlegger who had been selling the place and I'd sold a guy who had the room two or three weeks ago, a fellow who told me he was going to be there permanently, so I figured this guy was a roommate."

"Did he fall for it?" asked Perry Mason.

"I think he was falling for it, all right," Spear said, "but all the time I was sizing him up, and I saw that he had the same peculiar eyes, the same long, cat-fish mouth that the woman had I'd trailed over there. I'd got a good look at her when she paid off the cab driver. There couldn't be any mistaking that long upper lip and those eyes."

"You figure this guy was her brother?" Mason asked.

"Sure he was her brother, and I figured I was going to pull a fast one. I remember that her name had been Pender and that she came from Centerville. I could see that this bird wasn't going to do anything except listen to me sing my song and then slam the door in my face. I figured that if I could pull a good line on him, he'd take me into his confidence and loosen up. It was just one of those hunches that go across like a million dollars when they go across, and get you patted on the back as being a smart guy; and when they don't go across, they look like hell and get you fired. I didn't have time to think it over. I just played the hunch. I let my face light up with recognition and said, 'Why, say, don't you come from Centerville?'

"He looked at me sort of strange and gulped a couple of times and said, 'Who are you?', and I got a grin all over my face and said, 'Now I place you. Hell's bells, your name's Pender' and with that I stuck out my hand."

"What did he do?"

"There," said Danny Spear, "is where he fooled me. There's where he slipped one over on me."

"Go ahead," Mason said.

"I played him for a hick," Spear remarked ruefully, "and what a dumb boob I was! I was watching him like a hawk to see how he'd take it. For a moment, he was flabbergasted as though I'd knocked him off of the Christmas tree, and then all of a sudden his face lit up into a smile, and he started pumping my hand up and down, and said, 'Sure, buddy, I remember you now. Come in.'

"Well, he kept hold of my right hand with his right hand and pulled me in the door. He was grinning like Santa Claus on Christmas Eve. He kicked the door shut with his left foot, pumped my hand up and down two or three times, said, 'How are all the folks back home?' and crossed his left over to my eye with a sock that damn near put me out. He let go of my right hand then, and smacked me one in the kisser that smashed me back up against the closet door. I bounced back just in time to connect with one in the solar plexus that took all the joy out of life. I remember something coming up and smacking me in the face, and realized it was the dirty carpet."

"What did he do?" asked Perry Mason.

"Tore a pillowslip into pieces, stuck some rags down my mouth, tied my hands and feet, opened the closet door and stuffed me inside."

214

"Were you out?"

"Not clean out, but groggy. Don't make any mistake, whether I'd been out or not, there was no percentage in fighting that boy. He handled his fists just like the girl in your office handles the keys on the switchboard. Why, say, he juggled me around in the air like a Jap juggler tossing billiard balls."

"Go on," Mason said.

"After I was in the closet, he put on an act," Danny Spear went on ruefully, "and I'm damned whether I know if it was an act or not. Of course, when I saw what I was up against, I played 'possum and went limp as though I was out for keeps. I figured I might be able to twist my wrists a little and get some slack on the tie, so I pulled a dead flop. He tossed me in the closet as though I'd been a sack of grain he was putting in the barn. He closed the door and twisted the bolt — and, brother, let me tell you there's a strong bolt. It freezes that door into a wall as solid as a rock."

"What was the act he put on?" Mason asked curiously.

"Well, he went ahead with the packing up, and, believe me, he was in a hurry. He slammed open drawers and banged things into the suitcase and ran back and forth between the bed and the bureau like a rooster on a hot stove. About every two minutes he'd stop and call Garvanza three-nine-four-aught-one. He'd hold the phone for a minute or two and there wouldn't be any answer."

215

"That's the number of the Balboa Apartments," Mason said.

Danny Spear said, "I know it. He kept calling that number and asking for Miss Freeman."

"There was an answer then?"

"Yeah. Somebody answered at the other end all right, and he'd asked for Miss Freeman and wait awhile and then hang up. The closet door was pretty thin. I could hear every move he made and every word he said.

"What I'm getting at is that I don't know whether he knew I was listening and put on an act for my benefit, or whether he thought I was out, and was just talking, or whether he didn't give a damn one way or the other."

"I'm still listening," Mason said with a trace of impatience, "to find out just *what* you're getting at."

"Well, you see," Danny Spear explained, "I want you to get the picture, because it's important you see it just the right way. He kept packing and calling that number. Finally he got done packing. I heard the bed springs creak as he sat down on the edge of the bed. He called the same number again, asked for Miss Freeman, and then got her on the line. I heard him say, 'Hello, Doris, this is Oscar.' She probably told him not to talk over the telephone, because he told her the fat was in the fire and nothing made any difference now. He said that a detective had called on him and knew who he was. He gave her hell for being so dumb as to let a dick trail her to the hotel, and then he kept insisting that she told the two detectives who had called on her more than she'd admitted. She seemed to be all worked up, and after awhile he was soothing her and trying to quiet her down, instead of bawling her out, the way he'd started in.

"The thing that makes me suspicious about the conversation was that it was so long and so complete. They seemed to be gabbing over the telephone just as though they'd been farmers talking with the neighbors to while away a long evening, and, in the course of the conversation, she evidently asked him if he'd told her the truth. He started in and swore up one side and down the other that he'd told her the absolute truth, and he'd got as far as the door of Moxley's apartment and had rung the bell, trying to wake Moxley up, but that apparently Moxley had been asleep, because there wasn't a sound from the apartment. He said he figured the murder must have been committed before he got there. The girl evidently thought he might be trying to put sugar coating over the pill, and that he'd gone up to the room and cracked Moxley over the head. He kept denying it. They talked for darn near ten minutes.

"Now, that's the sketch. I give it to you complete, because it may make some difference. He may have put it on for my benefit. If he did, he was a darn good actor. If he was just sitting there, gassing with his sister, when he should have been taking it on the lam, he's just a hick.

You pay your money and take your choice. Figure him either for a dumb guy with lots of beef and a sudden temper, or a bird who's as fast with his mind as he is with his fists, and that's plenty fast."

Mason asked crisply, "What happened after that?"

"Well, they put that song and dance on over the telephone for a while, and then the guy told her that they were going to have to take it on the lam."

"Did he use that word?" Mason asked.

"Naw, he said that they had to start traveling. Evidently she didn't want to travel with him, but he told her they were in it up to their necks now, and it was sink or swim and there wasn't any good in separating, that if they separated it left two trails for the cops to follow and if they stayed together it only left one. He told her he was getting a taxicab and for her to have her things all packed up."

"Then what?" asked the lawyer.

"Then he dragged a bunch of baggage around, grabbed a bag or two and beat it down the corridor. I twisted and wiggled and finally got my hands loose, got rid of the bandages, and went to work on the door. I could have got out by making a racket or by smashing out the panels with my feet, but that would have brought a crowd, and I figured you wanted me to play them close to my chest. So I got out my pocket knife and whittled through the thin part of the panels, and took the rest of it out with one kick that didn't make too much noise. I was afraid to telephone from here because the calls apparently go through the desk, so I beat it down to the corner and telephoned the agency. Drake wasn't in, but I got one of the boys and told him to get busy and sew up the Balboa Apartments, to take a look at all of the railroad stations and to cover the airport. I gave him a description of the pair. He couldn't miss them very well, with the kind of mouths that run in that Pender family, and the guy would loom up like a mountain anywhere."

"Perhaps," Mason said, "they hadn't left the Balboa Apartments when you telephoned."

"I was hoping they hadn't," Danny Spear said, "because I'd pulled enough of a bonehead play for one day. I figured that if I could get on their trail and find out where they were going, it would be a good thing."

Mason said rather testily, "Why didn't you tell me this over the phone?"

"Because," Spear rejoined, "I had a choice to make. I only had one shot. I knew that seconds were precious. I figured I could call the agency and get them to pick up the trail while it was hot. I knew if I tried to explain to you over the telephone, I'd lose a lot of time. After I got the agency to working on the thing, I figured there was no use telling you all the details, because there was nothing you could do, and if I tried to tell it over the telephone, it wouldn't have made sense anyway, so I wanted to get you down here just as quickly as you could come, and then I figured you could use your own judgment. I take it you don't want these people stopped, do you?"

Perry Mason frowned thoughtfully, fell to pacing the faded, thin carpet. Slowly, he shook his head, said gravely, "No, I don't want them stopped. I want them kept going. I want to know where they are, so I can bring them back if I have to, but I want them kept moving."

Danny Spear looked at his watch. "Well," he said, "I'm sorry, but that's a clean breast of the whole situation. We can ring up the agency in half an hour and find out if the boys picked them up. Personally, I'd say it was a ten to one shot they did, because after they'd left the Balboa Apartments, it's a cinch they'd try a railroad train. They're the kind of people who figure nobody can catch up with a railroad train."

Abruptly Perry Mason grinned. "Well," he said, "let's get back to the office. Paul Drake will probably be there by that time."

Chapter 16

Judge Frank Munroe, of the Domestic Relations Department of the Superior Court, strode from his chambers to the bench, adjusted his glasses and peered down at the crowded courtroom. A bailiff intoned the formula which marked the opening of the court. Simultaneously with the banging of Judge Munroe's gavel, doors on opposite sides of the courtroom opened and officers brought Rhoda Montaine through the one door, Carl Montaine through the other. Both were in custody, Carl Montaine as a material witness, Rhoda Montaine as the defendant in a murder case. It was the first opportunity either had had to see the other since their arrest.

"The case of Montaine verses Montaine," said Judge Munroe. "John Lucas, a deputy district attorney, representing the plaintiff; Perry Mason representing the defendant."

Rhoda Montaine gave an involuntary exclamation, stepped swiftly forward. The restraining arm of the deputy barred her way. "Carl!" she exclaimed.

Carl Montaine, his face bearing the evidence of sleepless nights and worried days, clamped his lips in a firm line, held his eyes straight ahead, marched toward the chair which had been prepared for him, sat down beside the deputy, leaving his wife standing, with incredulous dismay in her eyes, her face ghastly white. From the courtroom came a low murmur which was silenced by the peremptory gavel of a bailiff. Rhoda Montaine walked blindly toward the chair which had been reserved for her. Her tear-dimmed eyes made it necessary for the deputy at her side to guide her with a hand at her elbow.

Perry Mason, spectator of the silent drama, said no word, made no move. He wanted the full force of what had happened to impress the spectators; and he was careful not to intrude upon the stage. It was Judge Munroe who broke the tension of the courtroom.

"Both parties," he said, "to this action are in custody. The defendant is charged with murder. It is rumored that the plaintiff will appear as a witness for the People in the murder case. The Court notices that the action is filed on behalf of the plaintiff by a counsel in the district attorney's office. The Court wishes to announce, therefore, gentlemen, that there will be no deviation from the issues in this case. The action before the Court is one to annul a marriage, on the ground that there was a prior husband living. Counsel of neither side will be allowed to cross-examine opposing witness for the purposes of eliciting information which may subsequently be used in the trial of People verses Rhoda

Montaine. Is that understood, gentlemen?"

Perry Mason bowed his head in silent assent. John Lucas flashed a glance of triumph at him. There could be no question but what the charge from the judge amounted to a distinct victory for the district attorney's office. Perry Mason could always have his client refuse to answer questions on the ground that the answer might incriminate her. The judicial admonition, therefore, amounted to a curtailment of Mason's right to cross-examine Carl Montaine.

"Call Carl Montaine as the first witness for the plaintiff," said Lucas.

Carl Montaine dug his hand into the shoulder of his father, who occupied a seat at the counsel table immediately adjacent to his son. The boy then marched with steady dignity to the witness stand, held up his right hand, was sworn, and then glanced inquiringly at Lucas.

"Your name is Carl W. Montaine?"

"Yes."

"You reside here in the city, Mr. Montaine?"

"Yes."

"You are acquainted with the defendant, Rhoda Montaine?"

"Yes."

"When did you first meet her?"

"At the Sunnyside Hospital. She was employed by me as a nurse."

"You subsequently went through a marriage ceremony with her?"

"Yes."

"Can you give the date of that?"

"The eighth day of June."

"Of this year?"

"Yes."

Lucas turned to Perry Mason with a wave of his hand.

"You may inquire," he said.

Perry Mason's smile was urbane. "No questions," he said.

The witness had apparently been carefully coached, in anticipation of a rigid cross-examination. Lucas had been in tense readiness to jump to his feet with an objection, should Mason ask any important questions. Both men showed their surprise.

"That's all," said Judge Munroe sharply. "Step down, Mr. Montaine."

Lucas was on his feet. "Your Honor," he said, "under the Code of Civil Procedure, we have a right to call the defendant to the stand for cross-examination as an adverse party, and in advance of any examination on the part of her counsel. I therefore desire to call Rhoda Montaine to the witness stand."

"Just what," asked Perry Mason, "do you expect to prove by this witness?"

Lucas frowned. "I don't believe," he said, "that it is necessary for me to disclose my plan for procedure nor the purpose of my examination."

"In view of the Court's statement," said Perry Mason, smilingly polite, "I was about to state that I thought we would stipulate whatever you wished to prove from this witness."

"Will you stipulate," asked Lucas, his voice harsh, driving and hostile, "that on the eighth day of June, when the defendant went through a marriage ceremony with Carl Montaine, she had previously been party to a marriage ceremony with another man; that this man's name was Gregory Lorton, alias Gregory Moxley, who was killed on the morning of June sixteenth of the present year?"

"I will," said Perry Mason.

Lucas showed surprise. Judge Munroe frowned thoughtfully. There was a rustle of motion in the crowded courtroom. "I also desire," said John Lucas, glancing at the Court, "to interrogate this witness as to the identity of a person who was buried in February of nineteen hundred and twenty-nine under the name of Gregory Lorton."

Perry Mason's smile became a grin. "In view of our stipulation," he said, "that *the* Gregory Lorton who was married to the defendant in this case was alive at that date, it becomes entirely immaterial in this action who it was that was buried under the *name* of Gregory Lorton. If you wish to pursue that inquiry in a criminal action, you have your right to do so. And, unfortunately, you also have the right to pursue that inquiry by giving out statements to the newspapers intimating that you suspect this defendant of having poisoned that individual."

Lucas whirled, his face red. "That insinuation is unjustified!" he shouted. "You can't . . ."

Judge Munroe's gavel banged on his desk.

"Counselor," he said to Perry Mason, "your objection is well taken. Your comments were entirely uncalled for."

"I apologize to the Court," said Perry Mason.

"And to counsel," suggested Lucas.

Perry Mason remained significantly silent.

Munroe looked from face to face. There was, perhaps, the faint twinkle of humor in his eyes. "Proceed," he said.

"That," said Lucas, "is our case," and sat down.

Perry Mason said, "Call Mrs. Bessie Holeman to the witness stand."

A young woman of perhaps thirty-two years of age, with tired eyes, strode to the witness stand, held up her right hand and was sworn.

"Did you," asked Perry Mason, "go to the inquest which was held over the remains of Gregory Moxley, alias Gregory Lorton, the man who was killed on the sixteenth day of June of this year?"

"I did."

"Did you see the remains?"

"I did."

"Did you recognize them?"

"Yes."

"Who was the man?"

"He was the man whom I married on the fifth of January, 1925."

The spectators gasped with surprise. Lucas half rose from his seat, sat down, then jumped up again. He hesitated a moment, then said slowly, "Your Honor, this line of testimony takes me completely by surprise. However, I move to strike out the answer as not responsive to the question, as incompetent, irrelevant, and immaterial. It makes no difference how many prior marriages this man, Moxley, might have had before he married Rhoda Montaine. He might have had two dozen previous wives living. Rhoda Montaine could have filed suit for annulment during his lifetime. She did not. With his death, she becomes a widow. In other words, her marriage is not subject to collateral attack."

Perry Mason smiled. "The law of this state provides that a subsequent marriage contracted by any person during the life of a former husband or wife of such person with any person other than such former husband or wife is illegal and void from the beginning. In the Estate of Gregorson, 160 Cal., 61, it is held that a void marriage *is* subject to collateral attack.

"Obviously, Gregory Lorton could not enter into a valid marriage with Rhoda Montaine as long as Lorton's prior wife was living. Therefore, the previous marriage of this defendant, being null and void, was no bar to a subsequent *valid* marriage to Carl Montaine."

"Motion to strike is denied," said Judge Munroe.

"Did you ever secure a divorce from the man who has been variously described as Gregory Moxley or Gregory Lorton subsequent to the fifth day of January, 1925?" asked Perry Mason.

"Yes."

Perry Mason unfolded a legal paper, presented it to Lucas with a flourish. "I show to counsel," he said, "a certified copy of the decree of divorce, and call to the attention of Court and counsel the fact that the decree of divorce was subsequent to the marriage of this defendant to Gregory Lorton. I offer this certified decree in evidence."

"It will be received," Judge Munroe said.

"Cross-examine," announced Perry Mason.

Lucas approached the witness, stared steadily at her and said, "Are you certain of the identity of this man you saw in the morgue?"

"Yes."

Lucas shrugged his shoulders, said to Judge Munroe, "That is all."

The judge leaned over his desk and said to the clerk of the court, "Bring me that one hundred and sixtieth California Reports, and volume sixteen of California Jurisprudence."

There was a restless silence in the courtroom while the clerk stepped into the Judge's chambers, returning with two books which the judge consulted thoughtfully. Judge Munroe looked up from the books and disposed of the case with a single sentence. "Judgment," he said, "must be entered for the defendant. The petition to annul the marriage is denied. Court is adjourned."

Perry Mason turned and caught the eye of the elder Montaine, an eye that was glittering and frosty. There was no expression whatever upon the face of the older man. John Lucas looked crushed. Carl Montaine seemed rather dazed, but C. Phillip Montaine retained his poise. It was impossible to tell whether he was surprised by the decision.

The courtroom buzzed with activity. Newspaper men sprinted for telephones. People milled into curious throngs, every one talking at once. Perry Mason said to the deputy who had Rhoda Montaine in custody, "I want to take my client into the jury room for consultation. You can sit in the door if you wish." He took Rhoda Montaine's arm, piloted her into the jury room, held a chair for her, sat across a table from her and smiled reassuringly.

"What does it all mean?" she asked.

"It means," said Perry Mason, "that Judge Munroe has held your marriage to Carl Montaine absolutely valid and binding."

"Then what?" she asked.

"Then," said Perry Mason, pulling the complaint from his pocket, "you are going to sue him for divorce on the grounds of extreme cruelty, in that he has falsely accused you of murder, in that he has betrayed the confidence you have made to him, in that he has, on numerous times and occasions, treated you in a cruel and inhuman manner. I have listed some of those times and occasions in this complaint. All you have to do is to sign it."

Tears came to her eyes. "But," she said, "I

don't want to divorce him. Don't you understand, I make allowances for his character. I tell
you, I love him."

Perry Mason leaned close to her, so that his
eyes were staring steadily into hers. "Rhoda," he
said in a low voice, "you've told your story.
You've given the district attorney a signed statement. You can't deviate from that story now.
You've got to stand or fall by it. So far, the district attorney hasn't been able to uncover the
person who actually *did* stand on the doorstep
and ring the doorbell of Moxley's apartment
while Moxley was being murdered, but I have
uncovered him. I have uncovered two of them.
One of them may be lying. On the other hand,
both may be telling the truth. The testimony of
either one will get you the death penalty."

She stared at him with consternation in her eyes.

"One of them," Perry Mason went on, "is Oscar Pender, a man from Centerville who was
trying to get money from Moxley. This money
Pender was to get for his sister. Moxley had
swindled Pender's sister out of her savings."

"I don't know anything about him," Rhoda
Montaine said. "Who's the other one?"

Mason's eyes bored into hers. He said slowly,
"The other one is Doctor Claude Millsap. He
couldn't sleep. He knew of your appointment.
He got up and drove to Moxley's house. You
were there. The lights were out. He rang the bell.
Your car was parked around the corner on a side
street."

Rhoda Montaine was white to the lips. "Claude Millsap!" she said, in a whisper.

"You got yourself in this mess," Mason told her, "by not doing what I told you. Now you're going to follow instructions. We've won that annulment case. Your husband can't testify against you. The district attorney, however, has given the newspapers signed statements covering your husband's testimony. He's held your husband as a material witness, where *I* couldn't talk with him; but he's let every newspaper man in town talk with him. Now then, we've got to combat that propaganda. We're going to file this divorce. I've drawn it on the theory that your husband was guilty of cruelty in telling a bunch of lies to the district attorney, lies that linked you with a murder of which you are innocent."

"Then what?" she asked.

"Then," he said, "it's going to make some nice copy for the newspapers, but the main thing is that I'm going to slap a subpoena on Carl Montaine, forcing him to attend at the taking of a deposition. Before the district attorney's office realized what has happened, they'll find that I've got Carl sewed up. If he doesn't change his story, you *may* get big alimony. If he does, it's going to look like hell for the D.A.'s office."

There was fear in her eyes as she asked, "Can they use this deposition against me in the murder case?"

"No."

"But," she said, "I don't want a divorce from him. I know he has weaknesses. I love him in spite of those weaknesses. I want to make a man out of him. He's had too much coddling. He's been taught to lean on his father and his ancestors. You can't change a man over night. You can't kick the props out from under him and expect him to stand on his own feet all at once. You can't . . ."

"Listen," he told her, "I don't care how you feel about Carl. Right at present, you're accused of murder. The district attorney is going to try and get the death penalty and back of the district attorney is a man who has a great deal of intelligence, a great deal of poise, and who is utterly ruthless. He's willing to spend any amount of money that is necessary to get you convicted and get you a death penalty."

"Who do you mean?" she asked.

"C. Phillip Montaine," he told her.

"Why," she said, "he doesn't approve of me, but he wouldn't . . ."

The officer in the doorway coughed suggestively. "Time's up," he said.

Perry Mason shoved the divorce complaint in front of her, held out his fountain pen. "Sign on that line," he said.

Her eyes stared appealingly into his. "Why," she said, "he's Carl's father! He wouldn't . . ."

"Sign," Mason said. The officer moved forward. Rhoda Montaine took the fountain pen. The fingers of her hand, brushing against the back of Mason's hand, were cold. She dashed off her signature, raised tear-moistened eyes to the officer. "I am ready," she said.

Chapter 17

Perry Mason's fingers drummed on the edge of his desk. His eyes, steady in their cold concentration, rested on Paul Drake's face. "Your man picked them up at the railroad depot, Paul?"

"Yes. He found them about ten minutes before the train time. He took the same train they did, wired me from a suburban stop. I got busy on the telephone and had operatives board the train at different points to give him reënforcements. We've kept the pair in sight ever since they started."

"I want them kept on the run," Mason said.

"That's what Della Street told me. I wasn't certain I got the message straight. I wanted to find out just *what* it was you wanted."

Mason said slowly, "I want them hounded, I want them frightened, I want them kept on the move. Every time they go to a place and register under assumed names, I want those names. I want photographic copies of the hotel register."

"You want them to know that detectives are on their trail?"

"Yes, but I want it done cleverly. I don't want them to think detectives are *too* close on their trail. I want them to think detectives are just blundering around, covering the various hotels with descriptions and that sort of stuff."

The detective smoked silently for several seconds, then blurted out, "I think you're crazy, Perry!"

"Why?"

"It's none of my business," Drake said slowly, "but this man, Pender, must have been on the scene at the time of the murder. He telephoned his sister and admitted that he rang the doorbell of Moxley's apartment at around quarter past two in the morning. He had a motive for killing Moxley. He had undoubtedly been threatening Moxley. Now, if, instead of getting this man on the run, you should have him arrested and turn the newspaper boys on him, he'd make a lot of favorable publicity for Rhoda Montaine."

"Then what?" Mason asked.

"Then the district attorney would be in a spot. You could demand that Pender be arrested. You could demand that the district attorney call him as a witness."

"Then what?"

"Why then," Drake said, "you'd have him before the jury and you could rip him to pieces. You could show that he came here to get money out of Moxley; that he did it by making threats. You could make him either admit that he was on the scene of the murder at about the time it happened, or else you could impeach him by showing the conversation he had with his sister. You could show the way he treated my operative."

Mason smiled. "Yes," he said, "I could do all those things. For a while I'd be sitting pretty. Then we'd go to trial. The D.A. would put Pender on the witness stand, let Pender admit that he called up Moxley and tried to get money out of Moxley, let him admit, if necessary, that he made threats to Moxley. Then he would have Pender testify that he went to Moxley's apartment sometime after two o'clock in the morning, that Moxley had told him he was going to meet Rhoda Montaine at two o'clock and that she would have money for him. Pender went to collect the money. That's only natural. And Pender would testify that he stood in front of the street door which opened on Moxley's stairway and rang the bell repeatedly and didn't get any answer.

"That would tie in with the testimony of the witnesses who lived in the other apartment house, and by the time Rhoda Montaine got on the witness stand and tried to swear that *she* was the one who was ringing the bell while the murder was being committed, the jury would put her down for a liar. Then the district attorney would start dangling that garage key in front of the jury, and Rhoda Montaine would draw a verdict of first-degree murder."

Drake nodded thoughtfully. "But," he said, "what's the idea of keeping those people on the run?"

"Sooner or later," Mason said, "the district attorney is going to realize the really vital point in this case. Some one *was* standing in front of the street door of Moxley's apartment ringing the bell, at the very moment the murder was committed. The testimony of the prosecution's main witnesses will establish that. Now, whoever that person was, he or she must be innocent of the murder, because, obviously, a person can't ring a doorbell on a street door and, at the same time, club a man over the head in an apartment on an upper floor and in the back of the house. On the other hand, the person who *was* ringing that doorbell isn't going to be anxious to come forward and admit being in the vicinity of the murder at the time it was committed, but when he is once run to earth by the district attorney, he's going to tell his story eagerly enough. Therefore, we have two people who are going to fight over that doorbell. One of them will be the person who actually was standing in front of the door, ringing the doorbell, and the other person will be the one who was murdering Moxley at the time the doorbell was ringing. Both of these people will insist that they were the ones who rang the doorbell.

"Rhoda Montaine has been the first one to advance her claim. It is weakened very materially by the presence of her garage keys in Moxley's apartment, but the jury may believe her, just the same. If, however, the district attorney can find some one who will go on the stand and swear positively that *he* was the one who was ringing the doorbell, it is going to weaken Rhoda Montaine's case."

Drake nodded. "If," Mason went on, "the district attorney gets hold of Pender, and Pender tells him his story, the district attorney will make him a star witness for the prosecution. I'll have to cross-examine him and try to prove to the jury that *he* is the murderer instead of the one who was really ringing the doorbell. Obviously, if I'm forced to cross-examine this man along the usual lines of simply trying to prove he's lying, I'm not going to get very far. The district attorney will have coached him and coached him carefully. But, if I can cross-examine him by proving to the jury that he fled over the country, using different aliases, leaving places in the dead of night, slinking about the country from city to city as a common criminal, I can brand his testimony as a lie. Now, that's what I'm doing with Oscar Pender, and incidentally, with his sister. I'm giving them an opportunity to impeach themselves before a jury. The more places that they go to and leave hurriedly, the more different names they take, the more attempts they make to disguise themselves and to conceal themselves, the more the jury is going to believe that they are the guilty ones. That's more particularly true because Pender will probably forget some of the places he went to and some of the names he used. If I can produce hotel registers to impeach his testimony, I can rip him wide open.

"Then," Drake said, "you intend to let the district attorney discover Oscar Pender eventually."

"At the proper moment," Perry Mason said, "I *may* let the district attorney get hold of Oscar Pender, but I want to have it in my power to produce him, or not to produce him, just as I see fit."

Drake nodded his head, said slowly, "You say there will be *two* people who will claim to have been on the scene of the murder, ringing that doorbell. One of them will be the murderer. The other one will be the one who was actually ringing the doorbell. We now have found these two people. One of them is Oscar Pender; the other one is Rhoda Montaine. Therefore, one of these people must be guilty of the murder."

A slow smile twisted Perry Mason's countenance. "Excellent reasoning, Paul," he said, "only it happens that there are *three* people who claim to have rung that doorbell."

"Three?" the detective asked in surprise. "Who's the other one?"

"I can't tell you, Paul, I can only tell you that he's a person the district attorney knows about. So far, the district attorney hasn't been able to get any admissions from him because this man is trying to protect Rhoda. Sooner or later they'll drag his story from him. That's going to put Rhoda in an awful spot.

"The district attorney will bear down heavy on this doorbell business, and *then* is when I will produce Oscar Pender. Then is when I will show his guilty conduct. Then is when I will show his motive. Then is when I will mix the whole case up so badly the district attorney won't know what it's all about, and the jury will get so hopelessly confused they'll let the two men fight it out and acquit the woman."

Drake stared thoughtfully at the tip of his cigarette. He half turned and raised his eyes to the lawyer's countenance. "I've stumbled on to something else," he said.

"What?"

"Some one is looking for Pender."

"How do you know?"

"We've had men watching the place where Pender stayed and the apartment that his sister occupied, just in case some other accomplice should show up. Yesterday evening a bunch of detectives came down on the place like flies coming to a syrup jar. They swarmed all over the place and moved heaven and earth, trying to find where Pender and his sister were."

Mason's eyes showed interest. "Police detectives?" he asked.

"No, they were agency detectives, and, for some reason, they seemed anxious to keep their activities from coming to the attention of the police."

"There were lots of them, Paul?"

"I'll say. Some one certainly is spending money on the case."

Perry Mason's eyes narrowed. "C. Phillip Montaine," he said, "is a dangerous antagonist.

I think he realized something of what I have in mind. I don't know how he got on Pender's trail. Perhaps it was the same way you did, Paul."

Drake said slowly, "You think old man Montaine is working up this case independently of the district attorney's office?"

"I'm certain of it."

"Why?"

"Because he wants to keep Rhoda Montaine from being acquitted."

"Why?"

"Because, in the first place," Mason said slowly, "if she is acquitted, she'll be his son's legal wife, and I think we'll find C. Phillip Montaine has some very definite plans for his son's matrimonial future."

The detective stared incredulously at Perry Mason. "That doesn't seem a strong enough motive," he said, "to cause a man to try to get a woman convicted of murder."

Mason's lips twisted in a grin. "That, Paul, is what I thought at the time, when C. Phillip Montaine approached me with a proposition to pay me a handsome fee for representing Rhoda if I would consent to place her in a position where her defense would be materially weakened."

The detective gave a low whistle. After a moment of thoughtful silence, he said, "Perry, where do you suppose Oscar Pender really was at the time Gregory Moxley was being murdered?"

"There's just a chance," Mason said, "that he

actually *was* standing in front of the street door, ringing the bell. That is one of the reasons why I would like to have enough ammunition in my hands when I cross-examine him to rip him wide open."

Drake's stare was steady. "You don't seem to have a great deal of faith in your client's innocence," he said.

Mason grinned, said nothing. Della Street opened the door, slipped into the room, glanced significantly at Paul Drake, and said to Perry Mason, "Mabel Strickland, Doctor Millsap's nurse, is in the outer office. She says she's got to see you at once. She's crying."

"Crying?" Mason asked.

Della Street nodded. "Her eyes are red and tears are streaming down her face. She can't stop them. She's crying so badly she can hardly see."

Mason frowned, jerked his head toward the corridor door. Drake slid over the arm of the chair, got to his feet and said, "Be seeing you later, Perry."

When the door closed on the detective, Mason nodded to Della Street. "Show her in," he said.

Della Street opened the door, said, "Come in, Miss Strickland," then stood to one side so the lawyer could see the sobbing woman grope toward the doorway. Della Street piloted her into the office, guided her to a chair.

"What is it?" asked Perry Mason. The nurse tried to speak, but failed, holding a handkerchief to her nose. Perry Mason glanced at Della

242

Street, who slipped unobtrusively from the office. "What's happened?" Mason inquired. "You can talk frankly to me. We're alone."

"You put Doctor Millsap on the spot," she sobbed.

"What happened to him?" Mason asked.

"He was kidnapped."

"Kidnapped?"

"Yes."

"Tell me about it," the lawyer said, his eyes wary and watchful.

"We had been working late at the office last night," she said, "almost until midnight. He was going to drive me home. We were driving along in the car when another car crowded us in to the curb. There were two men in it. I'd never seen either one of them before. They had guns. They told Doctor Millsap to get in the car with them and then they drove off."

"What kind of a car?" Mason asked.

"A Buick sedan."

"Did you get the license number?"

"No."

"What color was it?"

"Black."

"Did the men say anything to you?"

"No."

"Had they made any demands on you?"

"No."

"Did you report the affair to the police?"

"Yes."

"What happened?"

"The police came out and talked with me and went out to the place where our car had been stopped. They looked around but couldn't find anything. Then they made a report to headquarters, and then, apparently, the district attorney thought *you* had done it."

"Thought I had done *what?*" Mason asked.

"Grabbed Doctor Millsap so that he couldn't testify against your client at the trial."

"*Was* he going to testify against her?"

"I don't know anything about it. All I know is what the district attorney thought."

"How do you know what he thought?"

"Because of the questions he asked me."

"You were frightened?" asked Perry Mason.

"Yes, of course."

"What kind of a gun did the men have?"

"Automatics. Big black automatics."

Perry Mason got up from the desk, walked to the doors, made certain that they were closed, started pacing the office. "Look here," he said slowly, "Doctor Millsap didn't want to testify."

"Didn't he?"

"You know he didn't."

"Do I?"

"I think you do."

"Well, that's got nothing to do with his being kidnapped, has it?"

"I don't know," Perry Mason said thoughtfully. "I told him to take a sea trip for his health."

"But he couldn't. The district attorney served some papers on him."

Mason nodded. He strode up and down the office, watching the girl's quivering shoulders. Abruptly, he reached forward and snatched the handkerchief out of her hand. He raised it to his nostrils, took a deep inhalation.

She jumped to her feet, grabbed at his hand, missed it, clutched his arm, groped along the arm until she found his hand and tugged at the handkerchief. Mason held on to the tear-sodden bit of linen. She got one corner of it and tugged frantically. There was the sound of tearing cloth, and then a corner of the handkerchief ripped loose in her hands. Mason retained the biggest portion of the handkerchief.

The lawyer brushed the back of his hand across his eyes and laughed grimly. There were tears in his own eyes, tears that commenced to trickle down his cheeks. "So *that's* it, is it?" he said. "You dropped a little tear-gas into your handkerchief before you came into my office."

She said nothing. "Did you," Mason asked, staring at her with tear-streaked eyes, "drop some tear-gas in your handkerchief when you talked with the police?"

"I didn't have to then," she said, her voice catching in a sob, "they f-f-f-rightened me so that I didn't have to."

"Did the police fall for this story?" Mason inquired.

"I think so, because they thought the men might have been detectives you'd employed. They're tracing all of the Buick cars in the city to see if any of them are owned by detectives who might be working for Paul Drake."

Mason stood staring at her. "Damn this teargas," he said; "it blurs my eyes."

"I got an awful dose of it," she confided.

"*Was* there any automobile?" he asked.

"What do you mean?"

"Did any two men crowd you in to the curb in an automobile the way you said?"

"No. Doctor Millsap just went away. He wanted you to know that he wouldn't be a witness at the trial."

"If anything important develops," said Perry Mason, slowly, "could you reach him?"

"If anything important develops, you could telephone me," she said, "but be sure you talk plainly so I can recognize your voice, because otherwise I wouldn't believe it was you."

Perry Mason laughed, groped for a button on his desk and pressed it. Della slipped through the doorway from the outer office. "Della," said Perry Mason, "guide Mabel Strickland down to a taxicab."

Della Street gave a gasp. "My heavens, chief," she said, *"you're crying!!!"*

Perry Mason laughed. "It's contagious," he told her.

Chapter 18

Judge Markham, veteran of a thousand major criminal trials, sat in austere dignity behind the elaborately carved mahogany "bench." He stared down at the crowded courtroom, surveyed the patient, mask-like countenance of Perry Mason, looked over the alert, quivering eagerness of John C. Lucas, the trial deputy who had been selected to represent the rights of the people.

"The case of the People versus Rhoda Montaine," he said.

"Ready for the prosecution," Lucas snapped.

"And for the defendant."

Rhoda Montaine sat by a deputy sheriff. She was clad entirely in dark brown, relieved only by a white trimming at her throat and sleeves. The strain had told upon her, and her manner was nervous, her eyes were swift and darting as they shifted rapidly about the courtroom, but there was something in the tilt of her head, something in the set of her lips that proclaimed to even the most casual observer that, regardless of the strain, she would retain her poise and self-possession, even should the verdict of the jury be "murder in the first degree."

John Lucas glanced at the defendant and frowned. This was a dangerous attitude for any attorney to encourage in a woman who was accused of murder, far better to coach her to take advantage of all the prerogatives of her sex — to be feminine and weak; to apparently be on the verge of hysteria. A stern, capable woman might well commit murder; a feminine, delicate woman whose nerves were quivering from contact with a courtroom would be less likely to kill in cold blood.

The droning voice of the clerk called men to the jury box.

Lucas arose, made a brief statement of the nature of the case, looked up to Judge Markham.

"Under the law," said Judge Markham, "the Court is required to ask a few preliminary questions of the prospective jurors, touching their qualifications to act as jurors. Those questions may be supplemented by other questions from counsel." He turned to the jury and went through a ritual which was, so far as the selection of the jury was concerned, virtually without meaning.

He asked the jurors, in a tone of voice which indicated he was merely performing a meaningless chore, whether they had formed or expressed any opinion concerning the merits of the case; whether, if so, such an opinion would require evidence to remove, or whether, if they were selected as jurors, such opinion could be set aside and they could embark upon the trial of the case with a fair and open mind. As was to be expected, such questions brought out no disqualifications. The jurors, listening to the droning monotone of the judicial monologue, nodded their heads in silent acquiescence from time to time.

Judge Markham turned to counsel. "I am aware," he said, "that the legislature sought to expedite trials by providing that the Court should examine prospective jurors, and that this examination might be supplemented by questions asked by counsel. I am equally aware that within certain limits of propriety, an examination by counsel is far more efficacious than interrogations by the Court for the purpose of ascertaining the qualifications of jurors. The defense may inquire."

Judge Markham settled back in his seat, nodded to Mason.

Perry Mason got to his feet, turned to face the first juror who had been called to the box. "Mr. Simpson," he said, calling the juror by name, "you have stated that you can fairly and impartially act as a juror in this case?"

"Yes, sir."

"You have no bias, no prejudice one way or the other?"

"No, sir."

"You feel that you can treat the defendant in this case with fair impartiality?"

"I do."

Perry Mason's voice rose. His hands flung out

in a dramatic gesture.

"In what I am about to say, Mr. Simpson," he said, "there is no personal implication; it is a question which I consider it my duty to ask on behalf of my client. It is a question which is necessitated by reason of the fact that legal histories fairly swarm with instances in which circumstantial evidence has brought about convictions predicated upon a fortuitous chain of circumstances, circumstances which have subsequently been completely clarified and found to have no sinister significance whatever, yet circumstances which have, in the meantime, resulted in the conviction of an innocent person. Therefore, I ask you, Mr. Simpson, if through some fortuitous chain of circumstances, you should find yourself unlucky enough to be placed in the chair now occupied by the defendant, charged with the crime of murder in the first degree, would you, or would you not, be willing to trust your fate in the hands of twelve persons who felt toward you as you now feel toward the defendant?"

The dazed juror, listening to the dramatic array of words, getting the general idea without the specific meaning of each and every word impressing itself upon him, slowly nodded his head.

"Yes," he said.

Perry Mason turned to the other members of the jury. "Is there any member of this jury," he said, "who would not answer that question as

Mr. Simpson has answered it? If so, hold up your hand."

The other jurors had been waiting for the time when they would be singled out for a verbal heckling. Suddenly dazed by this swift turn of events, they looked from one to the other for mutual support. None of them fully understood the question. None of them felt like making himself conspicuous by holding up his hand.

Perry Mason turned to the Court with a triumphant smile. "Under the circumstances, your Honor, we could ask for nothing better than this jury. Pass for cause."

John Lucas jumped to his feet, his voice incredulous. "You mean," he asked, "that you're passing for cause in a murder case with no more examination than this?"

Judge Markham banged his gavel. "You heard the remark of counsel, Mr. Lucas," he said. But even the eyes of the magistrate sought Perry Mason's face in puzzled speculation. Judge Markham had seen enough of Mason's swift strategy in court to realize that the lawyer was playing for some master stroke, but he could not anticipate just what it was in this case.

John Lucas took a deep breath, swung his chair around and said, "Very well."

"You may examine the jurors," said Judge Markham.

And John Lucas proceeded to examine the jurors in detail. Very obviously he thought that Perry Mason had "planted" some very friendly person on that jury. Knowing the reputation of the man against whom he was pitted, Lucas saw no alternative other than to smoke this friendly juror out into the open; and he proceeded throughout the course of an interminably long afternoon to question the jurors as to their fairness and impartiality. And slowly the conviction was built up in the courtroom that Perry Mason, for the defense, had been satisfied to take the jurors' word for the fact that they were fair and impartial, but that the district attorney's office must heckle and browbeat them in an attempt to prove that they were liars. Before the afternoon had finished there was a distinct attitude of snarling hostility creeping into the manner of John Lucas.

Slowly Judge Markham's face relaxed. Once or twice, at some particularly flagrant example of mutual distrust between the questioner and the jurors, his face almost twisted into a smile, and, at time of the evening adjournment, he looked at Perry Mason with twinkling eyes.

John Lucas was still nagging at the jurors the next morning. By eleven o'clock he finished and passed for cause. Moreover, Lucas showed a recognition of the losing battle he had been waging by excusing four of the jurors under peremptory challenges. Whereas Perry Mason not only waived his peremptory challenges, but in doing so, commented that he had "been satisfied with the jury all along."

John Lucas had a reputation for mental agility

and a deep learning in the law. He had been selected by the district attorney to enter the lists against the hitherto invincible Perry Mason because of that quickness of mind. Lucas had embarked upon the battle with a grim determination that Perry Mason was not going to slip anything over on him, and this determination, so very apparent to every one in the courtroom, blinded the deputy district attorney to the impression he was creating upon the jurors.

Perry Mason, apparently, was trying to slip nothing over on any one. He was calm, serene and courteous, belying the reputation which had grown up about him of being a legal trickster, a juggler who could manipulate facts as a puppeteer manipulates his dummy figures. Court attachés who knew the dazzling technique of the lawyer realized that when he seemed the most innocent was the time when he would bear the closest scrutiny. But, to members of the jury, it seemed that Mason had a calm confidence in his case and his client, while the prosecution felt decidedly dubious.

The afternoon session opened with John Lucas showing the strain; with Perry Mason, suave, courteous, apparently confident that the innocence of his client would become plainly discernible from the testimony.

Officer Harry Exter was called to the stand. He testified with the belligerent emphasis of a police officer who defies counsel for the defense to try to rattle *him*. He was, he said, a member of

253

the police force of the city; was one of the officers who was assigned to a radio car beat in car
62; that at two twenty-eight A.M. on the morning
of June 16th, he had picked up a call over the radio; that, in response to that call, he had made a
quick run to the Colemont Apartments at 316
Norwalk Avenue; that he had entered the
apartment and found therein a man in an unconscious condition; that he had summoned an
ambulance and that the man had been removed; that, thereafter, the witness had remained in the apartment until a photographer
had arrived and taken a photograph; until after
fingerprint men had gone over the apartment
looking for fingerprints; that no one, save the police, had entered the apartment from the time he
arrived, that he had noticed a leather key container, in which were several keys, on the floor;
that they lay slightly under the bed on the carpet;
that he would know those keys if he saw them
again.

Lucas produced a leather key container, held
it toward Perry Mason, jingled the keys.

"Do you desire to inspect this, Counselor?" he
asked.

Perry Mason shook his head. He seemed utterly indifferent. The witness took the keys and
identified them as the keys that he had discovered in the apartment. The keys were introduced
as People's Exhibit A. The witness identified
photographs of the room in which the body had
been found, indicated the position of the body,

and, when he had testified to various details, was turned over to Perry Mason for cross-examination.

Perry Mason raised neither his voice nor his eyes. He sat slumped in his chair, his head bowed. "There was an alarm clock in the room?" he asked in a conversational tone of voice.

"Yes."

"What became of it?"

"It was taken as evidence."

"Who took it?"

"One of the men on the homicide squad."

"Would you know the alarm clock if you saw it again?"

"Yes."

Perry Mason turned to John Lucas. "You have the alarm clock?" he asked.

"We have it," said Lucas, puzzled.

"Will you produce it?" asked Perry Mason.

"When we are ready," John Lucas said.

Perry Mason shrugged his shoulders, turned his attention once more to the witness. "Did you notice anything about this alarm clock?" he asked.

"Yes."

"What was it?"

"The alarm had been set for two o'clock in the morning, or perhaps a minute or two before two o'clock."

"The clock was running?"

"It was."

"Look at the photograph," said Perry Mason,

"and see if the photograph, People's Exhibit B, shows the alarm clock."

"It does," said the witness.

"Would you mind pointing it out to the jury?"

There was a craning of necks as the jurors leaned forward and the witness, holding the photograph in his hand, pointed out the alarm clock.

"Might I ask to have the alarm clock produced now?" asked Perry Mason.

"It will be produced when we are ready to produce it," John Lucas remarked.

Perry Mason looked at Judge Markham. "I would like," he said, "to cross-examine this witness upon the alarm clock."

"The alarm clock has not been definitely brought into the case by the prosecution, as yet," Judge Markham said. "I think I will not force the prosecution to put on its case out of order. If, after the alarm clock is produced, you desire to examine this witness further, he may be recalled for further cross-examination."

"Very well," said Perry Mason listlessly, "I have no more questions."

John Lucas forged rapidly ahead. He called members of the homicide squad, members of the ambulance crew. He established the death of the man who had been taken from the apartment, introduced the poker which had been found in the apartment, with the gruesome stains of blood and the bits of hair adhering to the encrustations.

Perry Mason sat motionless, like some huge bear lying asleep in the sunlight and taking no notice of the circling approach of hunters. He asked no questions upon cross-examination.

Bit by bit John Lucas built up his case, and then he called Frank Lane to the witness stand. Frank Lane was a bright, alert young man of some twenty-five years of age. He testified to his name, address and gave his occupation as that of employee in a service station, giving the location of the service station and identifying it with reference to the residence of Rhoda Montaine. He was then asked if he had seen Rhoda Montaine on the morning of the sixteenth of June of the present year, and answered crisply in the affirmative.

"When?" asked John Lucas.

"At one forty-five in the morning."

"What was she doing?"

"She was driving a Chevrolet coupe."

"Was there anything peculiar that you noticed about that coupe?"

"Yes, sir."

"What?"

"The right rear tire was flat."

"What did she do, if anything?"

"She drove the car into the service station and asked me to change the tire."

"What did you do?"

"I jacked up the car, unscrewed the lugs, took off the tire, unscrewed the spare tire lugs and put it back on the right rear. Then, when I let the car

257

off the jack, I saw that the spare tire was nearly flat. I listened and heard air escaping from a small leak in the spare tire."

"Then what did you do?"

"I jacked the car back up, took off the spare tire and put in a new tube."

"Did you have any conversation with the defendant about the time?"

"Yes."

"What was it?"

"I asked her if she wanted me to repair the tube and she said that she was late for an appointment and that she couldn't wait. She told me to put in a new tube and repair the old one, that she'd call for it later."

"You gave her a ticket to serve as a claim check?"

"Yes, sir."

John Lucas produced a bit of numbered pasteboard. "Is this it?" he asked.

"That is it."

"What time did the defendant leave your service station?"

"At exactly ten minutes past two o'clock in the morning."

"Did you check the time in any manner?"

"I did, yes, sir. The time was checked in a book that I keep for entering repair work that is to be done by the day shift."

"And the defendant told you that she had an appointment to keep?"

"Yes."

258

"Did she say what time the appointment was for?"

"Two o'clock in the morning."

"Did she say where?"

"No."

John Lucas turned to Perry Mason with a sarcastic gesture. "Have you any questions of *this* witness?" he asked.

Perry Mason looked up at the witness, did not so much as move his body, but filled the courtroom with the booming resonance of his voice as he said, "The defendant drove into your station at one forty-five?"

"Yes."

"*Exactly* one forty-five?"

"Almost on the minute. It might have been a few seconds one way or the other. I looked at the clock when she drove in."

"She left at two ten?"

"On the dot."

"During the interval between one forty-five and two ten she was in your service station?"

"Yes."

"Watching you work?"

"Yes."

"Was she ever out of your sight?"

"No, she was there all the time."

"Is there any chance you're mistaken in your identification?"

"None whatever."

"You're positive?"

"Absolutely."

"That's all," said Perry Mason.

John Lucas called Ben Crandall to the stand. "Your name?"

"Benjamin Crandall."

"Where do you reside, Mr. Crandall?"

"At the Bellaire Apartments, 308 Norwalk Avenue, in this city."

"You resided there on June 16th last?"

"Yes."

"Were you in your apartment from midnight until two thirty on that date?"

"Yes."

"Are you familiar with the apartment known as Apartment B in the Colemont Apartments at 316 Norwalk Avenue?"

"Yes."

"I'll show you a diagram purporting to show the Colemont Apartments and also the Bellaire Apartments, and will ask you to designate your apartment on this diagram and also the position of Apartment B in the Colemont Apartments, with reference to your apartment." Lucas glanced up at Judge Markham. "I will state, your Honor, that I will subsequently connect up this map as far as its accuracy is concerned."

"No objections to the map or the questions," said Perry Mason.

"Proceed," said Judge Markham.

The witness pointed out the location of the two apartments. John Lucas produced a scale from his pocket. "There is, therefore," he said, making an elaborate show of extreme accuracy in applying the scale to the map, "a distance of less than twenty feet between your apartment and Apartment B in the Colemont Apartments, measuring in an air line."

Perry Mason shifted slightly in his chair. His deep voice rumbled across the courtroom. "That, your Honor," he said, "is acting, first, upon the assumption that the map is correct, and, secondly, upon the assumption that there is no difference in elevation between the two apartments. In other words, this map shows only a projected distance. It measures an air line between two apartments, so far as lateral distance alone is concerned; but does not take into account any slope or elevation between the windows of the two apartments."

Judge Markham looked across at John Lucas. "You have some side elevation map or sketch, Counselor?" Judge Markham asked.

Lucas bit his lip. "I'm afraid, your Honor," he said, "that I do not have such a map."

"The objection is sustained," said Judge Markham.

"Can you tell us how far it is, of your own knowledge?" asked John Lucas of the witness.

"Not in just so many feet or so many inches," said the witness.

There was a moment of silence. "*It is about* twenty feet?" asked John Lucas, plainly nettled.

"Objected to as leading and suggestive," said Perry Mason.

"Sustained," Judge Markham snapped.

John Lucas paused for a thoughtful moment. "Your Honor," he said, "I will withdraw that question. I will ask at this time that the jury be taken to view the premises so that they may see for themselves."

"There will be no objection on the part of the defense," said Perry Mason.

"Very well," said Judge Markham, "you may examine this witness as to any other matters and at three thirty o'clock the jurors will be taken to view the premises."

John Lucas smiled triumphantly. "Mr. Crandall," he said, "could you hear anything which took place in Apartment B in the Colemont Apartments early in the morning of the sixteenth day of June of the present year?"

"Yes."

"What did you hear?"

"I heard a telephone ring."

"Then what did you hear?"

"I heard a conversation, some one talking into a telephone."

"Do you know who was talking?"

"No, I only know that there was the sound of a voice — a man's voice — that it was coming from Apartment B in the Colemont Apartments."

"What was said in the telephone conversation?"

"He mentioned the name of a woman — Rhoda, I'm pretty sure the name was. He pronounced the last name so that I couldn't get it, but it had a foreign sound, ending with 'ayne' or

262

something like that — the way he pronounced it made it sound like a foreign name, but I'm not sure. He said that this woman was to call on him at two o'clock in the morning and give him some money."

"What did you hear after that?"

"I dozed off, and then I heard peculiar sounds."

"What sort of sounds?"

"The sounds of a struggle, a scraping and banging, the sound of a blow and then silence. After that I thought I heard whispers."

"Did you hear anything else at that time?" asked Lucas.

"Yes, sir."

"What was it?"

"The steady, persistent ringing of a doorbell."

"Was it repeated?"

"Yes, it was repeated."

"Can you tell me how many times?"

"No, it was repeated several times."

"When did that ringing take place, with reference to the sound of struggle?"

"During the time of the struggle, during the time the blow was being struck."

John Lucas turned to Perry Mason. "Cross-examine," he snapped.

Perry Mason straightened slightly in his chair. "Now, let's get this straight," he said. "You first beard the ringing of the telephone bell?"

"Yes."

"How did you know it was a telephone bell?"

"Because of the manner in which it rang."

"Just how was that?"

"It rang mechanically. You know how a telephone rings — a ring for a second or two, then two or three seconds of silence, then another ring."

"That woke you up?"

"I guess so. It was a warm night. The windows were open. I was sleeping very lightly. At first I thought the telephone was ringing in my apartment. . . ."

"Never mind what you thought," Perry Mason said. "What did you *do* and what did you *see* and what did you *hear?* That's all we're interested in."

"I heard the ringing of a telephone bell," said the witness belligerently. "I got up and listened. Then I realized the telephone was ringing in the apartment house to the north — the Colemont Apartments. I then heard the sound of a voice talking over the telephone."

"Then later on," said Perry Mason, "you heard the struggle?"

"That is right."

"And during the struggle you heard the doorbell?"

"That is correct."

"Wasn't it the telephone bell that you heard?"

"No, sir, absolutely not."

"Why are you so certain that it was not?"

"Because it was not the sound of a telephone bell — it was an entirely different type of bell. In the first place, there was more of a whirring sound to it. In the second place, it rang at longer intervals than a telephone bell rings."

Perry Mason seemed much disappointed by the answer. "Could you swear," he said, "that you were *absolutely certain* it was *not* the telephone?"

"I *am* swearing it."

"You are swearing that it was *not the telephone?*"

"Yes."

"You are as positive that it was *not* the telephone as you are of any other testimony you have given in this case?"

"Absolutely."

"Do you know what time this was?" asked Perry Mason.

"It was somewhere in the vicinity of two o'clock in the morning. I don't know exactly. Subsequently, when I became more wide awake, I notified the police. It was then two twenty-seven A.M. There had been an interval of perhaps fifteen or twenty minutes — I don't know exactly how long — I had been dozing."

Perry Mason slowly got to his feet. "Don't you know," he said, "that it is a physical impossibility for one who is in Apartment 269 of the Bellaire Apartments to hear the doorbell ringing in Apartment B in the Colemont Apartments?"

"It isn't an impossibility. I heard it," said the witness truculently.

"You mean you heard *a* bell ringing. You

don't know that it was the doorbell."

"I know it was the doorbell."

"How do you know it?"

"Because I recognized the sound of the ring. I know it was a doorbell."

"But you don't remember ever having heard the doorbell ringing in that apartment before?"

"No, this was a very hot night. It was a quiet, still night. There were no noises. The windows were all open."

"Answer the question," said Perry Mason. "You never heard the doorbell ring in that apartment before?"

"I can't remember."

"And you haven't listened to the doorbell since, in order to tell whether it was the doorbell that you heard or not?"

"No, I haven't. I didn't do it because I didn't have to do it. I know a doorbell when I hear one."

Perry Mason dropped back in his chair, smiled at the jury, a smile which was a scornful comment upon the testimony of the witness, but a smile, by the way, which brought no answering expression to the eyes of the jurors. "That," he said, "is all."

John Lucas took the witness for redirect examination. "Regardless of the measurements in feet and inches," he said, "you may state whether the distance is too great for you to have heard a doorbell."

Perry Mason was on his feet. "Objected to,

your Honor," he said, "as not proper redirect examination, as argumentative, as assuming facts not in evidence, as leading and suggestive. This witness has stated that to the best of his knowledge he never has heard a doorbell in this apartment. Therefore, it is not proper for him to state whether a doorbell could or could not have been heard. This is the conclusion for the jury to draw. Never having heard a doorbell ring, it is obviously impossible for him to tell whether he *could* have heard a doorbell ring. It is only a surmise on his part."

Judge Markham nodded thoughtfully, and said, "The objection is sustained."

Lucas frowned, and then said after a moment, "You were able to hear the telephone bell when it rang?"

"Yes."

"Was that bell distinctly audible or faintly audible?"

"It was distinctly audible. It sounded so plain that I thought it was my own telephone."

"In your experience," asked Lucas hastily, "are telephone bells and doorbells about equally loud?"

"Objected to," Perry Mason said, "as leading, suggestive, calling for a conclusion. . . ."

Judge Markham nodded and said decisively, "Counselor, the objection is sustained. The question is improper."

John Lucas thought for a moment, leaned toward one of the deputies at his side, and whis-

267

pered for several seconds. A look of cunning was on his face. Once or twice, as he whispered, he smiled. The deputy nodded. Lucas straightened in his chair, and said, "That's all."

"Recross-examination?" asked Judge Markham. Perry Mason shook his head.

"It is approaching the time heretofore fixed for an examination of the premises by the jury," Judge Markham said. "We will, therefore, take a recess at this time and we will proceed to the premises which will be shown to the jury. During such time no testimony will be offered or taken. Counsel can agree, themselves, as to certain matters which are to be pointed out to the jurors. The jurors will inspect those things and observe the premises. We will then return to court for further testimony. Cars are in readiness to transport the jury and the court officials to the premises. The Court will endeavor to do its part by having the trip made expeditiously, so that the case may continue its usual rapid progress." Judge Markham turned to the jurors. "During the trip which we are about to make," he said, "you gentlemen will remember the previous admonition of the Court and not discuss the case or allow any one to discuss it with you. Nor will you form or express any opinion as to the guilt or innocence of the defendant."

Chapter 19

Officials from the sheriff's office had paved the way for the examination of the premises by the jurors. The jurors stood in a body on the sidewalk, looked at the space between the two apartment houses. Upon stipulation of counsel, a deputy sheriff pointed out the windows of the Crandall apartment and also the windows of Apartment B in the Colemont Apartments. The jurors were taken up to the apartment where the murder had been committed. Deputies had previously arranged with Sidney Otis to have the apartment open for inspection.

John Lucas motioned to Judge Markham, drew him off to one side and beckoned to Perry Mason. "May we point out the door bell and press the button?"

"No objection," said Perry Mason.

A deputy sheriff pointed out the bell button. He pressed the button. The faint ringing of the bell could be heard in the upper apartment.

"Now," Perry Mason said, "if tests are being made with that doorbell, it should be removed, properly identified, and introduced in evidence."

John Lucas hesitated a moment. "We will do that," he said, "when we return to court."

He turned to the deputy sheriff. "What's the name of the present tenant of the apartment?" he asked.

"Sidney Otis."

"Slap a subpoena on him," ordered John Lucas in the majestic manner of a king who is accustomed to command and receive implicit obedience. "Bring him into court. And disconnect that doorbell and bring *it* into court."

"And now," said John Lucas in an undertone, "we'll take the jurors up to Apartment B in the Colemont Apartments, so they can look across into the windows of this upstairs apartment." He turned to the deputy sheriff, stared significantly at him. "You," he said "can be disconnecting that doorbell while we're up there."

It took two trips of the elevator for the jurors to reach the Crandall apartment, the elevator being packed to capacity both times. When the jurors had all been assembled and had crowded to the windows, which were open, and were staring across the space into the apartment where the murder had been committed, a whirring bell exploded the silence. There was an interval and then the bell rang again, long and insistent.

Perry Mason grabbed John Lucas by the arm, rushed him across to confront Judge Markham, said, out of earshot of the jury, "Your Honor, that is manifestly unfair. There was no stipulation that the doorbell was to be rung while the

270

jurors were assembled here. That's equivalent to the taking of testimony."

John Lucas kept his face innocent and guileless. "This," he said, "comes as very much of a surprise to me. I certainly didn't know that the bell was *going* to ring. I *did* instruct a deputy to disconnect the doorbell. Doubtless, in disconnecting it he pressed the button which caused it to ring."

Perry Mason said thoughtfully, "And I noticed you were engaged in a whispered conversation with him when the question was brought up in court as to whether it was possible for a witness to have heard the doorbell ring across the intervening space. And I noticed, further, that you gave the deputy a very significant look just before you left the other apartment house."

"Are you making an accusation?" Lucas flared.

Judge Markham said slowly, "That will do, gentlemen. We'll discuss the matter later. You have raised your voices, and it is possible for the jurors to hear what we are discussing."

"I am going to move," Perry Mason said in a low voice, "to have the jury instructed to disregard the ringing of that doorbell."

Lucas laughed, and his laugh was triumphant.

"You might strike it out of the records," he said, "but you'd never strike it out of the *minds* of the jurors."

Judge Markham frowned at him, stared at Perry Mason, and said in a low voice, "I'm very sorry it occurred, but undoubtedly the deputy district attorney is correct. Having occurred, there's nothing in particular that can be done about it. You can't erase from the minds of the jurors what they have heard."

"I had the right," Perry Mason said, "to use that as a point in my defense, to argue that it was a physical impossibility for the ringing of a door-bell to have been distinctly audible."

Despite his attempt to keep his features po-litely expressionless, there was a glint of triumph in John Lucas's eyes. "You can, of course," he said, "still argue the point."

Judge Markham shook his head firmly. "Gen-tlemen," he said, "this discussion will terminate immediately. If there should be any further dis-cussion, it will take place in court."

John Lucas nodded, moved away. Perry Ma-son hesitated. The doorbell rang once more in the apartment where the murder had been com-mitted, remained ringing for several seconds. John Lucas ran to the window and shouted, "Shut off that doorbell. The jurors weren't sup-posed to have heard it ring."

One of the jurors snickered audibly. Perry Ma-son clamped his lips in a firm, straight line. "Of course," Judge Markham said in a low tone of voice, "if you wish to have an investigation, Counselor, of any possible understanding be-tween the deputy and the district attorney's of-fice . . ."

Perry Mason's laugh was sarcastic. "You

know how much I'd find out," he said bitterly.

Judge Markham retained his judicial impassivity of countenance. "Is there any further inspection to be made?" he asked.

John Lucas shook his head.

"No," Perry Mason said curtly.

"We will then," ordered Judge Markham, "return to court. We can probably take some additional testimony before the evening adjournment."

The jurors elected to walk down the stairs rather than ride in the elevator. Waiting cars whisked them back to the courtroom, where they promptly took their places in the jury box. "Proceed," Judge Markham said.

"I will," said John Lucas, "call Ellen Crandall."

Ellen Crandall had dressed with care for the occasion. She moved forward, conscious of the eyes of the crowded courtroom. Her face held a fixed expression, an expression which evidently had been carefully practiced for the occasion. It was as though she wished the spectators to understand her appreciation of the gravity of the occasion, as well as the importance of the testimony she was about to give. Under the questioning of John Lucas, she testified to exactly the same set of facts that her husband had testified to, except that she had, perhaps, been more awake during the time of the struggle. She had heard the sound of the blow more distinctly, and she was positive that she had, following the sound of the blow, heard surreptitious whispers.

The hour for the evening adjournment found John Lucas just completing his direct examination. Perry Mason got to his feet. "After your Honor admonishes the jurors," he said, "I have a matter to take up with Court and counsel which concerns another phase of the case and should probably be discussed in the absence of the jurors."

"Very well," agreed Judge Markham, and, turning to the jury, said, "It appears that the usual hour of evening adjournment has been reached. The Court is not impounding the jury during the trial of this case, but wishes to impress upon you, nevertheless, that you have a responsibility as a part of the machinery of justice. The Court is about to adjourn until ten o'clock to-morrow morning. During that adjournment you will be careful not to discuss this case among yourselves, nor to permit others to discuss it in your presence. You will form or express no opinion concerning the guilt or innocence of the accused. You will refrain from reading any newspaper accounts of the trial, and you will promptly report to the Court any one who seeks to discuss this matter in your presence or any one who makes any advances to you."

The judge's gavel banged upon the marble slab on the top of his bench and the jurors filed from the courtroom.

When the jury had gone, Perry Mason arose and faced Judge Markham. "Your honor," he said, "Rhoda Montaine has filed suit for divorce against Carl Montaine. In connection with the proper preparation of that case for trial, it has become necessary for me to take the deposition of Carl Montaine; that deposition has been noticed for to-morrow. In order to facilitate matters, I have arranged that the deposition may be taken during the noon recess. It may, however, require a little additional time to complete the deposition, in which event I shall ask the indulgence of the Court."

John Lucas, sneeringly sure of himself, made an impatient gesture. "Counsel well knows," he said, "that the only object of that deposition is to go on a fishing expedition with one of prosecution's witnesses before that witness is put on the stand."

Perry Mason bowed mockingly. "A witness," he said, "who has been wet-nursed by the prosecution ever since the death of Gregory Moxley."

"Gentlemen," said Judge Markham, "that will do. Counsel is entitled to take the deposition of the witness if he wishes. That is the law. If the deposition is noticed for to-morrow, it will be taken up to-morrow."

"Under stipulation with the counsel who is representing Carl Montaine," said Perry Mason, "the deposition will be somewhat informal. It will be taken before Miss Della Street, my secretary, who is a notary public as well as an efficient shorthand reporter. Counsel for Carl Montaine and myself will be present. The deposition is a purely civil matter. I do not understand that Counselor Lucas will seek to be present. If . . ."

"I've got a right to be present if I want to," thundered Lucas.

"You have not," said Perry Mason. "This is purely a civil matter. You do not now appear as civil counsel for Montaine. Therefore it has been necessary for him to retain other counsel. The other counsel agrees with me that this is purely a civil matter, and . . ."

Judge Markham's gavel again banged on the desk.

"Gentlemen," he said, "this discussion is entirely out of order. Court will suit your convenience to-morrow in the taking of the deposition, Mr. Mason. Court is adjourned."

John Lucas, gloating in the triumph of a day during which he had built up a case against the defendant which Perry Mason had been unable to shake, smiled sneeringly at Mason and said in a voice loud enough to be heard over much of the courtroom, "Well, Mason, you seem to lack much of your usual fire to-day. You didn't get very far cross-examining the Crandalls about the doorbell, did you?"

Mason said politely, "You forget that I have not *finished* with my cross-examination."

The answering laugh of John Lucas was taunting.

Perry Mason stopped at a telephone booth and telephoned the hotel where C. Phillip Montaine, the Chicago millionaire, was registered. "Is Mr. Montaine in his room?" he asked.

After a moment he was assured that Mr. Montaine had not as yet returned to his room. "When he returns," said Perry Mason, "please give him a message from Perry Mason. Tell him that if he will arrange to be at my office at seven-thirty to-morrow evening I think I can arrange matters with him in regard to a property settlement in his son's divorce case. Will you see that he gets that message?"

"Yes," said the telephone clerk.

Perry Mason rang Della Street. "Della," he said, "I left a message for C. Phillip Montaine at his hotel, saying that if he would meet me at my office at seven-thirty to-morrow night I would arrange a complete property settlement between Rhoda and Carl. I don't know whether he will get that message. Will you ring him this evening and make sure?"

"Yes, chief," she said. "You won't be coming to the office?"

"No."

"Listen, chief," she told him, "Carl Montaine can't come to your office. The district attorney is keeping him in custody, isn't he?"

Perry Mason chuckled.

"That's right, Della."

"But you want C. Phillip Montaine to be here anyway, is that it?"

"Yes."

"Okay," she said. "I'll see that he gets the message."

That night the city editor of the *Chronicle*, examining the transcript of proceedings for the day, with the eagle eye of a newspaper man who had seen Perry Mason in action and who knew that lawyer's masterly technique of placing bombs in the prosecution's case timed to explode with deadly effect at the most inopportune moments, was impressed by the peculiar phraseology of Perry Mason's questions concerning the doorbell. He sent two of his best reporters out with instructions to corner the attorney and get an interview from him in regard to the significance of that particular phase of the case. The reporters, however, scoured the city and were unsuccessful. Not until court convened the next morning did Perry Mason put in a public appearance. Then, freshly shaven, with a certain jauntiness in his manner, he stepped through the swinging doors of the courtroom, precisely five seconds before court was called to order.

Judge Markham, taking his place on the bench, observed that the jurors were all present, the defendant was in court, and instructed Mrs. Crandall to once more take the witness stand for cross-examination.

Perry Mason addressed himself to the court. "Your Honor," he said, "it was agreed between counsel yesterday that the doorbell taken from the apartment where Gregory Moxley met his death would be received in evidence. I desire to cross-examine this witness concerning the sound of that doorbell, and have had an electrician prepare a set of dry batteries, properly wired with clamps which can be adjusted to the bell, so that I can ring the bell itself in court, so as to test the recollection of the witness as to the manner in which it was rung. The Court will remember that yesterday the husband of this witness testified generally to the sound of the bell as having been *'an entirely different type of bell. In the first place, there was more of a whirring sound to it. In the second place, it rang at longer intervals than a telephone bell rings.'*

"I have quoted, your Honor, from the testimony of Mr. Crandall, as it has been written up by the court reporter. Obviously, such testimony is merely the conclusion of a witness, and, in view of the fact that Mrs. Crandall has given similar testimony, I feel that I should be able to cross-examine these witnesses with the doorbell itself in evidence. In view of the fact that the bell has been brought to court, I ask permission of the Court to have this witness step down from the stand long enough to enable the prosecution to introduce its evidence, identifying the doorbell and making it available for such test."

Judge Markham glanced at John Lucas. "Any objections?" he asked.

John Lucas made a throwing gesture with his arms, spreading them wide apart as though baring his breast to the inspection of the jury. His manner was aggressively frank. "Certainly not," he said. "We are only too glad to put our evidence in in such a manner that it will assist coun-

279

sel for the defense in his cross-examination of our witnesses. We want counsel to have *every* possible opportunity for cross-examination." With a smirk, he sat down.

Judge Markham nodded to Mrs. Crandall. "Just step down for a moment, Mrs. Crandall," he said, and then nodded to John Lucas. "Very well, Counselor," he said in a voice sufficiently uncordial to apprise Lucas that further attempts to grandstand in front of the jury would meet with judicial rebuff, "proceed to introduce the doorbell in evidence."

"Call Sidney Otis," said Lucas.

The big electrician lumbered forward, glanced at Perry Mason, then glanced hurriedly away. He held his eyes downcast while he raised his hand, listened to the oath being administered. Then he sat on the edge of the witness chair and looked expectantly at John Lucas.

"Your name?" asked John Lucas.

"Sidney Otis."

"Where do you reside?"

"Apartment B, Colemont Apartments, 316 Norwalk Avenue."

"What's your occupation?"

"An electrician."

"How old are you?"

"Forty-eight."

"When did you move into the apartment which you now occupy?"

"About the twentieth of June, I think it was."

"You're familiar with the doorbell in the

apartment which you occupy, Mr. Otis?"

"Oh, yes."

"As an electrician you have perhaps noticed it more or less particularly?"

"Yes."

"Has the bell been changed or tampered with in any way since you occupied the apartment?"

Sidney Otis squirmed uncomfortably in the witness stand.

"Not since I *moved* into the apartment," he said.

"You say the bell has not been changed since you *moved* into the apartment?" John Lucas asked, puzzled.

"That's right."

"Had it, to your own knowledge, been changed or tampered with in any way *prior* to the time you *moved* into the apartment?"

"Yes."

John Lucas suddenly snapped to startled, upright rigidity. "What was that?" he demanded.

"I said it had been changed," said Sidney Otis.

"It had *what?*"

"Been changed."

"How? In what way?" asked John Lucas, his face taking on a slow flush of anger.

"I'm an electrician," said Sidney Otis simply. "When I moved into that apartment I put on a doorbell that I took from my own store."

There was an expression of relief apparent on the face of the deputy district attorney. "Oh, so you wanted to put on one of your own bells, is that it?"

"Yes."

"I see," said Lucas, smiling now, "and the bell that you took out when you installed yours you have kept in your possession, have you?"

"I kept it," said Sidney Otis, "but it wasn't a bell — it was a buzzer."

There was a tense, dramatic silence in the courtroom. Eyes of judge, jurors and spectators turned to the frank, honest face of Sidney Otis, then turned to stare at John Lucas, whose face, flushed and angry red, was twisting with emotion. His hands were gripping the edge of the counsel table so that the skin showed white over his knuckles. "When did you move into this apartment?" he asked ominously.

"About the twentieth or twenty-first of June — somewhere along in there."

"And just before you moved into the apartment, you changed the doorbell?"

"That's right. I took off the buzzer and put on a bell."

Lucas took a deep breath. "Look here," he said. "You're an electrician?"

"Yes, sir."

"Have you had occasion to go in the other apartments in that building?"

"No, sir."

"Then you don't know, as a matter of fact, that there are bells in the other three apartments, and that the very remarkable and single exception was discovered by you when you moved into your apartment and found a buzzer in it?"

"I don't know as I get just what you mean," Sidney Otis said, "but if you mean that my apartment was the only one that had a buzzer in it, you're wrong, because the other upstairs apartment had a buzzer."

"How do you know, if you've never been in the apartment? Did some one tell you?"

"No, sir, but you see, when I was putting on the bell in my apartment I started checking up on the wiring, and while I was doing that I pressed the button on the other apartments. I don't know what's on the two downstairs apartments, but on the other upstairs apartment my wife could hear the buzzer sounding when I pressed the button."

John Lucas snapped his mouth shut with grim determination. "I'm going to get to the bottom of this," he said. He whirled to a deputy sheriff. "Get out there and find if there are buzzers on those other apartments," he said, in a voice that was distinctly audible to the jury.

Judge Markham banged his gavel. "Counselor," he said, "as long as you are in court before this jury, you will confine your remarks to questions of the witness and comments to the Court."

Lucas was quivering with rage. He bowed his head in silent assent to the Court's admonition, turned to Perry Mason and, for a moment, could not trust his voice, then he said, after an abortive motion of his lips, "Cross-examine."

Perry Mason waved his hand in a gesture of dismissal. "Why," he said, "I've no questions. In fact, I find myself very much at a loss as to how to proceed because I had intended to make some tests with the doorbell. It now appears that *this* doorbell wasn't the one that was in the apartment when Moxley was killed."

John Lucas whirled to face the witness. "That's all," he said. "You're excused, Mr. Otis. I will call, if the Court please, as my next witness . . ."

"You forget," interrupted Perry Mason, "that Mrs. Crandall was on the stand for cross-examination. I had just started my cross-examination of her when she was withdrawn, in order to permit you to call Sidney Otis as *your* witness."

"Very well," said Judge Markham, "you may proceed with the cross-examination of Mrs. Crandall. Take the stand, Mrs. Crandall." Ellen Crandall again took the witness stand, looking very much bewildered.

"Directing your attention to the bell that you heard during the time when the sounds of struggle were coming from the apartment where the murder was committed," said Perry Mason, "are you prepared to state positively that that was not a *telephone* bell that you heard?"

"I don't *think* it was," said Mrs. Crandall.

"What are your reasons for saying that?"

"Because it didn't ring like a telephone bell. A

telephone bell rings a short ring, then there's a minute of silence and then another ring. It's a mechanical ringing, and it's a higher-pitched bell. This was more of a whirring sound."

"Now, then," said Perry Mason, "I don't want to trick you, Mrs. Crandall, and if it should appear that there wasn't any doorbell in that apartment, but that there was a buzzer, then it must, of course, be true that it *couldn't* have been the doorbell which you heard."

John Lucas got to his feet. "Objected to," he said, "as argumentative."

"The question may be argumentative," said Judge Markham, "but I am going to permit it. This is manifestly a fair method of cross-examination, even if the phraseology of the question may make it objectionable. The objection is overruled."

"I *thought* it was a doorbell," said Mrs. Crandall.

"Now, then," said Perry Mason, "I'm going to direct your attention to the photograph, People's Exhibit B, and show you that there is an alarm clock in that photograph. Isn't it possible, Mrs. Crandall, that the bell which you heard on the night of the murder, at the same time you heard the sounds of a struggle and conflict, *was the bell on the alarm clock?*"

Mrs. Crandall's face lit up. "Why, yes," she said, "it might have been. Come to think of it, perhaps it was. It *must* have been."

Perry Mason addressed the Court. "Now,

your Honor," he said, "I desire to cross-examine this witness by letting her hear the identical bell on this alarm clock. She has had her recollection tested by hearing the ringing of a doorbell in the apartment occupied by the victim of the homicide on the night of the killing. It now appears that that doorbell was not in the apartment at the time. It further appears, from the prosecution's own testimony, that the alarm clock was. I therefore insist that the prosecution shall produce this alarm clock here and now."

Judge Markham looked down at John Lucas. "Any objections?" he asked.

"You bet there's objection!" shouted John Lucas, getting to his feet. "We'll put on our case in any way we see fit. We're not going to be brow-beaten or tricked . . ."

Judge Markham's gavel banged repeatedly. "Counselor," he said, "sit down. Your comments are improper as argument or as statement. A request has been made that the prosecution produce an article which was taken from the room where the homicide was committed. This article is admittedly in the custody of the prosecution. In view of the testimony that has been introduced on the direct examination of this witness concerning the ringing of a bell in the apartment, I believe that it is within the legitimate bounds of cross-examination to ask this witness concerning *any* bell which was in the apartment, and to let her listen to it for the purpose of ascertaining whether it is the bell in question or not. I direct, therefore, that the alarm clock be brought into court."

John Lucas sat rigid. "You have the alarm clock in your possession?" asked Judge Markham.

"The sheriff has it," said John Lucas, speaking with an effort. "And, your Honor," the enraged prosecutor said jumping to his feet, indignation giving him sudden loquacity, "you can see the manner in which this whole thing has been manipulated. We were trapped into breaking into the cross-examining of Mrs. Crandall, in order to be confronted with the surprise which counsel on the other side apparently anticipated. Now, with the witness confused by this spectacular development which I have had no chance to thoroughly investigate, she is rushed along in her cross-examination without the opportunity of conferring with counsel for the prosecution. . . ."

Judge Markham's voice was stern as he said, "Counselor, your remarks are improper and are out of order. You will be seated." Judge Markham turned toward the jury with the admonition, "The jury is instructed to disregard the remarks of counsel," then, turning to the bailiff, "bring that alarm clock into court."

The bailiff stepped from the courtroom. There was a moment of silence, then the hissing sibilants of excited whispers, the sounds of rustling garments as people squirmed in an ecstasy of excitement. From the back of the courtroom came a sharp, hysterical giggle.

Judge Markham's gavel commanded silence.

There followed a period during which comparative silence was restored, but occasional whispers crept into the tense atmosphere, vague, indefinite sounds, impossible to locate, yet surreptitiously adding to the emotional tension.

The deputy sheriff brought an alarm clock into court. Perry Mason looked at the alarm clock, turned it over in his hands. "There's a label pasted on this clock, if the Court please," he said, "stating that it is the same clock which was taken from the apartment of Gregory Moxley on the morning of June sixteenth of this year."

Judge Markham nodded.

"I take it," said Perry Mason, "that I may use this in my cross-examination of the witness?"

"In view of the fact that it was produced by the prosecution in response to an order of this Court directing the prosecution to place in your hands the identical alarm clock which was taken from that room," said Judge Markham, "you may use it. If the deputy district attorney has any objection he will make it now." John Lucas sat very straight and very erect at the table assigned to counsel for the prosecution. He made no sound, no motion. "Proceed," said Judge Markham.

Perry Mason, the alarm clock in his hands, approached the witness stand. "You will observe," he said, handing the alarm clock to Mrs. Crandall, "that the alarm is set for two o'clock. You will further notice that the clock has now

288

stopped. It has, apparently, run down. I will also call to the attention of the Court and counsel that the alarm seems to be run down."

"It would," said John Lucas sarcastically, "naturally have run down. No one would have heard it ring in the sheriff's office at two o'clock in the morning."

"There need be no argument," said Judge Markham. "What is it you wish to do with the alarm clock, Counselor?"

"I wish to wind the alarm," said Perry Mason, "turn the hour and minute hands of the clock so that it may definitely be ascertained when the alarm was set. I want the witness to hear the sound of the alarm, and then she can testify whether that was the bell which she heard."

"Very well," said Judge Markham, "you will wind the alarm clock and set the hands under the supervision of the Court. Mr. Lucas, if you wish to step up to the bench while counsel is winding the clock you are invited to do so."

John Lucas sat rigid. "I refuse to have anything to do with this," he said. "It is irregular, a trick of counsel."

Judge Markham frowned at him. "Your remarks, Counselor," he observed ominously, "come very close to being contempt of court." He turned to Perry Mason. "Step up with the alarm clock, Counselor."

Perry Mason suddenly dominated the courtroom. Gone was all the indifference of his former manner. He was now the showman, putting on a headline act. He bowed to the judge, turned to smile at the jury, stepped up to the bench. He wound up the alarm, turned the hands of the clock slowly. When those hands registered two minutes before two, the alarm whirred into action.

Perry Mason set the clock on the judge's desk, turned and walked away, as though satisfied with what he had done. The alarm whirred for several seconds, then paused for an appreciable interval, then whirred again, paused and once more exploded into noise.

Perry Mason stepped forward and shut off the alarm, turned to Mrs. Crandall and smiled at her. "Now, Mrs. Crandall," he said, "since it appears that it *couldn't* have been the *doorbell* that you heard, since you are equally positive that it wasn't the *telephone* bell that you heard, don't you think that the bell you heard *must* have been that of the alarm clock?"

"Yes," she said dazedly, "I guess it must have been."

"Are you sure that it was?"

"Yes, it must have been."

"You're willing to swear that it was?"

"Yes."

"Now that you think it over, you're as certain of the fact that it must have been the bell of the alarm clock which you heard ringing, as you are of any other testimony you have given in this case?"

"Yes."

Judge Markham picked up the alarm clock, inspected it frowningly. He toyed with the key which wound the alarm, suddenly started drumming his fingers on the bench. He frowningly surveyed Perry Mason, then turned to regard the alarm clock with a scowl. Perry Mason bowed in the direction of John Lucas. "No further cross-examination," he said, and sat down.

"Redirect examination, Counselor?" asked Judge Markham of the deputy district attorney.

John Lucas got to his feet. "Are you now swearing positively," he shouted, "in contradiction of your previous testimony, that it was not a doorbell which you heard, but the bell of an alarm clock?"

Mrs. Crandall looked somewhat dazed at the savagery of his attack. Perry Mason's laugh was good-humored, patronizing, insulting. "Why, your Honor," he said, "Counselor has forgotten himself. He is seeking to cross-examine his own witness. This is not *my* witness; this is a witness on behalf of the prosecution."

"The objection is sustained," said Judge Markham.

John Lucas took a deep breath, keeping control of himself with an effort. "It was this alarm clock which you heard?" he asked.

"Yes," said the witness with a sudden truculent emphasis.

John Lucas sat down abruptly. "That's all," he muttered.

"Your honor," said Perry Mason, "may I recall Mr. Crandall for one question on further cross-examination?"

Judge Markham nodded. "Under the circumstances," he said, "the Court will permit it."

The tense, dramatic silence of the courtroom was so impressive that the pound of Benjamin Crandall's feet as he walked up the aisle to the witness stand sounded as audible as the pulsations of some drum of doom. Crandall resumed the witness stand. "You have heard your wife's testimony?" asked Perry Mason.

"Yes, sir."

"You have heard the alarm clock?"

"Yes, sir."

"Do you," said Perry Mason, "desire to contradict your wife's testimony that it was the alarm clock she heard, or . . ."

John Lucas jumped to his feet. "Objected to!" he said. "Argumentative. That's not proper cross-examination and counsel knows it."

Judge Markham nodded. "The objection," he said, in tones of grim severity, "is sustained. Counsel will keep his examination within the legitimate province of orderly questions. Counsel must well realize the impropriety of such a question."

Perry Mason accepted the rebuke meekly, but withal, smilingly. "Yes, your Honor," he said quietly, and turned to the witness. "Now, I'll put it this way, Mr. Crandall," he said. "It now appears from the physical facts of the case that you *couldn't* have heard a doorbell, and, inasmuch as you have stated positively that it *wasn't* a telephone bell which you heard, don't you think it *must* have been this alarm clock which you heard?"

The witness took a deep breath. His eyes moved around the courtroom, locked with the steady eyes of his wife, who sat in an aisle seat. John Lucas made an objection in a voice which quivered so that it almost broke. "Your Honor," he said, "that question is argumentative. Counsel is carefully making an argument to this man, and incorporating that argument as a part of his question. He keeps dangling the wife's testimony in front of the husband. It's not the way to cross-examine this witness. Why doesn't he come out and ask him fairly and frankly, without all these preliminaries, whether he heard a doorbell or whether he didn't hear a doorbell."

"I think, your Honor," Perry Mason insisted, "that this *is* legitimate cross-examination."

Before Judge Markham could rule on the point, the witness blurted a reply. "If you fellows think I'm going to contradict my wife," he said, "you're crazy!"

The courtroom broke into a roar of spontaneous laughter, which Judge Markham could not silence, despite the pounding of his gavel. After the tense drama of the previous situation, the spectators welcomed a chance to find some relief from the emotional tension. When some semblance of order had been restored by Judge Markham's threat to clear the courtroom if there were any further demonstrations, John Lucas said in a voice that was like the complaint of a wronged child to its mother, "That's just the point that Mason was trying to drill into the mind of this witness. He was trying to make him realize the position he'd put his wife in if he didn't testify the way Mason wanted him to."

"Well," said Judge Markham, with a smile twisting the corners of his mouth, despite himself, "whether that may or may not have been the case, it now is apparent that the point *has* at least occurred to the mind of the witness. However, I will sustain the objection. Counsel will ask questions which are free from argumentative matter."

Perry Mason bowed. "*Was* it a doorbell that you heard," he asked, "or *was* it an alarm clock?"

"It was an alarm clock," said Crandall, without hesitation.

Perry Mason sat down. "That's all the cross-examination," he said.

"Redirect examination?" asked Judge Markham.

Lucas walked toward the witness, holding the alarm clock in his left hand, shaking it violently until the sound of metal tinkling against metal was audible throughout the courtroom. "Are you going to tell this jury," he said, "that it was *this* alarm clock that you heard?"

"If that's the alarm clock that was in the room," said the witness slowly, "that was the one I heard."

"And it wasn't a doorbell at all?"

"It couldn't have been."

Lucas looked at the witness with exasperation on his face. "That's all," he said.

Crandall left the stand. Lucas, holding the alarm clock in his hand, turned and walked toward the counsel table. Midway to the table he paused as though he had suddenly been struck with some idea. He raised the alarm clock, stood staring at it, then whirled to face Judge Markham. Indignant words poured from his lips.

"Your Honor," he said, "the object of this examination is apparent. If this alarm was set for five minutes before two, and the alarm was ringing at the very moment when Gregory Moxley was murdered, the defendant, Rhoda Montaine, can't possibly have been the one who was guilty of that murder, because the testimony of the prosecution's own witnesses shows that she was not at the scene of the murder at that time, but, until some ten minutes after two o'clock, on the morning when the murder was committed, was in a service station where she was under the eyes of an attendant who has carefully checked the time.

"Now, your Honor, in view of that fact, it appears that the most important part of this whole situation hinges upon the question of whether the alarm on this clock had been *shut off,* or allowed to run down. Now I notice that counsel for the defense took that clock from the hands of the deputy sheriff. I notice that he *said* that the alarm was run down, but there's no proof that it *was* run down. It would have been an exceedingly simple matter for counsel to have manipulated that lever while he was winding the alarm clock and turning the hands. I, therefore, suggest that all of this evidence be stricken out."

The Court motioned Perry Mason to silence, stared steadily at John Lucas.

"You can't strike out that evidence," he said, "because the witnesses have now testified positively that it was the alarm clock that they heard. Regardless of the *means* by which they were induced to make such a statement, they have made it, and the testimony must stand. However, the Court desires to state, Mr. Lucas, that if counsel had desired to safeguard the interests of the People against any such manipulation of the alarm clock, counsel was afforded that privilege. The Court specifically invited counsel to step up to the bench and watch counsel for the defense while he was winding and setting the clock. As I remember the situation, your attitude was that of a sulky child. You sat at the counsel table sullen and sulking, and refused to participate in the safeguards which were offered you by the Court. The Court is administering this rebuke in the presence of the jury, because your accusation of misconduct on the part of counsel for the defense was made in the presence of the jury. The jury are instructed to disregard the comments of both Court and counsel, so far as having any probative weight in this case is concerned. The *means* by which a witness is induced to make a statement are controlled by the Court. The effect of the statements made by witnesses are for the jurors."

John Lucas stood, face white, his hands clenching and unclenching at his sides. "Your Honor," he said in a voice which was barely audible, "this case has taken an unexpected turn. I, perhaps, deserve the rebuke of the Court. May I ask, however, that a continuance be granted until to-morrow morning?"

Judge Markham hesitated, glanced dubiously at Perry Mason, and asked, "Is there any objection on the part of the defense?"

Perry Mason was smilingly urbane. "So far as the defense is concerned, there is no objection whatever. As counsel for the prosecution remarked, earlier in the case, the prosecution desired that the defense have *every* opportunity to present its case. Now it gives counsel for the defense equal pleasure to assert to the Court that it desires the prosecution to have every opportunity to try and make out a case against this defendant — *if it can.*"

Judge Markham placed a hand to his lips, in order that the jury might not see any possible quivering at the corners of his mouth. "Very well," he said. "Court is adjourned until to-morrow morning at ten o'clock. During the interim, the jury will remember the admonition of the Court, and not discuss the case, or permit it to be discussed in their presence, nor form or express any opinion as to the guilt or innocence of the defendant."

And with that, Judge Markham whirled about in his chair, and strode to his chambers, his robes fluttering behind him. But there were those among the spectators who caught a glimpse of the judicial profile just as it turned into chambers, who subsequently swore, with great glee, that the judge wore a very human grin which stretched from ear to ear.

Chapter 20

The lights of Perry Mason's private office beat down upon the mask-like countenance of C. Phillip Montaine, the granite-hard features of Perry Mason. Della Street, obviously excited, held an open notebook on her knee. "Have you seen your son this afternoon, Mr. Montaine?" Mason asked.

Montaine's face was inscrutable, his voice well-modulated and slightly scornful. "No," he said, "you know that I have not. You know the district attorney has him held in custody as a material witness, that no one can see him."

Mason said, almost casually, "Wasn't it *your* suggestion, Mr. Montaine, that he be kept in custody?"

"Certainly not."

"Doesn't it impress you as being rather strange," Mason suggested, "that despite the fact the district attorney knows he cannot call Carl Montaine as a witness because of the law which provides a husband cannot be called as a witness against a wife, the district attorney should keep Carl locked up as a material witness?"

"I see no particular significance connected

with it," Montaine said. "Certainly, I have had nothing to do with it."

"I was just wondering," Mason said, "if there wasn't something back of all this; if, perhaps, some one were not trying to keep me from giving Carl a vigorous cross-examination." Montaine said nothing. "Did you know that I saw him this afternoon?" Mason inquired.

"I know you were to take his deposition in a divorce action, yes."

Perry Mason said slowly and impressively, "Mr. Montaine, I am going to ask Della Street to read to you what happened at the deposition." Montaine started to speak, then checked himself. His face was as a mask. "Go ahead," said Perry Mason to Della Street.

"Do you wish me to read just what I have here in my notebook?"

"Yes."

"Both the questions and the answers?"

"Yes, you can read just what you have there."

" 'Q.: Your name is Carl W. Montaine? A.: Yes.

" 'Q.: You are the husband of Rhoda Montaine? A.: Yes.

" 'Q.: You understand that Rhoda Montaine has filed a complaint for divorce against you, charging you with cruelty? A.: Yes.

" 'Q.: You understand that one of the allegations of that complaint is that you falsely accused her of the murder of Gregory Moxley? A.: Yes.

" 'Q.: Was the accusation false? A.: It was not.

" 'Q.: You repeat that accusation then? A.: Yes.

" 'Q.: What grounds have you for making such an accusation? A.: Plenty of grounds. She tried to drug me in order to keep me in bed while she went to keep an appointment with Moxley. She sneaked her car out of the garage, committed the murder, returned, and crawled into bed as though nothing had happened.

" 'Q.: Isn't it a fact that you knew all about Moxley prior to the time your wife slipped out at two o'clock in the morning? A.: No.

" 'Q.: Now, wait a minute. Isn't it a fact that you retained a so-called shadow to follow your wife; that this shadow followed her to my office on the day before the murder; that the shadow trailed her to Gregory Moxley's apartment? A.: (The witness hesitates, fails to answer.)

" 'Q.: Go ahead and answer that question, and remember you're under oath. Isn't that a fact? A.: Well, I employed a person to shadow her. Yes.

" 'Q.: And, when your wife left the garage around one thirty in the morning, there was a flat tire on her car, was there not? A.: So I understand.

" 'Q.: And the spare tire had a *nail* in it, did it not? A.: So I understand.

" 'Q.: But the air had not entirely leaked out of that spare tire? A.: I guess that's right. Yes.

" 'Q.: Now, will you kindly tell us, Mr.

Montaine, how it would be possible for a *spare* tire on the back of a car, elevated some three feet from the ground, to get a nail in it, unless that nail had been driven into it? A.: I don't know.

" 'Q.: Now, when your wife returned her car to the garage, she couldn't get the door closed, is that right? A.: Yes.

" 'Q.: Nevertheless, when she *left* the garage, it was necessary for her to both open and close the sliding door? A.: Yes, I guess so.

" 'Q.: You don't have to guess. You know, don't you? You heard her open and close the door. A.: Yes.

" 'Q.: Now, that door closed freely when she left the garage? A.: Yes.

" 'Q.: And isn't it a fact that the reason the door wouldn't close when your wife tried to close it the second time was that the door caught on the bumper of your automobile, which was also in the garage? A.: Yes.

" 'Q.: Therefore, isn't it a fact that your automobile must have been moved during the time your wife's car was absent from the garage, and when it was returned to the garage it wasn't driven in quite far enough to clear the door? A.: I don't think so.

" 'Q.: Isn't it a fact that you knew your wife was going out at two o'clock in the morning? A.: No.

" 'Q.: You admit that you looked in your wife's purse and found a telegram signed "Gregory"? A.: Yes, that was afterwards.

" 'Q.: And isn't it a fact that on that telegram the address of Gregory Moxley was written? A.: Yes.

" 'Q.: And didn't you know that your wife intended to go to an appointment with Gregory Moxley? Didn't you determine that you would be in the house where Gregory Moxley resided, in order to see what was taking place between your wife and Moxley. Isn't it, therefore, a fact that you planned to delay your wife after she started so that you would have sufficient time to arrive first on the scene? Didn't you, therefore, let the air out of the right rear tire on her car and drive a nail into the spare tire, making a slow puncture, so that the tire would be flat, but its condition would not be apparent until after it had been put on the car? Didn't you then, after your wife had dressed and left the garage, and while she was at the service station getting the car repaired, jump into your car, and drive to Gregory Moxley's apartment house? Didn't you climb up the back stairs and enter the adjoining apartment on the second floor on the north? Didn't you secrete yourself there until your wife came to keep her appointment with Moxley? Didn't you then climb over the rail separating the back stoops or porches, enter the kitchen in the Moxley apartment, hear Moxley demanding that your wife should get money, even if it became necessary for her to poison you and collect the insurance? Didn't you hear your wife state she was going to telephone me? And then the sounds of struggle? And didn't you, in a sudden panic, lest your name and the name of your family should be dragged into such a mess and bring disgrace or fancied disgrace to your father, pull out the master switch on the switch box in the back of the said apartment, thereby plunging the apartment into darkness? Didn't you then dash into the Moxley apartment, hearing the sound of a blow, and then hearing your wife run from the apartment? Didn't you sneak into the room where Moxley had been, striking a match to see what had happened? Didn't you find Moxley just getting to his feet, having been dazed by a blow which had been struck him on the head with a poker? Didn't you, thereupon, acting upon impulse, pick up the poker, strike Moxley a terrific blow over the head, felling him to the floor? Didn't you, thereupon, start to walk down the corridor, striking matches as you went, the matches being those that you had picked up from a smoking stand in Moxley's apartment? Didn't you then encounter another person in the corridor? A man who had been ringing the doorbell, had received no answer, and who had, therefore, gone around to the back of the house and effected an entrance in the same manner that you had done? Wasn't that person a man named Oscar Pender, from Centerville, who had been trying to force Moxley to give money to his sister? Didn't you two hold a whispered conversation, and didn't you explain to the said Pender that you were both in a very dangerous position?

Didn't you state that you had found Moxley dead when you entered the apartment, but that the police would never believe you? Didn't you, therefore, seeking to cover your tracks, take cloths and wipe all fingerprints from the door-knobs and the weapon of death? Didn't you, thereupon, start to the back of the house, and didn't you then think that perhaps your wife might have run out through the back door and have climbed into the corridor of the adjoining apartment? Didn't you, therefore, walk down the said corridor, striking matches to give you illumination, and, when you found the corridor was empty, returned to the Moxley stoop, and having used the last of the matches, toss away this empty match container? Didn't you then throw back the master switch which turned on the lights once more in Moxley's apartment? Didn't both you and Oscar Pender then hastily leave the premises? Didn't you jump in your car, drive hurriedly home, beat your wife there by a matter of seconds, and, in your haste, neglect to put your car far enough in the garage so that both doors would move freely? You could move the door back of your car freely back and forth, but when both doors were pushed over from the other side of the garage one of them would lock into position on your bumper, and isn't that the reason your wife couldn't get the garage door closed?

" 'A.: My God, yes! And I've kept it bottled up so long that it's nearly driven me crazy. Only, you're wrong about the killing. I turned out the lights to give Rhoda a break and then I was afraid he might overpower her. I heard the sound of a blow in the dark. I heard some one fall. I struck matches and groped my way through the rooms. I found Moxley on his feet. He wasn't badly hurt, but he was in a murderous rage. He started for me. The poker was lying on a table. I dropped my match, grabbed the poker, and swung in the dark as hard as I could. Then I called to Rhoda. She didn't answer. I didn't have any more matches. I groped around in the dark, and it was then I dropped the garage key and car keys. I must have pulled the leather container out of my pocket. I didn't know it at the time. Then some one else struck a match. That was Pender. The rest of it happened just as you said. I gave Pender money so that he could skip out. I didn't intend to accuse Rhoda at the time. It wasn't until I was almost home that I looked for my garage keys and realized what had happened.

" 'Q.: So then you left the garage unlocked, put your car away, went to your bedroom, and, as soon as your wife came in and went to sleep, you got up, opened her purse and took out *her* garage key and the keys to the cars; and it was *her* leather key container that you showed to me in my office. Is that right? A.: Yes, sir, that's right. I thought Rhoda would claim self-defense and a jury would believe her. I came to you before I went to the police because I knew you could get her off.

" 'Q.: And, as I understand it . . .' "

Perry Mason raised his hand. "That, Della," he said, "is far enough. Never mind the rest of it. You may leave us."

The secretary shut her notebook, vanished into the outer office. Mason faced C. Phillip Montaine. Montaine's face was white. His hands gripped the arms of the chair. He said nothing. "You have," Perry Mason remarked, "undoubtedly read the afternoon papers. It's been rather clever of you, Montaine, not to attend the trial, but, of course, you know what has happened. The prosecution's own witnesses have given Rhoda Montaine an alibi. A jury will never convict her.

"I believe what your son said," Perry Mason remarked slowly, "but a jury wouldn't — not after the way he's behaved in this case, not after the way he tried to get out from under by shifting the blame to Rhoda's shoulders.

"I know something of Carl's character. I learned it from talking to Rhoda. I know that he's impulsive and I know that he's weak. I know that he fears your disapproval more than anything on earth. I know that he values his family name because he has been taught to value it.

"I know that Moxley needed killing, if ever a man needed killing. I know that your son has never faced any real crisis in his life by himself. He has always had you to lean on. I know that when he first went to Moxley's apartment, he did so because he thought his wife was having an affair with Moxley. After he realized the true facts, he acted upon impulse, returned home in a panic and realized that he had left his garage key in Moxley's apartment. He had left the garage unlocked when he took out his car, and he had sense enough to leave it unlocked when he returned, so that Rhoda would find it unlocked. He knew by that time he had left his keys in Moxley's apartment and he had made his plan to steal Rhoda's keys so that it would appear her key container was the one left in the apartment. When it came down to a real test, your son didn't have guts enough and didn't have manhood enough to stand up and take it on the chin. He passed the buck to Rhoda.

"If your son had had simple manhood enough to have gone to the authorities and told his story, he could doubtless have made out a case of self-defense. As it stands now, he can't do it. No one will believe him. Personally, I don't blame your son for the killing. I do blame him for trying to pass the buck. You're the one that I blame. I'm satisfied that you either knew what had happened or suspected what had happened. That was the reason you came to me and tried to get me to weaken Rhoda's defense by letting your son testify against her and by tying my hands so that I couldn't rip into him on cross-examination. Frankly, that was one of the first things that aroused my suspicions. I couldn't understand why a man of your character and intelligence would try to bribe me to let a client get a death penalty. I couldn't figure what motive would be powerful enough. And then I suddenly realized the only motive that *could* have been strong enough to have made you play your cards that way. That motive was a desire to save your son."

Montaine took a deep breath. "I'm licked," he said. "I realize now that I made fatal mistakes in the training I gave Carl. I know that he isn't a particularly strong character. When he wired me that he was married to a nurse I wanted to find out what sort of a woman she was. I wanted to find out in such a way that I could convince my son of his mistake and, at the same time, hold the whip hand over the woman. Therefore, I came to this city while my son thought I was still in Chicago. I had her shadowed night and day. I was kept advised of every move she made. My men were not regular detectives. They were confidential investigators whom I kept constantly in my employ."

Mason puckered his brows thoughtfully. "Why," he said, "the man who shadowed her from this office was the rankest kind of amateur."

"That, Counselor," Montaine said, "was one of those peculiar coincidences which upset the most carefully laid plans. When Rhoda Montaine left your office she was shadowed by my man. That man was so shrewd even Paul Drake never suspected him. But remember that Carl, also, had become suspicious. *He* had hired a so-called private detective, who was little more than an amateur, to shadow Rhoda. By the use of that shadow he had discovered something about Doctor Millsap — I don't know just what."

Mason nodded slowly. "Yes," he said, "as soon as Carl told me about Doctor Millsap I felt certain he must have acquired the information by the use of a detective."

"One of my detectives," Montaine went on, "was on the job when Rhoda left the house to keep her appointment with Moxley. He tried to follow her, but she gave him the slip. Remember, it was late and the streets were almost deserted? He didn't dare to follow her too closely. When he lost her, he returned to the house and concealed himself. He was in time to see Carl return to the garage, park his car and enter the house."

"You knew, of course," Mason said, "the importance of this?"

"As soon as my detective made a report to me," Montaine said, "I realized the deadly significance of the information. By that time it was too late to do anything about it. The newspapers were on the street, and Carl had gone to the police. You see, I slept late that morning and my detectives didn't awaken me to give me the information. I had left orders that I wasn't to be disturbed under any circumstances. That was the first really serious blunder this detective had ever made. He obeyed orders."

"And," Mason said, "of course, *he* didn't ap-

310

preciate the deadly significance of what he had discovered?"

"Not until after he read the later editions of the newspapers," Montaine said. He made a shrugging gesture with his shoulders. "However, Counselor, all of this is beside the point. I am in your hands. I presume, of course, you want money. Do you want anything else? Do you insist on communicating these facts to the district attorney?"

Perry Mason slowly shook his head. "No," he said, "I'm not going to tell the district attorney anything. This deposition was privately taken. I won't talk, and Della Street won't talk. The attorney who represented your son *can't* talk because he's bound professionally to protect Carl. It might, however, be a good thing if you would give him a rather substantial retainer to defend Carl in the event it should become necessary.

"Now, then, in regard to money: I want money for the work I did for Rhoda Montaine. I want you to put up that money. That, however, is a minor matter. The main thing I want is money for Rhoda."

"How much money?" Montaine asked.

"Lots of it," Mason said grimly. "Your son did her an irreparable wrong. We can forgive him; he was a weakling. But you did her an irreparable wrong, and, by God, we can't forgive you! You're an intelligent man and a strong man, and you're going to pay." Perry Mason's eyes burned steadily into those of the multi-millionaire.

C. Phillip Montaine took out his checkbook. His face was utterly without expression. His lips were compressed into a thin line. "It would seem," he said, "that both my son and myself have, perhaps, taken too much credit because of our ancestors. It would seem to me that it is up to some one to redeem the family."

He took his fountain pen from his pocket, unscrewed the cap, deliberately signed two checks in blank and passed the signed checks over to Perry Mason. "You," he said in a voice that was steady, although his lips were trembling, "can assess the fine, Counselor."

Chapter 21

Late morning sun, streaming through the windows of Perry Mason's private office, fell across the big desk in splotches of golden light. The lawyer fitted a key to the exit door of his private office, flung open the door and stood to one side, motioning to Rhoda Montaine to enter. The woman's face showed the strain under which she had been laboring. Her cheeks, however, were flushed with color. Her eyes were sparkling. She stood by the desk, looking about the office. Tears came to her eyes. "I was thinking," she said simply, "of the last time I saw this office — how independent I was, how I tried to lie to you, and the things that have happened since. And, if it hadn't been for you, I'd have been convicted of murder."

She shuddered. Perry Mason motioned her to a seat, and, as she sank into the big leather chair, dropped into his swivel chair and reached for a cigarette.

"I can't begin to tell you," Rhoda Montaine said, "how ashamed I am of myself. It would have been easier for you if I had followed your instructions. I knew that I was in an awful mess, but you could have worked me out without much trouble if I'd only had sense enough to put myself in your hands and follow your instructions.

"But the district attorney kept commenting about the fact that *some one* was standing downstairs ringing the doorbell while Gregory Moxley was being murdered. I knew that the district attorney could prove that I was in the neighborhood at about the time the crime was being committed, so I thought that all I had to do was to swear that I was the one who had been ringing the bell and stick to it."

"The trouble with that line of reasoning," Mason said smilingly, "is that everyone else figured the same way."

He opened the drawer of his desk, took out a check and handed it to her. She stared at it with wide, incredulous eyes. "Why!" she said, "why — what's this?"

"That," Mason told her, "is something that C. Phillip Montaine did by way of squaring things with you. Legally, we'll call it a property settlement between you and Carl Montaine. Actually, it represents a penalty that you assessed against a rich man for losing his moral perspective."

"But I don't understand," she said.

"You don't have to," he told her. "Furthermore, Mr. Montaine paid my fee, and I don't mind telling you that he paid a generous fee. So that this money is net to you, with one exception. There's one payment you've got to make."

"What is it?"

"This Pender woman," Perry Mason said, "married Gregory Moxley under the name of Freeman. Gregory took her money. She came here to collect it. Her brother came to help her. I haven't any sympathy for her brother, but I have for her. It was necessary, as a part of your defense, to get them on the run and keep them on the run. Therefore, I want you to pay her back the money Gregory took. It's all in that check. I figured it out when I fixed the amount of the check."

"But," she said, "I don't understand. Why should C. Phillip Montaine make a check to me? And why should he make it for any such enormous sum?"

"I think," Perry Mason said, "you'll understand a little better when you read the deposition of your husband, which was taken yesterday."

He pressed a call button on his desk and almost immediately the door to the outer office opened. Della Street rushed across the threshold, paused when she saw Rhoda Montaine, then came forward with outstretched hands. "Congratulations," she said.

Rhoda Montaine took her hand. "Don't congratulate me, congratulate Mr. Mason."

"I will," Della smiled, and, turning, gave the lawyer both of her hands, stood for a long moment looking into his eyes. "I'm proud of you, chief."

He disengaged one of her hands, drew her to him, patted her shoulder. "Thanks, Della."

"The district attorney dismissed the case?" asked Della Street.

"Yes, they were licked. They threw up their hands. . . . Did you write up that deposition, Della?"

"Yes."

"I want Mrs. Montaine to read it, and then I want you to destroy it."

"Just a minute," Della said.

She gave his hand a quick squeeze, stepped to the outer office and returned with sheets of typewritten paper.

"Read these," Perry Mason told Rhoda Montaine. "You can skim through the first part and concentrate on that long question and the answers that come after that."

Rhoda Montaine started reading the deposition. Her face lighted with interest, her eyes moving rapidly from side to side as they read down the typewritten lines.

Della Street stood at Perry Mason's side. Her hand touched his arm. Her voice was a half-whisper. "Chief," she said, "was that doorbell business on the square?"

He smiled down into her troubled eyes. "Why?" he asked.

"I've always been afraid," she said, still using the same low tone, "that some day you'd go too far and some one might make trouble for you. You see . . ."

His laugh interrupted her. "My methods," he said, "are unconventional. So far they've never been criminal. Perhaps they're tricky, but they're the legitimate tricks that a lawyer is entitled to use. In cross-examining a witness I have got a right to use any sort of test I can think up, any sort of a build-up that's within the law."

"I know," she told him, speaking with low-voiced rapidity, "but the district attorney is resentful. If he could prove that you even went to that house without the permission of the owner he'd have you arrested. He'd . . ."

Perry Mason gravely took a folded paper from his pocket. "You might," he said, "file this among our receipts." She stared at the folded paper. "A rental receipt," the lawyer explained, "for the building at 316 Norwalk Avenue. I thought I'd make an investment in real estate."

She stared at the paper with wide eyes. A smile of slow, satisfied comprehension gave her face a whimsical expression. "I should have known," she said softly.

Rhoda Montaine jumped to her feet, threw the deposition on the desk. Her gloved hands were clenched. Her eyes stared at Perry Mason with burning scrutiny. "So *that's* what they did!" she said.

Perry Mason nodded slowly.

Rage showed in her eyes. "I'm cured," she said slowly. "I wanted to get a man who was weak and mother him. It wasn't that I wanted a mate. I wanted a child. A man can't be a child. He can only be weak and selfish. Carl didn't have nerve enough to stand up and take it. He tried to blame the murder on me. He stole the keys from my purse, reported me to the police, framed a murder on me, and his father tried to get me convicted to spare his son. I'm cured. I'm finished."

Perry Mason watched her, said nothing.

"I had decided," she went on, speaking rapidly now, "that I'd never touch a cent of the Montaine money. I'd intended to give Carl's father his check back. Now . . ." She paused, her nostrils dilated, her shoulders heaving. Then her eyes sought those of Della Street. "Can you," she asked, "get me some one on the telephone?"

"Why, surely, Mrs. Montaine."

Slowly the hard look faded from Rhoda Montaine's eyes. There was a wistful tilt to her mouth. "Please," she said, "call Doctor Claude Millsap for me."